NIGHTMARES
UNHINGED

TWENTY TALES OF TERROR

PRAISE FOR NIGHTMARES UNHINGED

"Featuring an impressive line-up of speculative fiction luminaries—Mario Acevedo, Jason Heller, Jeanne C. Stein, Steve Rasnic Tem, Warren Hammond, etc.—this stellar collection of twenty nightmare-inducing short stories is appropriately titled: it's a check-underneath-the-bed-before-you-go-to-sleep kind of anthology."

—PAUL GOAT ALLEN

"Poe, Lovecraft, King—step aside for the new kids on the block who bring goose bump horror and pit-of-the-stomach dread to stories of the modern world and the future. Ebola in the heartland, an Iraq veteran with a problem, a high school bully who gets his due, a librarian with an exclusive clientele, a far-future alien race that delights in cruelty–the stories in *Nightmares Unhinged* deliver creepy surprises, sweat-inducing fear and chilling revulsion. These are stories by masters at their peak, stories you will still be thinking about long after you've laid down the book."

—JESÚS TREVIÑO, director of *Star Trek Voyager, Star Trek Deep Space Nine* and *Babylon Five*

"The sheep you so desperately count into slumber are about to sharpen their teeth, burrow into your brain and infest your dreams."

—MARK HENRY, author of *Battle of the Network Zombies*

"What is fear? It is many different things for each individual. What Joshua Viola has done in this anthology is touch on every exposed nerve one might have. Like a master chef in his kitchen, Viola manages to put together a delicious dish of 'Macabre Under Glass.' Some of the dishes may be challenging and new to your palette, but it is a many splendored meal with each course displaying its own variety of flavors. It was truly satisfying and yet, now, I am hungry for more even though I have a terrible time sleeping with such a full belly."

—**JONATHAN TIERSTEN**, actor *Sleepaway Camp*

"With a delicious story for seemingly every fear, *Nightmares Unhinged* features a treasure of writers—both established and rising—who know how to peel away all layers of protection and dig into your deepest phobias. These stories will leave you fascinated, vulnerable, and truly considering leaving your bedroom light on at night. If you are looking for short story horror at its creative peak, *Nightmares Unhinged* is a must-read."

—**CARTER WILSON**, author of *The Comfort of Black*

"This collection of chills by Colorado authors takes a retro, *Twilight Zone* approach to horror and offers it in a distinctly Western mood. There's a nostalgia to this book's type of creepy; fans of old-fashioned, midnight horror will enjoy. Best read after dark."

—**STANT LITORE**, author of *The Zombie Bible*

"Get ready for blood, terror and the unexpected in *Nightmares Unhinged*, a devilish anthology from a cast of superb writers."

—**MIKE BEFELER**, author of *Mystery of the Dinner Playhouse* and *The Paul Jacobson Geezer-Lit Mystery Series*

"Recommended doses of terrific and terrifying tales, *Nightmares Unhinged* is the perfect remedy for feeling just a little too cozy and secure."

—**J.L. ABRAMO**, award-winning author of *Gravesend*

"Less a collection of stories and more a warning list of places never to be—the library, fields with scarecrows, Mexican bars, the dentist, work parties, your neighbour's house, and if you're male and play golf, don't you ever, ever go looking for your balls under a bridge. A lot safer to just stay at home and read this book."

—**PAUL CAMPION**, director of *The Devil's Rock* and VFX Artist for *The Lord of the Rings Trilogy, Constantine* and *Sin City*

"From the moment you open *Nightmares Unhinged*, it chokes the air from the room and leaves you holding your breath until you finally close its pages. Unfortunately, no matter how hard you try, you'll never get rid of that sinking feeling it will leave with you."

—**JOSH DANFORTH**, Celldweller Productions

"*Nightmares Unhinged* has stories that will frighten even the most thick-skinned reader."

—**CAT ZINGANO**, UFC Bantamweight Number One Contender

NIGHTMARES UNHINGED

TWENTY TALES OF TERROR

EDITED BY JOSHUA VIOLA

FROM THE TWISTED MINDS OF

Mario Acevedo

Edward Bryant

Dustin Carpenter

Sean Eads

Keith Ferrell

Warren Hammond

Jason Heller

Gary Jonas

Stephen Graham Jones

J.V. Kyle

Aaron Michael Ritchey

Jeanne C. Stein

Steve Rasnic Tem

Joshua Viola

& Dean Wyant

HEX PUBLISHERS

NIGHTMARES UNHINGED
TWENTY TALES OF TERROR

Edited by Joshua Viola
Copyedits by Matthew Wayne Selznick and Jennifer Melzer

Art Director: Joshua Viola
Cover design by Joshua Viola and Erica Schaub
Cover illustrations by Aaron Lovett
Interior illustrations by Aaron Lovett
Typesets and formatting by Dustin Carpenter
Assistant Typesetting by Matthew Floyd

A Hex Publishers Book

Published & Distributed by Hex Publishers, LLC
PO BOX 298
Erie, CO 80516

www.HexPublishers.com

Print ISBN-10: 0985559098
Print ISBN-13: 978-0-9855590-9-0
Ebook ISBN-10: 0996403906
Ebook ISBN-13: 978-0-9964039-0-0

First Edition: September 2015

10 9 8 7 6 5 4 3 2 1

Printed in the U.S.A.

CONTENTS

FOR MELANIE

"May the merciful gods, if indeed there be such, guard those hours when no power of the will, or drug that the cunning of man devises, can keep me from the chasm of sleep. Death is merciful, for there is no return therefrom, but with him who has come back out of the nethermost chambers of night, haggard and knowing, peace rests nevermore."

H.P. Lovecraft, "Hypnos"

TERRORS IN THE NIGHT

STEVE ALTEN

There's a difference between a night terror and a nightmare. A nightmare is a scary dream; sometimes it awakens us, or our moaning disturbs a significant other who shakes us awake. I have a reoccurring nightmare of standing in the shallows as a twenty-story wave approaches and my legs are heavy as lead.

A night terror is death reaching for you in your dreams. It is a nightmare unhinged. You can't outrun it, it owns your ass. It whispers in your ear and you freak. The response is electric: you shoot up in bed and release a blood-curdling scream that causes anyone within fifty feet to call the cops. And the fear is so real, you can't remain in the room; you physically need to get out.

I've had one night terror in my life (during a sleepover when I was eighteen), and it's stuck with me ever since. I was in a dark alley, alone, only not alone. Something was following me. When it whispered into my brain, I jumped from bed and sent my friend in the next bed over clutching at his heart, hyperventilating. Another friend, who was sleeping on the sofa downstairs, rushed into the bedroom expecting to find a murder. It was five in the morning and we stayed up the rest of the night–in another room. It took the first friend an hour before he could speak.

I suppose I'm grateful to have experienced the night terror, as it's influenced several characters in my books. Jonas Taylor (in the *MEG 20th Anniversary Special Edition*)

suffers severe night terrors (who wouldn't with a seventy-foot Megalodon after your butt?). His son, David, must deal with a similar ailment in *MEG: Nightstalkers* (it's not easy being the son of a Taylor or any of my lead characters).

Nightmares Unhinged is an exciting premise for an anthology, and there are contributions here from some terrific writers. I'm especially proud of the work Josh Viola accomplished in the task of editing the manuscript. Josh and I first worked together back in 2010 on his debut novel, *The Bane of Yoto*. He was a quick study and a brilliant artist, and it's rewarding for me to watch his success.

Sleep well.

Steve Alten, Ed.D.

www.SteveAlten.com

INTRODUCTION
RECLAIM YOUR FEARS

JOSHUA VIOLA

H ave you ever awoken bathed in a cold sweat? Or found your arms in a death grip around your pillow? Ever rush to turn on the lights in the middle of the night?

Chances are, you've just had a nightmare.

Nothing gets the heart racing like a *good* bad dream.

Sometimes nightmares do more than just frighten us. Sometimes, they tear our psyches from their hinges and shatter all sensibility, leaving us with just one option: cut and run.

But there's no escaping fear. Fear haunts until it's confronted.

Fear is human.

Evolution made us this way. Our brains are primed for it. It's in our bones. Nightmares tap into our most basic emotions and force us to face them.

For most of us, the old terrors lurking in the dark corners of our minds fade away in adulthood. Fear is no longer the boogie man hiding under the bed, or monsters lurking in the closet. It's worrying about the mortgage, and whether or not there'll be enough money left for gas and groceries.

Even so, our *fascination* with the boogie man remains. We are, as a species, attracted to the rush of adrenaline it provides. Whether it's the thrill of jumping from a plane or watching a scary movie, horror acts as a coping

mechanism. A whetstone to sharpen our senses in order to survive the mundane.

Fear is necessary.

Modern society has turned our terrors into entertainment. We put ourselves in frightening situations to satisfy evolutionary urges. We constantly seek reminders of those old feelings. Those fears.

And those old feelings and fears inspired this anthology.

It was delightfully terrifying putting *Nightmares Unhinged* together with the help of such a talented group of writers, some new, and some you might've read before. In the pages that follow, you'll discover stories of horror. Of dread. Some gross, some hilarious. And some that are just plain weird.

Now... allow yourself a moment to reclaim your fears, to relive those thrills, and bask in the triumph of conquering them.

It's time to get scared again.

THE
BROLLACHAN

STEVE RASNIC TEM

THE BROLLACHAN

STEVE RASNIC TEM

Brenda didn't want Granny Adamina telling Lillie stories about the brollachan. Lillie was a lonely child, and too precocious for her own good, and Brenda didn't need one more thing to worry about in her complicated life. She was a single mother with a young teenage girl to raise. But Adamina didn't listen to anyone or anything but her own heart, and that old heart sometimes told her the most bizarre things.

"The brollachan, he has nae shape," Adamina said in her raspy Scots whisper. "Until he needs one. Oh, except the bairns." She raised a finger like a bent oak twig. "Well, their bairns might hae webbed feet–who can say fur sure? A dale mare common are the bogles, the wee dark clouds that float along the edges of the forest like smoke. Wee, but evil. If ye look close enough, ye can see the two bright red eyes floatin' inside, like burnin' coals."

When she was little, Brenda would curl up on the rug in front of the fireplace and listen to the old woman's tales. Granny would laugh at this and call her *Kitty*. "I hae another tale fur ye, Kitty," she'd say, and laugh at her little pun.

So many things her granny said were doubtful, but still had the power to fill Brenda with dread. "Ah, ye best stay close tae the hoose, lassie. Dinnae ye ken that the brollachan has an appetite fur the minds of the human bairn? Ye stay away from strangers–ye never know if they be hiding a brollachan inside! They see ye, and they be

takin' way that kitty mind of yours. They'll come steal it, hide deep ben ye, or maybe just leave ye an empty shell!"

Home had been a small farm in Virginia on the edge of an old-growth forest. They'd raised chickens, grown apples and berries. Brenda had loved it, as far as it went–it just didn't go far enough. She'd wanted the color and excitement of town, and to spend more time with kids her own age.

Granny Adamina came over from Scotland after Brenda's father died in a trucking accident. She barely remembered him; she'd been six at the time. She did remember Adamina's arrival, however: a large lady full of color and a funny way of talking, so different from her own mother, who would be distant and grim-faced all the rest of her days.

Brenda never really believed Adamina's stories, but her granny told them with such conviction they did give her pause. When she was younger she didn't mind staying close to home, just in case. At least it was beautiful there. But any time she saw a hint of a smoke cloud she would wonder, and search for the eyes inside. But what about the milky early morning fog that threaded its way through the ragged edges of the trees? Might that hide brollachan too? And the way her mother was after her father died, the emptiness in her eyes–could a brollachan have done that, gone in and just scooped her out? It was all too scary to think about. Even if the brollachan were real, she didn't want to know about them.

Her life changed completely when they stopped homeschooling her and sent her to the junior high in town. Granny Adamina didn't know much more than farming and her spooky tales of the old country. And Mother could barely talk to her now, much less teach her, and, anyway, she died before Brenda got out of high school. Mother's last week living was spent staring at the ceiling with her eyes full of fog.

The first thing wee Brenda learned about in the new school was boys. She was always a little scared of them, and soon discovered that very few seemed to have her best interests in mind. They might break your heart without a second thought. And the way they filled her mind and took it over sometimes, so she could barely think a sentence without one of them nasty boys sneaking his face inside, could any brollachan do worse than that?

"You don't have to believe everything Adamina says, you know." Brenda could feel Lillie's eyes on her, but couldn't return her gaze. Her own child had always made her feel uncomfortable, the way she was always watching, but never revealing what she felt about what she saw. "I mean, you need to respect her, but some of her stories..."

"She says you got pregnant with me because you didn't listen to her stories."

Brenda looked up, then, scowling, "She said that?"

"Not in those exact words, but yeah, that's what I think she said, pretty much." Lillie said it with a kind of half-smile. Was she enjoying this? Brenda might have been this aggravating as a teenager, but if so, she didn't remember.

"Granny Adamina said lots of things to me growing up, most of it nonsense. I got pregnant with you because I was young and stupid, and Adamina never said anything that might have made me smarter, believe me. Still, I'm glad I did. I'm glad I have you." *Most of the time*, she thought, and made herself smile for her daughter. But Lillie gave her nothing in return. In fact, Lillie turned her back and returned to the sanctity of her bedroom. She didn't quite slam the door, but she'd learned the art of shutting it just loudly enough to be infuriating.

Brenda sat on the couch, seething. The perverse power of teenagers was they knew you loved them but they could make you act like you couldn't stand them, which gave them permission to hate you, or at least act like they did. The end result was you were miserable either way. And they *knew* this, despite their pretense of innocence. Sometimes it seemed Lillie ate Brenda's misery for breakfast and long before dinner she was hungry for it again.

She'd never really known how to handle her, but Brenda knew she couldn't do it in rural Virginia with just Adamina to advise her. At least in a city like Richmond there were job opportunities and possible resources for her quiet and strange child.

Brenda hated going to sleep angry, and Lillie always showed up later with something nice to say. Brenda chose to believe that this meant Lillie cared about her feelings, even though there was scant evidence for that.

That night it only took a half hour before Lillie came to her with that patented apologetic look pasted on her face. "Sorry, I guess I'm just in a grouchy mood today." Lillie then gifted her with a quick, perfunctory hug.

"That's okay, sweetheart. Guess I haven't been the happiest person today either." Which was a complete fabrication. Brenda had been fine before the argument.

"Can I go out with Caitlin and Ann? They want to go to a movie, or something."

"Do I know them?"

"Of course you do—they're my friends."

Brenda felt sure she'd never heard those names before. And Lillie didn't have many friends, none really, at least that she'd heard of lately. But the empty look on her daughter's face was heartbreaking—it was clear she didn't expect Brenda to say yes. "But it's a school night."

"I finished my homework *hours* ago. I almost never go out."

Which wasn't quite true, was it? Lillie *never* went out. She reminded Brenda of herself as a child, but Brenda had had no choice—she'd lived deep in the country, alongside those woods. Lillie was supposed to have a better chance here in the city.

"Maybe, maybe. But I want to meet them. Don't just rush out until I've talked to them."

Lillie nodded blankly and went to her room. *She wasn't even excited,* Brenda thought. *What does that child think about all day?*

Seconds after Lillie left the room the grating sound of Adamina's voice issued from her bedroom. "Ye let the wean walk aw over ye. Jings! The gob on that wan! Ye cannae ken what goes on inside the lassie's haid. Dinnae be an idiot!"

"I'll see them first. I'll talk to them before I let her go out."

"Gonny invite 'em in? It be the guid thing to do. But watch em canny fur their evilness."

Brenda twisted her head. Granny had her door cracked only a couple of inches, just enough to hear, and say a few nasty words through. She rarely came out of there anymore. Adamina hated the city. Brenda

thought the woman was even more scared of the city than she had been of that old Virginia forest full of boogies and brollachan.

"Adamina, they're just young girls. I'm not raising my daughter to be scared of everything like I was, afraid to go out, afraid to go anywhere by myself."

"But ye did, didnee ye? And leuk whit happened tae ye! Keep the lassie safe! Dinnae be sairy efter!"

Brenda had seen the handsome young man before, but she'd never been close enough to approach him. He was usually walking quite fast, as if he were afraid of what might be living in the woods, or perhaps he was returning from some job or other, and had promised to return to his family by a certain time. So surely someone like that was dependable, not wanting to worry the ones who loved him, and so wouldn't be a danger at all, especially if he was scared of the woods like she was. He was just like her then, and not so experienced in the world, that he could still feel some fear when he was out and about. But still a bit braver than she, to be out so regularly, which was an attractive quality.

After seeing him from afar for weeks, she was surprised one late afternoon to have him step into the path beside her. She had no idea where he had come from, but his clothing was rough and dark, so maybe the shadows from the nearby trees had obscured him.

She made a small yelping sound, and he sighed. "Oh, don't say you're afraid of me. No one is ever afraid of me." His voice was soft and shy, so soft in fact she wondered if perhaps he didn't use it much. She could barely hear him.

"I just didn't see you, was all. I'm certainly not afraid of you." Which wasn't completely true, and she wondered why she was lying, unless it was because she was feeling extremely attracted to him, and she really didn't know anything about boys at all, and she didn't want the truth to ruin things, as it so often does.

He tilted his head ever so slightly and smiled at her. It confused her, because all of his face didn't appear to move at the same speed. His eyes and his too-wide smile smeared through the late afternoon dimness,

and the reddening sunset gleamed across his gaze. Was this what love-at-first-sight felt like? She had no idea. She was suddenly giddy with fear.

"There's nothing to be afraid of." He said it so quietly, no louder than the voice inside her head. "Whatever the old folks say, I promise not to bite."

He may have kissed her then, she wasn't sure. She'd never been kissed before, and had no idea what it was supposed to feel like. She remembered he whispered something into her lips, and the whisper traveled down her mouth and into her throat, and later when she woke up in the woods the whisper was inside her belly trying to speak to her, but she couldn't understand most of the words.

Adamina had looked at her oddly when she got home. Brenda claimed a stomachache and a desperate need to lie in bed. Could Adamina see it in her face? Brenda had always imagined they could see it in your face afterwards. And when she examined herself in the mirror it seemed her complexion might be slightly darker than it had been before, as if some storm had gotten into her skin, and one eye was slightly bloodshot, and as she would later discover, always would be.

They all said she went wild after that. They couldn't control her in school. But she'd just been trying to shake herself back into normal again, into some semblance of happiness, but her efforts were useless. She would never be the same. She would always hear his whisper inside her.

Adamina never let her forget her mistake, of course, and tormented her with strange singing, and teas made from a variety of foul herbs. Brenda was never sure of the purpose of it all–Adamina just said, "fur ye betterment, d'ye no ken?" Of course Brenda didn't believe her, but tried it all anyway, desperate for a betterment that never came.

Then when Lillie came, Adamina and her mother withdrew Brenda from school in shame.

Caitlin and Ann came up just as Brenda had requested, and Lillie even had them sit down so Brenda could talk to them, but not without a sidelong glance that clearly begged *don't embarrass me*. It was an encouraging sign; she was completely unaccustomed to that sort of sociability from her daughter. And the girls were neatly dressed and very polite.

"So how did you girls meet?"

Ann and Caitlin looked at each other, and then at Lillie, who appeared studiously quiet and even distracted, as if she'd just stumbled into a conversation she wasn't interested in.

Ann spoke up, but lazily, as if half-asleep. "Oh Caitlin and I have known each other forever. Lillie... she's the new girl, right? I'm not sure when she started at our school."

Caitlin interrupted, looking slightly anxious. "Just because... because we don't have classes together, doesn't mean we can't be friends. It's good, it's good..." She stared at Ann as if seeking help.

"To have somebody new, somebody different," Ann said. Ann glanced at Lillie then, raising an eyebrow. She appeared to mumble something silently to herself. Lillie had no reaction at all. "Lillie's different."

Brenda let them go, not without misgivings. She hugged Lillie fiercely as they left, but true to form, Lillie didn't hug back.

For months after her encounter with the dark young man along the edge of the woods, Brenda would return there, even though the place terrified her more than it had before. She didn't feel like she had any choice–part of her would always belong in that borderland between the forest and the plowed fields owned by the human bairn. It was fall, and the woods didn't hide much. The silhouettes of skeletal limbs and trunks made an intricate black lace against the gray sky. She'd scan this complicated backdrop for signs of him, and though there would be the occasional red gaze, the body swollen and smeared, they belonged to deer gasping out gray clouds of breath, or the fat rabbits sitting on their haunches, staring at her rudely with their angry eyes. Her handsome young man had disappeared back into his own mysterious history.

The girls returned hours after they'd promised, past midnight. Brenda was so shocked when she'd let them into the door she forgot her own anger over their lateness. Caitlin's beautiful curly blonde hair now appeared limp and unwashed. And her eyes were so caked with dried makeup that had been so sloppily applied it was hard to determine what the intention had been. Ann's makeup was minimal–in fact it appeared fiercely scrubbed off. It was the clothing that was the main problem. Her

jeans were now stained and faded, her top too tight and almost shredded around the hem. Had she changed after they'd left?

Both girls had little bruise marks on their necks. Hickies, unmistakably. Love bites. At least Lillie's pale skin proved clear.

In fact Lillie appeared much the same as before they'd left, although a bit more leery. Brenda pulled her aside. "Are those girls intoxicated on something?"

"They're, they're just silly, Mother. They're really not too bright, once you get to know them. They really need a keeper. They can't be trusted out alone."

Brenda sent both girls back to their homes in a taxi. She turned her attention to Lillie, but Lillie wanted to talk about other things.

"So what was he like, my dad?"

Brenda sighed–Lillie didn't look exactly resentful, but worse, hers was a face that appeared to expect little. "It's embarrassing–I've told you before. I didn't know him very well."

"You must have had an impression. What about him attracted you?"

"He was quiet. I liked that. I guess he didn't feel like he had to talk all the time. He didn't feel like he had to fill every silence. I admired that."

"So he didn't talk much?"

"No, it wasn't like that exactly. He talked, but it was just so nice, the way he talked. It's corny, but it was like the words went right past my ears and straight into my heart. It wasn't like I heard his words, but that I felt them. Like I'd felt them all of my life."

"But he left you."

"But he left me with you, so it wasn't like he really ever left at all."

"He burrowed deep inside you then?"

Brenda stared at her. "I wouldn't exactly put it that way, but yes, it was something like that. It wasn't as if he were gone, but that he was hiding inside me."

"You know, I'd like it if somebody loved me like that." Before Brenda could answer Lillie left the room.

But I do, honey, I do love you like that, Brenda whispered to the empty room. It was true. Lillie was lodged inside her forever.

Brenda was awakened the next day by an early morning phone call. "It's Barbara, Caitlin's mom. We need to talk."

Brenda thought it might be an apology, some revelation about what Caitlin had done, how she wasn't a proper companion for anybody. But what the woman said was, "You need to keep Lillie away from my daughter."

"What? My daughter did nothing. Those girls–"

"The girls tell me they don't even know your daughter. She just approached them one day in a grocery store. They don't even go to the same school!"

"I don't understand why they would say that–"

"I don't know what Lillie does, but they tell me they lose time when they're with her. They're not even aware of what they're saying. I don't know about any of that, but obviously this so-called friendship isn't working out." The woman hung up.

He may have kissed her then, she wasn't sure. He promised not to bite.

"Oh Lillie," Brenda whispered to nothing.

Later she found her in Adamina's room. The old woman was cold and still. Lillie turned her head, and just like her father, her red gaze, her too-wide smile, smeared.

FANGS

J.V. KYLE

FANGS

J.V. KYLE

He didn't think he had a problem, but he had to admit he developed a... *taste* for it. For them–for their blood and what it contained.

Be honest, he told himself as he moved slowly through the shadows. It wasn't the blood–there was blood everywhere. Everyone he passed–those who looked at him and those, far larger in number, who saw something or sensed something and averted their eyes–had blood. Blood could be found everywhere. Blood wasn't the problem.

The problem–if it was one, he reminded himself–was that once he'd drunk from a particular source, he wanted more. And more than that. And–

Tonight.

He would get all he wanted, and start, he felt sure, getting control of the–

It *wasn't* a problem.

At least not one he couldn't handle. Tonight, he would handle it.

He sank into a pool of deep shadows and stood there for a moment, catching his breath. His heart raced at a pace unseemly for one of the undead.

The hell of it was that it all came about by accident. An accident of timing, or location, or whatever. He was looking to feed in a new part of the city. He wasn't looking for new blood–that joke had been told a century ago. But over the centuries, he learned to change his feeding grounds with some frequency. Wouldn't do to take too

many drinks from the same neighborhood. That was a rookie mistake, and he was no rookie.

So he sought new territory, a fresh herd. He'd worn out his self-imposed welcome near the schools that held night classes, factories that had late night shift changes, and the same for the club district and the dive bars. Funny thing about the club district, about the patrons of bars in general, none of them had ever gotten to him the way this had. He could sink his fangs into a vein flowing with blood alcohol levels that would get them locked away by even the most lenient of judges. The alcohol he consumed along with the blood had no effect on him–he could drink his fill and still walk a straight line to his next victim.

Same with the kids coming from the clubs. Coke, weed, X, meth, crack back in the day, even heroin–nothing. Oh, a small buzz once in a while, and now and then something like a bigger one, but on the whole, *nada*.

But this–*this* was different.

He'd come across it by accident.

It happened when he was lowering a young woman to the ground, her flushed cheeks from a night of partying going pale after he drained her. He let her down gently, placing her head on a discarded newspaper. And as he did so, he saw the bold line at the bottom of an ad:

EVENING HOURS 7-10 TUES-THURS, NO APPOINTMENT NECESSARY

He made note of the address–not a good neighborhood, which was a very good sign–and as soon as the sun was gone the next day, he began his surveillance. It didn't take long to add the place to his list of feeding grounds.

The rhythms of the business were not hard to discern. Its low-rent address told him who the practitioner catered to, what sorts of clientele the office served. That made no difference: he'd fed upon wealthy and poor over the centuries, nobles and serfs, bankers and laborers. The blood of the bottom 1% satisfied him as deeply as that of the top.

Besides, he told himself the night before his first meal, it spoke well of the clientele that they would use some of their limited resources–and time; if they were coming to such a service at night their days were

doubtless filled with dead-end jobs. He felt certain they all dreamed of finding a job with benefits–if you had insurance, you didn't have to come to a place like this. Some of them probably left and went on to third shift jobs, working until dawn.

Like me, he thought with a chuckle.

The night of the first feeding was cool, clear and moonless. It looked to be a slow night, but by eight thirty he'd selected his prey. A slender woman, mid-twenties he guessed, dressed in a uniform from some fast food chain or other, walking swiftly, a cloth pressed to her right cheek. She entered the building where the practitioner had his office.

A bit more than an hour later she emerged, still holding a cloth to her cheek, but moving more slowly.

He let her get half a block deeper into the shadows before he made his move.

He took her quickly, one hand over her mouth, the other pressing hard at the small of her back to tilt her backward; bending her and sinking his fangs into her throat the instant their needle-sharp points were fully extruded.

He knew from the first sip something was different. There was a tang, a hint of sweetness to her blood, a quality that flowed into him along with the nourishment that seemed to reach into his brain and cast him... not adrift–he had far too much self-control for that–but certainly afloat. He felt as though he were floating somewhere above reality. He could see himself as he finished feeding, draining the last drops of life from the young woman.

He was struck and, to be honest, touched, by the woman's final gesture. She had not struggled, and he saw a certain sleepy resignation in her eyes as he fed. But when he removed his hand from her as she died, she opened her mouth and slowly, almost sensuously, ran the tip of her tongue over her teeth, managing a slight smile as her life left her.

After disposing of her body in a culvert far enough from the hunting ground, he made his way back to his lair. The strangeness that had come into him with her blood lingered through his journey back to his sleeping place. He enjoyed it–he savored it, in fact. He had never felt anything

quite like it, a numbness that was nonetheless filled with awareness and sensation. He slept dreamlessly through the next day, his first dreamless sleep in a century, and awoke at twilight refreshed and wanting–

More.

Worried–fearing–the quality had been unique to the young woman, and that it died with her, he returned to his waiting place near the night office.

It was almost ten before he found his next victim, a portly man in a cheap suit who put up no struggle, and whose blood was even more highly laced with the special quality the woman's blood had given him. Stronger, richer, more redolent of dreamless sleep, more powerful.

A larger dose.

Only his experience and instincts kept him from drifting off before reaching his hideaway. Once there, he slept as he had never slept in centuries. When he awoke he knew he wanted–

More.

It was the anesthetic, of course. By the time he awakened after the sleep following his third meal–a young man of average weight who provided him with a medium, by what little criteria he possessed, dose of dreamlessness–he knew it with certainty.

What he didn't know–yet–was what to do with the knowledge.

The plan took two nights–and two meals–to formulate. Neither meal was wholly satisfying: the first night's blood held only the lightest dose; the second's, none at all. He dreamed for the first time in more than a week. But he also awakened knowing what he must do.

He waited in the shadows until nearly ten, until the last of the night's trade emerged from the office. For an instant he was tempted to defer his plan for another evening–the woman emerging from the office would make a lovely meal. He could tell by the slow, unsteady way she walked she was full of the stuff. It would be easy to–

No.

He had taken five here already. Those, combined with the night's activities, would spoil these hunting grounds for him. He would have to move on.

But not until he paid his own visit to the practitioner.

Once the woman rounded the corner and was out of sight, he left the shadows and walked to the office door. Another woman, in a white uniform, approached from inside just as he entered.

"Oh," she said, evidently startled. "I–we're closing."

He pressed a hand to his left cheek. "I'm in some pain," he said. "I was hoping–"

"I'm sorry," the woman said. "We're–"

"Jean?" a man's voice called from the corridor that led off the waiting room. "What is it?"

"A walk-in," she said. "I've explained we're closing, Doctor."

"I think we can squeeze one more in," the doctor replied. He stepped into the corridor and nodded. "Put him in room three. You can take down his information and give him a preliminary look. Then go ahead and lockup. I'll be in shortly."

The doctor stepped back into a room. There was the sound of a door closing.

"This way," the woman said. "Follow me."

He could already smell what he had come for–its scent clung to the woman in white, wafted in minute traces through the air.

The dental technician seated him in an examining chair in a windowless room, flanked by the tools of the practitioner's trade. The many-armed mechanical assistant with its drills and brushes and attachments, the spit-bowl with its constantly swirling jet of water, the paper-covered tree with its array of shiny instruments, and–

The tank.

The tank with its flexible tube that culminated to a simple mask–the mask that had covered the mouths and noses of those whose blood had delivered him to dreamless sleep.

The dental technician leaned over him and said, "Open please."

The scent of the gas clung to her clothes, her skin. He could smell it even through the latex gloves she'd donned for the examination. He breathed deeply and looked up at her. The technician's neck was long

and graceful, her steady pulse showing in her throat. He felt his fangs beginning to extrude.

"Please open," she said again, more firmly, almost wagging the long-handled dental mirror at him.

He opened and she placed the mirror inside his mouth, moving it from one side to the next in search of a reflection he knew she wouldn't find.

After a moment, the technician said, "Huh." She showed a small frown and tapped the mirror, lightly, against each of the fangs. "I'll have to get the doctor to take a look at this. He'll be right in." She left the room and closed the door behind her.

He was able to sit still for only a moment before twisting in the dental chair and leaning close to the tank.

Slowly, unable to resist, he lifted the mask and held it to his mouth and nose, breathing deeply, taking into himself every atom of the gas that lingered on the interior of the mask.

It wasn't enough.

He reached with his right hand for the valve at the top of the tank. He would twist it just a little, just enough to take the edge off. Not too much–he wouldn't take too much–not when he had the dentist and his technician to deal with. He would take a whiff, just a whiff and no more, and then he would feed upon the dentist and the technician, and then–

He would leave, and take the tank with him.

He twisted the valve, savored the hiss as the gas began to flow, held his breath for an instant, then opened his nostrils slightly, felt the sweet bite of gas and couldn't help himself.

He breathed deeply once, twice, a third time before mustering enough strength to close the valve. He drained the mask of the last of the gas, then slumped back in the chair.

I have a problem, he thought, and would have laughed were it not for the need to gather all of his instinct and experience to deal with what he must do before leaving and returning to the safety of his lair.

He tried to lift himself from the chair when the door opened and the dentist entered, followed closely by his technician.

The dentist beamed at him, and turned to the young woman.

"You see!" the dentist said. "None of them can resist. Your kind just don't have it in you, do you, my friend?"

The dentist stepped close and leaned down.

"Can't move, eh?" he said softly. "Too bad–the door's made of silver. I'd have liked to have seen your face when you made *that* discovery. But not to be, not to be."

In the chair, the patient felt dreamlessness calling to him, drawing him in. There was nothing he could do.

"You're my sixth, you know," the dentist said. He took a small vial from the pocket of his jacket and held it close to the patient, rattling its contents: ten perfect fangs. "Yours will be eleven and twelve–an even dozen for my collection!"

He placed the vial back in his pocket, and took two latex gloves from a box on the implement tray.

"Now," the dentist said cheerfully, "would you hand me my extractors, Jean?"

BE
SEATED

KEITH FERRELL

BE SEATED

KEITH FERRELL

I

The chair had belonged for more than five decades (that I know of) to A_____, whose true name, because it would be known to a majority of you, and known *well*, notoriously, to a substantial percentage of that majority, shall only be hinted at here. If you know the person of whom I write, you will understand my circumspection. If you know him well, you are undoubtedly thinking I have said too much even in these few words.

But I have a wish to have my say, and if I am unwilling to use his full name, I will endeavor to hold back nothing else. I am not afraid of A_____. What can he do at this point? Kill Me? Hardly.

He was, as you will see, fond of me.

2

I never sat in that chair while A_____ was present, nor have I seated myself in it for more than a second or two since it came into my possession. It was A_____'s territory alone, from the carved, clawed feet at the bases of its sturdy, gently curved legs, to the leather upholstery of its seat and back, to the broad armrests upon which A_____ never chose to rest his arms. No one among his guests ever saw him place a fingertip upon the armrests. Perhaps he did so when he was alone.

But when there was someone present, A_____ kept his hands in constant motion, gesturing, finger-pointing, clapping his palms together for emphasis (not applause; none of us who knew him could imagine ever receiving his applause), never resting, never settling for so much as an instant upon the armrests.

Those in attendance to him, though, gave the armrests of their own, lesser chairs a workout. We held on tight once the Friday evening show began.

Once, a woman of my acquaintance, drawn to A_____'s circle by her own interests and proclivities, was invited to join one of A_____'s Friday evening salons by someone other than me. *Salon* was A_____'s word for the gatherings; those who attended, and those who only heard rumors, gossip, whispers, had other names for them.

I never found out if my acquaintance had a word for what she witnessed that Friday night. She was immobilized from the moment A_____ began the incantations that played so large a part in the evenings. I watched as my acquaintance gripped the armrests of her chair. Her knuckles grew white with the force of her grip, her shoulders shook as she sought to hold on harder and harder, as though she felt that relaxing her hands even an iota would result in her being ripped from the chair in which she sat, and flung from it, from the room, perhaps from the very world itself.

She would not let go of the armrests, not even after A_____ had completed the evening's rituals and the dark reverences that accompanied them, and descended from the point high above the table to which he and his chair had floated. He watched the rest of his guests with a mixture of bemusement and annoyance as we gathered around my acquaintance and endeavored to pry her fingers loose from the arms of the chair, an exercise that took several minutes and came close to removing all bemusement from A_____'s demeanor.

When we finally got her hands free, and lifted her from the chair-her clothing, a silk blouse and cotton slacks, were sodden with sweat-her eyes remained open and unblinking, focused on A_____. She continued to stare at him until we lifted her and carried her from the room.

My acquaintance never spoke again after what she saw, and is to this day residing in a home for the mentally disabled. She has developed an ability to work with wicker, reweaving the seats and seatbacks of chairs, but only those lacking armrests.

3

Why did I attend the salons?

Why, after the first one, after I knew what took place in A____'s presence, did I continue to attend, to sit with others in obeisance to A____ and his ceremonies? I knew what he was–why did I continue to go to him?

I have asked myself those questions countless times, always on my way to a gathering of the salon, and more intensely afterward. The questions were rarely far from thoughts in the times between salons, but only recently have I settled upon an answer that I find acceptable if far from satisfactory:

Why did I assume I was given any choice?

4

How many salons did I attend over the years while A____ was in residence in our community?

I could answer that question with relative ease: I keep a detailed daybook of my appointments, expenses, activities, events and occasions, dalliances and diversions (fewer of those than my own reputation would seem to promise).

I could go through the pages of my daybooks, one for each year of the past half century. I could tally the salons. I could arrive at a number.

I won't, for I am already in possession of a better answer, and a more accurate one.

I never missed one of A____'s salons; not once in fifty years did he host a gathering at which I was not present. No one else could boast such a total, such a display–a *demonstration*–of devotion.

The number in total, the tally of my attendances?

One.

Looking back, I can see now that there was only one salon: a single Friday night gathering, and it never ended until A_____ left our community and abandoned our communion.

5

A_____ gave us no warning, no hint, no intimation that he would be leaving us. Why should he have? Did any of us really think or even hope that he might show *us*, for whom he held such cordial contempt, any small courtesy?

Of course not.

He was with us and then he was not.

6

We discovered his absence on a Friday night, of course. There were no new guests in attendance, only the seven of us who had been members of the salon since the beginning.

As was our custom, we waited on the broad stone patio that ran the entire length of the left wing of A_____'s home. We waited, as we had waited there every Friday, until we all were gathered. Pleasantries were exchanged–the same pleasantries as were exchanged every Friday, which I now see was always the same Friday. The pleasantries touched upon the weather–we waited outside even on the most inclement of winter evenings, the better to be warmed by the great fire in A_____'s hearth, the even greater stagecraft emanated from him in his chair–and the passing of the seasons, and how untouched by their passing we all seemed to be.

And we were untouched. Fifty years of the same Friday evening and as though not one instant had elapsed since A_____ arrived.

We all knew why, but none of us said so, nor even skirted the broaching of the subject. We could look at each other and see that we had not aged.

None of us was willing to show the others a close enough or sharp enough gaze to let on that we also knew where our aging had gone, in whom it now dwelled.

7

When we were all in attendance and entered the house, we knew immediately that this, at last, would be a different Friday night.

There was no long table and sideboard spread with delicacies and wines and liqueurs, coffee and teas. A_____always set a bountiful repast. I was rarely hungry before the Monday following a Friday night salon.

There was no fire in the hearth, although the evening was chill for September.

There was no chair with its great carved clawed feet, although all of the other furniture remained in the room in which the salons were held.

There was no A_____.

8

We waited for over an hour before daring to leave the great room and explore, for the first time, the rest of the home. None of us, I believe, was searching for A_____. We had no expectation of finding him slumped at a desk, or disabled in bed or bath. We knew already that he was gone.

We found nothing.

The other rooms were completely empty, and gave no evidence of ever having been furnished or inhabited. There was no dust anywhere, no cobwebs.

Nothing.

9

If you followed the news, even tangentially, you are aware that a letter arrived at the local police department the following morning, carefully and beautifully handwritten. I had no doubt that it was written with a quill pen, but also no doubt that the pen was dipped in ink, not blood, as some of the more sensational news stories–and virtually all of the local gossip–implied.

The letter confessed–*boasted* is the word I, and all of the others who had known A_____, would have used–of certain long unsolved murders and disappearances, providing details that could only have been known to the person who committed the crimes. There was no doubt that the killer had written the letter.

But there was even less doubt that the killer *could* have written the letter, for some of the crimes had taken place more than a century in the past.

The letter was signed, with a flourish, simply A_____.

10

There was another letter, one the authorities knew nothing of, and it arrived, along with an immense packing crate, at my home on the first Friday after A_____ departed.

This letter, too, was beautifully handwritten, though far briefer than the one the police received. This one had no crimes to be accounted for, or at least none the police would have any interest in or understanding of.

The letter read:

I have felt for a time the desire for a change of venue, and as is my nature, I have decided to act upon my desires.

We will not meet again, as I suspect you already know, but in my absence I wish for you to have this not small token of my affection and esteem for you, my most loyal and unfailing of attendants.

A_____

The packing crate contained the chair, of course. I knew that without opening it and did not, in fact, open the crate for nearly three weeks after signing for its delivery.

Once I did open the crate, I was startled to find how perfectly the chair fit into my parlor. It had seemed larger in A_____'s home and the great room the chair dominated.

In my home it seemed smaller. Only after I sat in it for the first time did I realize that it was not smaller at all, but rather was perfectly suited for my own shape and size.

For me.

II

I waited another week before sending out the first of my invitations, writing each of them carefully and by hand, though with a fountain pen.

Of the six invitations I sent out, I received six responses in the affirmative.

Which did not surprise me.

12

Nor was I surprised, and certainly not displeased, when my guests congregated on my porch, each clearly willing to be present before entering my home.

Inside, by my fireplace, I warmed my hands and made no move to ask any of them in early. There was time.

Soon enough, and without hesitation or regret, I would take my seat and assume my place of honor before those I invited to join my salon.

THE
MAN
WHO
KILLED
TEXAS

STEPHEN GRAHAM JONES

THE MAN WHO KILLED TEXAS

STEPHEN GRAHAM JONES

B aylock heard about it on the radio first: Jackson, Mississippi had fallen.

America was coming down like dominoes.

It was unconfirmed, but there were reports the cough had made it to Lincoln, Nebraska, as well, and there was talk on top of that about Air Force bombers gliding through the clouds on silent wings. Because maybe a solid line of chemical fire could stop the cough from spreading.

The good news was that the animals weren't carrying it yet. Baylock knew that as soon as a cat or a squirrel showed up bloody-mouthed and hollow-eyed, though, well, that was it for the human race, pretty much. Only way to fence a cat or a squirrel in is to shoot it, but good luck with that.

Baylock's guard booth wasn't really a booth. It was a flatbed equipment trailer with a sixteen-foot camper rolled up onto the tracks where the backhoe was supposed to ride. They'd picked the trailer because, cocked sideways, it was long enough to bar the whole road. If you had a truck with mud tires, Baylock figured you could probably chug your way around the tongue of the trailer over in the ditch, but that would be a narrow pass between the tongue and the fence, and forty-inch lugged tires, they like nothing better than spooling up eighty or a hundred feet of barbed wire before you can get your foot out of the accelerator.

The ditch on the back side of the trailer was clogged with a bushy oak Baylock had chainsawed to pieces, day one.

The road was the Myrtis Texas Line Road, at least on the maps that went into that much detail. East of McLeod, South of Texarkana. For Baylock, before he'd grown up and started working, it had always just been Lake Road: what his dad would drive one Saturday a month, to take them fishing in Louisiana.

Standing guard over it now, late in the day so his shadow could be dramatic, *epic*, Baylock felt a little like Bowie and Crockett at the Alamo. He had drawn a line in the sand and was looking over it, saying this far but no more. It was one of hundreds of lines drawn by the new militia, roused into action by the radio broadcasts. But–and he wouldn't say this to anybody, except maybe his brother Stubs, and only then deep in the night, a pyramid of cans on the tailgate–what he really felt like was that he was protecting his childhood. He was preserving all those Saturday morning drives, his dad letting him and Stubs ride in back after they were out of sight of the house, where their mom couldn't call them back.

Back then Stubs had still been Reddy, after their dad, but even at ten he was already due to lose the two outside fingers on his left hand. He was already due to be Stubs for the rest of his life.

Baylock didn't even like fish, unless it was fried in a deep fryer with cornmeal, and even then he required ketchup and an open mind.

It never had been about the fish, though.

Baylock kicked at a dandered-up spider web running down from the flatbed's trailer to the side of the tire. It gummed on the toe of his boot.

Jackson had fallen, the radio had said. And Jackson was the gateway to Louisiana.

Shreveport would be next. And then, at twenty-eight, Baylock would become an only child. And not an uncle anymore either. Or a brother-in-law.

Just a guy standing with a deer rifle on a flatbed trailer.

So far he'd only had to shoot into the blacktop in front of three cars and one truck.

The radio broadcast had told him and the rest of the militia to pop the radiators as warning, to show they were serious about this quarantine, but he couldn't bring himself to strand anybody in this heat.

If the cars or trucks *kept* coming, then the militia was cleared to shoot through the windshield. For Texas.

She'd survived Spain and Mexico and the United States.

Now if she could just hold her breath until November, when the cold would tamp down the cough. But the cough was more of a grass-fire, Baylock could tell. He wasn't a doctor or a scientist, but he knew that when you're caught out in the open with the wind pushing smoke at you, what you had to do was pull up all the yellow grass around you, then ball up on the bare dirt that's left, hide your eyes and your hair. If you were lucky, the fire would just scorch you when it passed by, not bake you like a potato.

Florida was littered with potato husks.

That was where it had all got going. Spilling up from a cruise ship, as near as anybody could tell.

It started as just some redness at the edges of your eyes, and a cough you never would have thought to pay attention to.

That was just what you could see, though. What you could hear.

Inside, it was turning you to slurry. The closest thing to compare it to–they didn't say this at the meetings at the Baptist church or on the radio broadcasts, but Baylock had seen it enough times to know–was parvo, like a dog'll get.

Baylock had had to put two dogs down with that in his life, both of them inside a single year, because parvo works its way into the dirt, and doesn't leave.

And now Jackson, Mississippi had it.

Now I-20 had it.

The cough had hit a main artery.

Baylock squinted east along the blacktop, the butt of his rifle planted on the toe of his boot so the rubber pad wouldn't crud up on the hot asphalt.

His and Stubs' dad had always told them that there was a monster alligator living in Black Bayou Lake. And then he'd push the three of them out in the little aluminum boat, and the grim way he looked over the bow, like he was watching for those two leathery eyebrows to crest the surface of the water–eyebrows two *feet* from each other–Baylock's heart would thump so hard in his chest he didn't know if it was joy or terror. He didn't know if he wanted to see Moss Head float up beside them like a giant dirty log someday, or if he wanted him to stay a story.

Looking east toward the lake, now, he was thinking about that giant gator spider-walking like they do, like trying to touch the front and back feet together on each side, each step. Moss Head's toes would be spread wide for grip in this strange, alien world, his mouth open from the effort. Open and ready for whatever.

It made Baylock's heart thump all over again.

If cats and squirrels weren't carrying the cough yet, it was a fair bet reptiles weren't either. But if Moss Head was abandoning his ancestral home, there had to be a reason, didn't there? Would it mean the west side of Jackson, Mississippi had tried to beat it out of town at the last moment, fifty thousand cars battling for pole position, and the bridge had collapsed over the lake, clogging those waters with the dead?

But wouldn't that be a buffet for Moss Head?

Unless he knew better. You don't live two hundred years by being stupid.

Baylock pulled the rifle up to his shoulder, found the crosshairs in his scope, imagined pushing one single slug through the right eyeball of a giant gator. The shot that saved Texas. He'd go up on the wall with Sam Houston, with Stephen F. Austin, with whoever that astronaut had been. They'd measure Moss Head by how many yellow stripes he stretched out between, and the stink of his rotting corpse would keep Mississippi's refugees from Texas.

Here, a dragon had fallen.

Here, a knight killed a dragon.

If Moss Head couldn't pass, then who could?

Baylock pulled his finger against the trigger guard, made the sound effect with his lips, then lowered the rifle to study the road.

There was still nobody.

It meant the bridge *had* fallen. Maybe the Army had bombed it, even, like they had I-10 west of Tallahassee. If they were smart they'd bombed it, Baylock corrected. If they really wanted to keep the east east, the west west. If the bridge was still standing, Baylock would have been drilling slugs into the tacky blacktop ever since lunch. Since he hadn't, that meant the Army was on his side. That he was on theirs. That the radio broadcast hadn't been lying about armed citizens' obvious duty.

Baylock went back into the trailer. He balanced a once-frozen burrito onto the camp stove. It involved peeling the paper off and re-wrapping the burrito in foil and turning it every thirty seconds. The trick was getting the center warm enough. But that had always been the trick, even at a gas station microwave at two in the morning. In between one of those turns, he keyed open the two-way's mic, said, "Lake Road Post, checking in."

Lonny was sitting right there, said back, "Check." If not for his wheelchair, he'd probably have Baylock's post.

"Heard from Thomas?" Baylock asked.

Thomas was the south post. He claimed his two-way had been janky from day one, but, too, Baylock knew he'd brought a .22 as well as a real rifle, so he could plug squirrels out in the trees.

"He's good," Lonny said, clipping his words short like always, like that would save Baylock's battery.

"Six hours," Baylock said, signing off.

"Midnight," Lonny said back, and then, because there was no one to say otherwise, Baylock allowed himself a second beer of the day and sat on the edge of the trailer in the unforgiving sun, his legs swinging like a kid, and ceremoniously ate the burrito.

This was good, he told himself.

He'd been thinking about calling in to work this week anyway.

Now, now there wasn't even going to *be* any work. Nobody was going to be ordering pipe and two-hundred pound drill bits for a generation or

two, he figured. The world was about to get a lot more hand to mouth. If you knew where to find the deer, if you knew where the good watering holes were, well: it was all going to matter in a new way, now. A better way.

But first they had to keep Texas Texas.

The rest of the world might go to hell, but Texas would stand strong.

Baylock went on patrol. It didn't say to do this on the radio. It was something he'd figured out himself, tying his empty beer cans on baling wire and unspooling that wire through the trees, so an alarm would ring if anybody tried to swing wide on foot. You couldn't space the cans out, though, he'd found. Even if you put gravel in them. They rattled great when you shook them by your ear, then not at all on the wire. What you had to do was tie the cans in clumps, like wind chimes. That way they'd clink against each other, their hollow spaces full of sound. When Baylock got asked to say something for the radio broadcast, he was going to tell about the cans, and then everybody would be doing it.

He should have thought to bring some plastic owls, too, like you use to guard a stand of grapes. People are spooked by an owl watching them. Superstitious. They'll keep turning to clock that owl, and then walk right into a tangle of wire and cans.

Next time. Next plague.

Baylock smiled, covered it with the crook of his hand like there was anybody to catch him being evil.

A third beer, then. He deserved it.

The supply run was coming on Sunday anyway.

Baylock howled something that didn't even count as a word out into the last part of the day.

Another howl answered him.

Baylock stood, wary, not completely sure he wasn't imagining this. Was that something that happened, when you hadn't talked to another soul face-to-face for six days in a row? Did you start making up voices, to keep the lonely away?

If so, Baylock's imaginary friend, he sounded just like him.

He scanned the road, the trees.

No one, nothing. No car, no truck, no tank. No monster gator flopped up from legend onto the unsuspecting bank of the world.

But it hadn't been any damn echo, either.

Baylock squinted what he considered his gunfighter squint, nodded so it would appear he'd decided something, that he was resolute, and then right when he stepped down from the flatbed there was a hard *whap* behind him, that turned his step-down into something between a fall and a jump and a yip.

He looked back. There was a new perforation in the camper. A bullet hole, drilled right through what he knew had been his silhouette one single step ago.

Baylock hit the asphalt on reflex, his skin crawling with crosshairs, and rolled back under the trailer, keeping his rifle between him and this shooter.

Three feet to his left, the rear set of the thick-walled trailer tires popped at the same instant, and then the report of a rifle rolled down the road.

The trailer tilted just enough for Baylock's beer up there to tip over, spill down over the edge.

Then the front set of dually tires of the trailer burst as well, both at once again.

It was deafening, left Baylock where he couldn't pinpoint where the reports might be coming from. That both tires were popping at once, though, that meant the shooter was lying down as well, that he had a straight-through line, that he was shooting level with the blacktop.

That he was right at Baylock's level.

He kicked deeper under the flatbed. He was trembling. It was stupid enough he heard himself laugh once, a quick bark that sounded almost like crying–the same sound he'd once heard a woman make at a funeral.

He shimmied deeper under the trailer, knees of his pants be damned. Deep enough he could feel sunlight on the heels of his boots.

Now he was a dog hiding under the coffee table.

Better than a *shot* dog, though.

Twenty minutes later, the sun bobbing on the horizon, just after Baylock had rolled over sideways to piss in a runnel that tried to come back on him, a fifth or sixth grader came walking up the yellow stripes, his hands held up the whole way. No rifle, no pack. Just a sandy-headed kid, his face dirty above the paper mouth-masks everybody was supposed to be wearing.

Still.

Baylock leveled the gun against the boy and shot just to his right, close enough that the kid had to have felt the suck of air.

The boy flinched like anybody would and fell to his knees, jarring his slight frame, but he kept his arms up, like he was insisting on something here.

"Go back, go back!" Baylock yelled from his dark cave.

He was yelling it for him and for the boy both.

This wasn't any dragon of an alligator.

This was worse.

If the boy kept walking–*don't, don't*, Baylock tried to will down the yellow stripes–then Baylock wasn't going to have any choice. This was his station, this was his post, this was his place to guard. He was the last line. It was the boy, or it was Texas.

But still.

Putting one through a kid, Baylock already knew it wasn't a thing he'd ever be able to shape into words proper. Instead he'd swallow it down deep and keep it there until it grew into a tumorous pearl he would choke on someday, trying to spit it up.

If he got to live that long, that is.

If the cough didn't spore up from the boy's chest when Baylock shot him. If the wind didn't catch those germs, sigh them over the state line.

"*Go away!*" Baylock called out.

The boy was crying, and he'd peed his pants. He'd been walking for days, it looked like. Ever since the news washed up from Florida, probably.

Goddamn those cruise ships. Fucking Petri dishes of the water, Baylock knew. All the radio stations were saying it, how we should have known better.

It was too late for that now, though.

Now there was the boy. Now there was this day. Now there was this part of the road.

"Where's the gun?" Baylock called out.

The boy just shook and cried and blubbered something Baylock couldn't get heads nor tails from.

And then he coughed once inside his paper mask, twice, and doubled over from it.

Baylock closed his eyes.

There *was* a dragon here today.

Baylock *did* have a duty to fulfill.

He scooted forward on his elbows, stabbed his rifle out past the flattened tire, his head just past the lip of the trailer now, and he settled the delicate crosshairs on the boy like he'd known he was going to have to. Like he either hoped every other guard along the state line was having to do, or like he hoped no one would ever have to do again in the whole history of man.

"I'm sorry, kid," he said, and just as he started to empty his lungs the way his brother had taught him more than half a lifetime ago, a cold finger pushed into the hollow at the base of his skull.

Baylock hissed through his teeth, straightened his trigger finger back out.

"You're the father," Baylock said, seeing it all now–the bait, the trap. How they'd gotten past roadblock after roadblock. Why they'd shot the tires out: so the trailer wouldn't move over his head, after they drove him under it. So it wouldn't shift when whoever this was climbed up onto it.

It had just been a waiting game. One Baylock had never been going to win.

"Guess I'm more than just his father," a voice Baylock knew said back, but he had to peel through half his childhood to pin it down.

"Stubs?" he said, and rolled over to be sure.

Stubs.

Baylock hadn't seen him in probably two years, but you don't forget your big brother.

But neither do you forget a rifle barrel nestling into the base of your skull.

Stubs clumped down from the trailer, his hair wild, his clothes rags, his rifle held clear of his leg to keep it from going off. Meaning it really had been ready to.

He lowered a hand to Baylock, to haul him up.

"Of all the gin joints," he said. "Or'd you plant yourself out here special to welcome me? What other road would I come home by, right?"

"You got out," Baylock said, still trying to make this make sense.

"If you can call it that," Stubs said. "We'll know about this time next year, reckon?"

Baylock nodded, shrugged. This was all still too much. He needed to sit down.

"How?" he said, leaning against the trailer with his butt. It had been a few inches too tall for that before.

"How'd we clear out of the Shreve?" Stubs asked.

Baylock nodded. That would be a start, anyway.

"By not being there," Stubs said. "Had the boy out shining flash-lights on suitcases"–spotlighting alligator, a trick their dad had taught them–"when I tried to tune in the game."

"They canceled it," Baylock said, rubbing at his lips with the back of his hand.

"Sounds like *we're* the ones getting canceled," Stubs said.

Baylock leaned over to spit, then rubbed it into the asphalt with his boot. "You mean you've been hoofing it the whole way here?" he said.

"Hook, crook, whatever it took," Stubs said. "And we're coming home, let me tell you. That's what you do in times like this. You get to where matters."

Baylock scratched a spot below his right eye and studied the boy out there who must be Sawyer.

"I didn't even recognize him," he said.

"They grow fast, this age."

"What about Gracie, and Anna, and Rocko?"

Stubs didn't answer, and that was answer enough.

"So they put you out here?" Stubs said, impressed, either with Baylock or with his own luck.

"Volunteered," Baylock said, shrugging like it was nothing.

"And you gonna fall for this bullshit trick again?" Stubs said, reaching around to slap Baylock on the back of the head, make him twelve years old again.

Baylock shook it off.

Sawyer was still out there, hands up, mask over his mouth. For all he knew, his dad was negotiating their passage with some stranger, Baylock figured. For all he knew, the rifles were still in play.

"What's procedure for y'all now?" Baylock said, about Sawyer. "What comes next in this little operation?"

"We're in uncharted territory," Stubs said. "You're unconscious at this point. Just conked, not shot. We're loading up your beef stew in Ziploc bags, and taking your batteries, some water. And then we're gone. You wake up to stand watch another day. To stand *better* watch."

Baylock nodded. It felt like he was buying time, here. Like he was stalling.

"You know what this cough does to a person?" he said, peering up at his big brother.

"I know what it does to the *world*," Stubs said, no joke to his voice at all. "But no, we were ahead of it, I guess. Haven't seen it first-hand."

They stood there. There wasn't much else to say.

"So you going to offer us a drink, or we got to ask?" Stubs said, hopping up to sit on the trailer, his rifle leaned against it now.

"I heard him cough," Baylock said, pointing down the road with just his forehead.

"It's part of the act," Stubs said.

"I could have shot him."

"And I could have shot you. Tragic day all around."

"Tragic month."

Stubs raised his three-fingered hand to Sawyer, waved wide, bringing him in.

Sawyer stood, visored the setting sun from his face.

"He's a good kid," Stubs said. "Except for the parts that are like me."

Baylock studied his nephew. He was edging in a few steps at a time, unsure.

"It's your uncle Bay-Bay!" Stubs yelled, his hands cupped around his mouth.

Sawyer cocked his head over like letting the words drain in. But he'd heard. He lowered his mouth. His smile was still there. It was the same one Stubs used to get before a football game on a Friday night. Not because he played, but because that was when all the fights happened, under the stands.

"Listen," Baylock said, the first part of a speech he had no idea how to finish, "I'm not supposed–"

Before he could get into it, Sawyer had stopped again, was bent over, one hand on his knees, the other barreled in front of his mouth, to cough through. It was dry, hacking, deep.

"No," Stubs said, sliding down from the trailer, his whole body on alert for the next cough.

"Not him," Baylock said, his voice almost breaking.

When Stubs turned to Baylock, his eyes were already full.

Baylock had to look away, the lump in his own throat swelling to burst.

"Just go back," Baylock said in a voice he had to fake, taking his rifle under the action, hiking it up to his hip like a proper guard.

Stubs was breathing hard now, from the mouth.

It made him cough too.

Baylock turned to him slow, his rifle between them.

"But you stayed ahead of it," he said, in what he knew was a little brother whine.

"This is just–" Stubs said, but couldn't finish, even had to unfurl a bandanna from his pocket to cough into.

The bandanna had been white with black design. Now it had red design too. Days of it.

And when he shook it open, a bottle of Visine tapped down onto the ground.

No, it fell between them like a bowling ball. Like an anvil.

When Baylock looked up to Stubs about this, he was looking into Stub's upturned rifle.

"We just want to go home, Bay," he said, still coughing.

"I can't–" Baylock said, his own rifle coming up, the iron sight under Stubs's chin.

"You're protecting *what* anymore?" Stubs said around the rifle, and then Sawyer was there, edging in next to his dad, Stubs lowering an arm around the boy's shoulders.

"Texas," Baylock heard himself say. "I'm protecting Texas."

"You think there's state lines anymore?"

Baylock didn't have an answer.

"When was the last time you heard from anybody in town?" Stubs said. "It's already there, man. It's probably been there for a day or two."

"I can't let you pass," Baylock said, clicking the safety off.

"Come *home* with us," Stubs said. "I just want to see the place one more time, man."

Baylock breathed in, breathed out, the infection swirling into his lungs, he knew.

What if Stubs was right? What if town was already coughing?

But what if it wasn't.

"Let me just–" Baylock said, stepping back all at once, taking his rifle with him. "I've got a radio, I can just..."

He didn't finish because he was already climbing up onto the trailer.

"Do what you need to, little brother," Stubs said, Sawyer still clamped to his side, and Baylock left them like that, stepped through the small door of the camper.

Because his eyes weren't adjusted, he had to feel around on the counter, spill the forks and spoons onto the floor then try to step around them.

Before keying the mic on the two-way open he shut his eyes, in prayer. That Lonny would answer. That someone not coughing would answer. But then, the mic open so he could announce himself, he shut it again, dropped it onto the counter.

He pulled himself back to the still-open door, so what he feared could be just that: him being afraid; him not trusting his brother.

Him not being the guard he'd promised to be.

There was no one standing on the Louisiana side of the trailer now. Just Stubs's rifle, leaned up where he'd been.

Baylock raced around to the side of the camper.

Stubs and Sawyer were booking it down the center stripe, their inside legs moving together like a potato sack race at the fair, Stubs having to carry Sawyer every few feet when he near fell down from coughing.

"No," Baylock said, and then looked down to the rifle he didn't remember having picked up on the way through the door. "Stop," he said, but it wasn't loud enough for Stubs and Sawyer to hear.

He was talking to himself.

But he was doing it anyway, through his tears.

Because it was kinder, he settled the crosshairs on the back of Sawyer's head first. The scope had enough magnification that Baylock could see all the way back to when Stubs first brought Sawyer around, before the kid was even a year old. He could see all the way back to Sawyer at five, sitting in the bed of his granddad's parked truck, Stubs back there with him, telling him this was where him and his punk little brother used to ride on weekends, going fishing. Back when the truck ran.

Back before everything.

"No, no, no," Baylock said, and pulled the trigger before he could stop himself.

The rifle bucked against his shoulder once, with finality, and Sawyer's face splashed out ahead of him and Stubs, the red mist hanging in the air like a last breath. Like a last cough.

Baylock raised the rifle to chamber another round.

What he was ready for was leading Stubs as he zigged and zagged down the blacktop.

It wasn't happening like that, though.

Stubs was on his knees, had caught Sawyer before he could even fall all the way. He was holding what had been Sawyer's head to his chest, holding tight enough that the inside fingers of his three-fingered hand were going into the new cavity, even.

"Reddy James Baylock," Baylock said, in respect, in farewell, in thanks, and then he pulled the trigger again.

Twenty years ago, his brother had lined their dad's beer cans on the top rail of the fence, to teach Baylock how to shoot.

Baylock never forgot.

His shot caught Stubs right at the hinge of the jaw, right in front of the ear.

Because going sideways through a skull is less of a job than pushing through from the front—animals are made to charge, are built to take abuse from the front—and because a slug from a deer rifle is so fast, Stubs didn't even get thrown to the side, slapped to the asphalt.

He just wavered there, holding his son, his mind somewhere else now. His mind splashed over the center stripe of Lake Road.

Baylock turned away before he could fall. He collapsed against the other side of the camper, pushing the rifle as far away from him as he could, until it clattered off the side of the trailer.

He was crying through his mouth, through his eyes, through his face.

And then he stood all at once, with resolve.

He went back into the camper, pulled the mic hard to his mouth, closed his eyes to make it really count, and said, "Anybody there? Anybody? Lonny?"

He released the button, let the empty static roll in, wash over him.

His hand was shaking, his nose was running, and his lips were trembling.

"Lonny?" he said again, weaker, pressing the mic into his forehead now.

Static. Nothing. It was making Baylock breathe too deep. It didn't mean he was getting too much air, though. There wasn't enough air in the world anymore. There weren't enough brothers, either. Enough nephews.

He took a step away from the radio and the forks on the floor scattered ahead of him and he caught himself on the counter, realized he was throwing up a few moments after it was already happening.

It was only when he became aware of a sound that he realized he'd been deaf since shooting.

It wasn't a sound so much as a feeling, though.

He looked up, wiped tendrils of vomit away on the back of his arm, the fingertips of his other hand still to the floor of the camper.

What they transmitted up to him was a trembling, a vibrating–an *engine*.

Baylock smiled, knew who it was going to be: his dad. His and Stubs's dad.

They were going to the lake, weren't they? Was it Saturday already? It was, yes. Definitely.

Baylock pulled himself up into the bright doorway, was going to climb down into that pickup bed and go with, he knew. He was going to shut his eyes against the wind, the truck going faster and faster.

Maybe he would learn to like fish this time.

No, he *would* like fish this time, he told himself, and stepped out into the last of the sunlight to keep that promise.

The road leading out of Texas, it was empty.

The one behind him still had two bodies slumped together, holding onto each other. One without a face, one with a hole plowed through from ear to ear.

Baylock looked past them, though.

"Dad," he said, and jogged a couple of steps like he'd just missed the truck.

He went off the side of the trailer, bloodying his knees and his hands, his chin and right shoulder, but it didn't register. He stood just as fast, the smile on his face red now, and he loped on ahead, for home, not stopping at the bodies, only slowing down a rifle shot or so later, when the coughs racked up from deep inside him, spattering dark splotches onto the back of his arms, driving him down onto his hands and knees to try to get it all out, his back humping over from the effort, his eyes feeling like they were going to burst, his shadow in the ditch not his own anymore, but the dark outline of a monster, a beast from the deep, one coming west hand over hand, into Texas.

Far above a buzzard floated in lazy circles, a taste on the air it knew.

SCARECROWS

JOSHUA VIOLA

SCARECROWS

Joshua Viola

"**T**hat's mine," Cody said, hoping he sounded tough–if he did, maybe he wouldn't have to take them on. "Give it back."

The tough tone didn't work. "Newbie wants his little cap back," Rich, a senior and the biggest of two kids said, sneering. He held Cody's cap high, higher than Cody could reach.

"Give it back to me now," Cody said.

"Or what?" said Joey, the other kid. He was smaller than Rich, but not by much, which still made him bigger than Cody. "You gonna fight Rich for it? Be a big mistake, cap-boy. Maybe the last one you'd get to make. Ain't that right, Rich?"

Cody felt his stomach tighten, and hoped he wouldn't puke. He felt tears trying to rise too. Cody thought puking would be better than crying, but he didn't want to do either, not in front of those assholes. All he wanted was to get his cap back.

His dad's cap. It had the Atlanta Braves *A* on it, but they never called it the Braves cap. It was the *Chemo Cap*. Cody had been with his dad, not long after Dad's hair started falling out. He'd helped Dad pick it out. For a while they'd thought about something with a funny or positive saying on it, or a stupid drawing, but finally Dad had thrown an arm around Cody's shoulders and pulled him close.

"Y'know, Code, my man," he'd said, "let's go with Atlanta. Once we've got this thing beat, I'll treat you to the Braves in the World Series next year. All four games. They're going to sweep it. I've got a feeling."

The Braves didn't even make it to the postseason the next year, but they still did better than Cody's dad. He didn't make it even close to the start of the season. Last thing he did was put that cap on Cody's head. Cody never took it off, except he had to today–first day of school in a new town, and no caps allowed in class. But the minute the bell rang and he got outside, he'd put it on. Didn't even have time to get it settled just right–Dad wore it tilted a little to the left, and so did Cody–before Rich grabbed it.

"Well?" Joey said, his voice hard. "You gonna fight Rich for it or not?"

"No need to fight," Rich said, still holding the cap high like a pennant in a game of capture the flag.

"No," Cody said, "there isn't."

"Watch your tone," Joey said.

"Easy now," said Rich. "Let's all just settle down a little while I explain to–"

Cody waited a split-moment before saying, "Cody."

"Right. To Cody here that he doesn't have to fight for his little cap. Not that fighting would do him any good anyway. But there's no need. We're going to give Cody a chance to *earn* his cap back. Got a little job that even he ought to be able to handle."

"What kind of job?"

Rich leaned close, his nose almost touching Cody's. "Be at the baseball field tonight at midnight. Not one minute later."

Rich stood up and made a show of putting the cap on his own head. "If you're too scared to show up, don't sweat it. I sorta like the way this feels."

"Looks good on you, too," Joey said.

"Midnight," Rich repeated before he and Joey walked off laughing.

Cody waited until he was sure they–or anybody else–couldn't see him before ducking around the far corner of the school, finding some bushes, and puking his guts out behind them.

Cody snuck out his bedroom window and made it to the baseball field with a couple of minutes to spare before midnight. Rich and Joey were already there, leaning against Rich's red Mustang at the edge of the outfield. Rich was wearing the Chemo Cap. Cody hated the way the cap looked on him–it made him feel like he'd let his dad down. But he kept his anger hidden and walked straight to the two assholes.

"I want my cap back," he said. "What's the job?"

"Gonna set the night on fire," Rich said, lifting a gasoline can and shaking it.

Cody could hear the gas sloshing. When he stepped closer he could smell it. The smell made him want to hurl, but he was done with puking. He looked at the cap on Rich's fat head. He was ready to do anything to get it back. Now, watching Rich put the gas in the trunk, he wasn't so sure.

"Get in," Rich said. "Front seat–between us."

Cody got in. Rich started the car while Joey climbed in on the passenger side, digging Cody in the ribs with a hard elbow as he did. Cody gave him one back, more to see what would happen than to do any damage, and was surprised when Joey didn't do anything.

Rich put the car in gear and peeled across the outfield, the tires kicking up divots. Cody hoped there weren't any cops around–it was bad enough that Mom moved them to the sticks, farm country, to be near her sister, and bad enough had already been made worse by Rich and Joey, and would undoubtedly take another downward turn or two whenever they got wherever they were going. He didn't need a cop tagging him, along with Rich and Joey, for vandalism.

But there weren't any cops, or even a school night watchman nearby to hear Rich peel off, so they got away clean. Rich drove fast and had them outside the town limits in a few minutes, picking up speed as they headed out into farmland.

"You know about the Corn Witch?" Rich said.

"Jeez!" said Joey with a nervous laugh. "Gives me the sheebie jeevies just hearing that name."

"*Heebie jeebies*, you dumb shit," Rich said, no nervousness at all in his laugh. Only contempt.

"Heebie jeebies, okay then," Joey said. "Gave me them, too."

"Good. Have some more. Corn Witch. Corn Witch. Corn Witch."

"What's a Corn Witch?" Cody asked.

Rich raised his eyebrows and grinned, the Chemo Cap rising as he did, his face spooky in the dim light from the dashboard instruments. Cody hated him wearing that cap.

"Not what," Rich said. "*Who*."

"All right, whatever," Cody said. His voice sounded tougher. "Who's the Corn Witch?" He turned to Joey and said directly to him, "Stupid name. Corn Witch." He was sure Joey flinched when he said it.

"You won't think it's stupid if she ever gets hold of you," Joey said. "Will he, Rich?"

"No," Rich said softly. "He sure won't."

"Why's that?" Cody said.

"Because she hasn't fed for a while. For a *long* while."

"She'll be *real* hungry," Joey said.

"So what is it you want me to do? Burn the witch at the stake?"

"You couldn't get close enough," Rich said. "Nobody ever has."

"Never," said Joey.

"Why not?" Cody asked.

"She's... *protected*," Rich said.

Cody listened.

"She lives in an old house, a hundred years old, maybe two. She's lived there as long as anybody can remember, and maybe longer than that. Nobody knows because nobody's ever been to it. You can't get close because of the... *scarecrows*."

Rich said the word in what he must have thought was a spooky voice, but he just sounded dumb to Cody.

"She has a circle of scarecrows around her house, and they... protect her."

"Scarecrows?" Cody said, making the word sound as unspooky as possible. He thought about laughing out loud, but didn't.

"You heard me," Rich said. "And you'll see them in about five minutes, and you'll know what I mean, so just shut up until we get there."

The house was old, dark—power and telephone lines ran along the road, but made no trip to the house; *the Corn Witch lives off the grid*, Cody thought—set back from the road and surrounded by cornfields nearing harvest. Rich pulled the car onto the shoulder and wasted no time getting out. Cody followed. Joey took his time, and Cody suspected Joey would have preferred to stay in the car.

Rich popped the trunk and got the gas can; handed it to Cody. "Come on," Rich said, and stepped into the field, moving slowly among the tall stalks. Cody followed him close, but Joey held back several steps.

Cody's eyes adjusted to the darkness of the nearly moonless night by the time they reached the first scarecrow. Squinting, Cody saw the silhouette of another in the distance, and beyond that, the barest hint of another. He turned his head the other way and saw the same figures, links in the chain of scarecrows that surrounded the house.

Cody stepped closer to the nearest scarecrow. It looked like it had been there a long time. Somebody put a lot of trouble into making it, and had made it to last.

Rich tapped Cody on the shoulder and handed him a lighter. "Burn it down," he said. "Burn the fucker to the ground and you'll be one scarecrow closer to getting your little cap back."

Cody put the gas can on the ground and reached out to the scarecrow. He felt something like a shock when his fingertips touched the rough, weathered fabric that covered the straw and corn shucks the scarecrow was stuffed with. The stuffing rustled and crackled, dry—it would burn fast. Cody pressed his hand more firmly against the scarecrow and the shock gave way to a warmer current of memory:

Cody and his father watching *The Wizard of Oz* when he was a little boy. Cody told his dad the scarecrow was his favorite. "Mine, too," Dad

had said. "Always has been, always will be." That was Dad, always had been, always would be–didn't need a cap for that.

"Burn it!" Rich said.

Cody reluctantly took his hand from the scarecrow and turned to face Rich. Joey was a few steps back–he wasn't going to get close to the scarecrow even before it was on fire.

"Burn it!"

"No," Cody said. He dropped the lighter on the ground.

"What?"

"You heard me. I said no. Fuck this. Keep the hat."

"You pussy. Scared little pussy! You ain't getting the cap back, and you're gonna be walking back to town."

"Beats riding with a couple of shits like you two," Cody said, and took a step past Rich.

"Burn it, you pussy," Rich said again.

Cody turned to him. "You want it burned, asshole, burn it yourself. Or are you afraid of the Corn Witch? Is that it? Too scared to burn it yourself? Who's the pussy in this field? Not me."

Cody stepped past Rich again. He heard the gas sloshing in the can when Rich picked it up, but didn't look back, just got ready to haul real ass in case Rich did something truly stupid like trying to douse him. Cody didn't think Rich would light him, but he wasn't completely sure, and was ready to run.

"You think I'm scared?" Rich said, almost shouting. "You think *I'm* the pussy? I'll show you who's the pussy."

The scent of gasoline grew stronger and Cody heard it splashing.

"Joey," Rich said. "Grab that lighter and give me a hand."

"Come on, Rich," Joey said. His voice weak. "Let's get out of here. I thought I heard something. Let's just go."

"Jesus! *Two* pussies walking back to town! Either get over here and give me a hand or you're walking!"

Joey didn't move.

Cody stopped beside Joey and turned to look at Rich. "Let it go," he said. "Keep the fucking cap and leave the scarecrows alone."

"Fuck the both of you," Rich said, and thumbed the lighter to life.

The scarecrow burst into flames when Rich waved the lighter under its chin.

Rich took a quick step back to keep from being burned, but he didn't move fast enough.

Engulfed in flames, the scarecrow's arms reached out and grabbed Rich. Blazing hands lifted him from the ground. Cody had never heard anything as horrible as Rich's screams.

The scarecrow raised Rich's writhing body high above its head and shook him hard three times.

Rich was still screaming when it threw him into the circle of scarecrows. Something dark and immense rose up and took Rich from the sky before he landed, and a moment later the screams stopped.

Cody and Joey ran.

Rich's car keys must have been in his pocket, so Cody and Joey walked back to town. It took them until nearly dawn, but neither of them spoke a word the whole way, any more than either of them had looked back to see how long the scarecrow flames illuminated the sky.

Cody snuck into his bedroom, but couldn't sleep. When he heard his mother stirring, he went through his own motions, showering, dressing, and getting ready for school. He told her he thought he'd ride his bike to school today, and she said she thought that sounded like a good idea.

Rich's Mustang was still parked on the shoulder of the road when Cody got to the cornfield. Cody laid his bike on the ground and stood still for a moment. In daylight it was easy to see how the scarecrows encircled the house. Cody took a deep breath and walked into the field.

The scarecrow, when he found it, showed no signs of having been burned. The fabric wasn't scorched, the arms, covered with flames last

night, bore evidence only of years–How many? Decades? Centuries?–of sunshine and rain, hot weather and cold, growing seasons and winter seasons.

There was no sign of the gas can, and Cody felt sure there would be no sign or trace of Rich anywhere in the field.

The only difference, the only thing that told Cody this was the scarecrow he'd seen last night, was the Atlanta Braves baseball cap that rested on its head.

Cody looked at the cap for a long moment, then reached up to adjust it so that it was tilted slightly to the left, the way that cap was meant to be worn.

The bike ride back to town didn't take anywhere near as long as the walk the night before.

走狗

ZǑU GǑU

MARIO ACEVEDO

走狗

ZǑU GǑU

MARIO ACEVEDO

The chime sounded, confirming the atmosphere checks were complete. Lights above the airlock flashed green, and the inner and outer doors of my Duzmier shuttle slid open. The planet's musty, stale air flooded the shuttle's exit foyer.

My nerves tingled with anticipation. Fellow astronauts have been interned for eight years here on Tau-Sigma Four, prisoners of our ill-fated war against the Duzmier. It was my job to start the process of bringing them home. I wondered in what state of health I'd find them, and what kind of reception awaited me.

I stepped into the murky, artificial light of the landing bay. A tall, slender man waited for me at the end of the ramp, and beside him, a standard helper robot balanced on its uni-roller. I recognized the man from the dossier Space Command provided. Ambassador Timothy Roach. Ambassador being a lofty term that Roach's kind bestowed upon themselves. The rest of us humans called them Zǒu Gǒu, Chinese for lackey, which better described their role between us and our Duzmier masters.

Though standing at an imposing 1.9 meters in height, Roach seemed unremarkable and meek. Zǒu Gǒu were typically portrayed as scheming, gnomish men, as traitors often are.

The tattered brim of a cap shaded his face, and weary blue eyes peered from within swirls of wrinkled skin on sunken cheekbones. A bedraggled mustache drooped

from the corners of his mouth. His thin frame sagged forward and gave the appearance of wasting away. His hands were gnarled and his fingernails chipped and grimy like a mechanic's, not what I expected from a servile bureaucrat.

His brown outfit was decidedly vintage. Oddly, he carried a pistol holstered to his waist. I smirked, as Zǒu Gǒu were fond of parading about like petty warlords.

Eight years ago the Duzmier arrived in our little neighborhood of the Milky Way. They tore through our solar system like avenging gods, seemingly omnipotent in their huge, gleaming ships. And for all our technology and pride, we humans were like pests in their newly found garden. Our defenses were as useless as gnats attacking a battleship. After six months, their conquest completed, the Duzmier armada moved on. Earth was left behind, a colonized wreck, our civilization broken and traumatized.

In the aftermath, people like Roach chose to accept the scorn of their fellow humans for the chance to ingratiate themselves at the feet of our alien overlords. Some ambassadors presided over the richest districts on Earth and lived like pampered royalty. Others, such as Roach, were assigned enclaves on distant, isolated planets.

Eleven months ago the Duzmier issued the repatriation order: their prisoners were to be collected and returned to Earth, which was why I was here.

I stepped down the ramp toward Roach. His gaze zigzagged from my face to my epaulets and down my body. His eyes lifted back to my face and he allowed a disarming grin. "My apologies, Colonel…"

"Colonel Amanda Nuñez," I replied.

"I know it's impolite to stare, but it's been a long time since I've had a visitor." He spoke with a stilted inflection, his English blended with a medley of accents from his library files. "Welcome to my humble corner of the Duzmier Empire, Amanda."

"Colonel Nuñez," I corrected to remind him I was here on official business.

His eyes cut to my left breast. "What is that insignia?"

"Chief Flight Surgeon Astronaut."

"Ahhh," he gasped in appreciation, betraying an ambassador's fascination with military accoutrements. "A colonel and a doctor. I am honored."

Like a true rat, his words were dishonest, his attitude contemptuous.

"If you don't mind, Ambassador, we have work to do," I said.

He led me down the steps of the boarding ramp. The interior of the landing bay looked like it hadn't seen recent use. Dust and oily patches covered the hydraulic servos that worked the roof panels and the docking cradle my ship had settled into.

Roach started out the door, and we tramped through a long corridor. The robot trailed at our heels like an obedient dog. From what I remembered during the landing approach, this corridor connected the landing bay with the main building, the only structures on the planet.

Once in the main building, I detected a greasy smell permeating the musty odor. Assorted machinery–lathes, presses, welding torches–rested on brick plinths. Tools and piles of junk littered the concrete floor, itself cracked and stained. Twisted ropes and rusted chains dangled from gantry hoists. Stacks of lumber and piles of sawdust added to the neglected, rustic ambiance. Though the building was large, it appeared more a cavernous maintenance shed than a prison.

I assumed a lot of repair work was going on. I hadn't thought what kind of custodial duties occupied Roach, who was posted here alone as an agent of the Duzmier. But I didn't imagine he did all the work himself, especially as he had scores of trained and highly capable astronauts at his beck and call.

I looked for evidence of the prisoners, either the astronauts themselves, or their bunks or possessions, but all I saw were broken-down machinery and discarded odds and ends.

He led me into his living quarters. The room brought to mind the lobby of a rundown hotel, furnished with scarred chairs and tables. The shabby carpet was rutted from years of Roach's footfalls. Scratches and dings marred the walls. Only a few of the overhead lights worked.

What caught my eye were pieces of wood assembled into abstract sculptures; Roach's doing, I was sure. They were bizarre works–some the

height of tables, others scraping the ceiling–parts going every which way and daubed in bright, random colors. The sculptures gave the impression of thoughts bursting in all directions but going nowhere, of desperate frustration. One resembled stocks to hold someone bent forward at the waist with shackles for the ankles and a neck hole, but strangely, nothing to restrain the prisoner's hands. I considered the assembly a metaphor for Roach's predicament here, and I realized he was at the heart of all things, a very lonely man.

But that was his problem. I wasn't here to psychoanalyze him. My mission was to evaluate the astronaut prisoners and relay my report to the repatriation team.

We passed through the living quarters and out a reinforced door to an empty lot. The glare reflecting off the smooth dirt blinded me. Roach and I donned sunglasses. Grassy, rolling hills dotted with trees surrounded the compound. This growth must've supplied the lumber.

Thankfully the air smelled fresher. A tall wire fence marked the perimeter of the lot, and in the distance, storm clouds gathered above the horizon. As I scoped out the compound, I still saw no evidence of anyone besides Roach. "Where are the prisoners?"

"Soon," Roach replied, evasively.

"What do you mean 'soon'?"

"Within a half hour. Then you'll see them."

Sensors and stun projectors topped the fence posts, facing outward. My mission briefing indicated the planet was a safe haven for the captives, not a concentration camp.

"Why do you need the fence?" I asked. "Isn't it just you and the prisoners?"

"It's a little more complicated than that," he replied without looking at me.

"Explain it then."

He gestured toward a hover cart. "When I show you, then you'll understand."

His vague answers only stoked my loathing of him. Maybe the gun on his hip was more than decoration.

The robot circled past us and clamped into a large bracket at the front of the cart. Roach and I occupied the center seats and buckled into safety harnesses. Like everything I'd seen so far, the cart bordered on junk. Rust-rimmed holes marked where rivets and bolts had broken loose and fallen away. Strips of tape and crudely applied patches mended the tattered upholstery.

Roach gestured with his hands, and a holoscreen materialized in front of us. A blinking orange light marked our position on the translucent map. Blue lights glowed in a cluster about three kilometers northeast of our location.

"Watcher drones," he said.

"For the astronauts?"

Roach didn't respond, and his silence infuriated me. But there was little I could do. He answered to the Duzmier, not to me or any other human.

Our cart lurched upward, skimmed over the fence, and cruised in the direction of the watcher drones. I studied the passing vistas, amazed by the progress that Duzmier terraformers made on this planet. It was originally just a rock and a few oceans of sterile water. What they made of it was nothing short of impressive.

We were on the southern tip of an island chain the size of Japan, which was overgrown with grasslands, dense thickets, and adolescent forests. I hadn't been told if the Duzmier transplanted fauna as well as flora. If so, the creatures may have mutated into something dangerous, but that didn't square with why the astronauts were outside the perimeter.

It didn't make sense.

We levitated over a wide, shallow valley, carpeted in lush pastures. The valley floor sloped toward a lake. The scene was surprisingly pastoral and serene but I couldn't shake my misgivings.

About a hundred meters above the rise, a small dot floated: a watcher drone. It glided toward us. A second one climbed to the left. Then a series of human heads appeared along the crest of the rise, men and women. Their heads bobbed up and down, rising, then exposing shoulders, then

chests, then complete bodies. They galloped naked over the rise like a herd of two-legged mustangs.

And they had no arms!

My nerves froze ice cold in horror and disbelief. Some of their torsos rounded smoothly from shoulders to upper rib cage. Others bore the bony nubs of clavicles that marked where their arms had been lopped off. Patches of armpit hair decorated their shoulders.

The cart drifted out of their way, and the runners stampeded past. We followed close beside the horde at an altitude of about five meters.

Manes of thick hair flopped on their heads, and woolly pubic hair covered their crotches. The men wore beards. Their complexions varied from bronze to ebony. Aside from the lack of arms, they were all excellent, toned specimens of the human form and sprinted with the athletic, effortless grace of wild animals. A few flicked glances in our direction.

Without warning, the group veered to the left, moving *en masse* like a school of fish. They darted to the right, again in perfect syncopation.

They thundered for hundreds of meters, never losing speed, never tiring. Nearing the lake, they slowed to a trot, then halted in the meadow along the water's edge. The herd milled on the grass, sweat glistening on their sleek bodies. Though their torsos bellowed from the exertion, none looked spent. The men loosed streams of piss. A couple of the women lowered into half-squats and also pissed.

I tallied their numbers, counting forty-five men and twenty-seven women. I recognized tattoos on many of them, confirming that this feral mob of armless and naked humans were my astronauts. I needed several moments to process the abominable scene–though I shouldn't have been shocked as the Duzmier committed many ghastly acts to us humans before. At last I managed to ask, "What happened?"

"An experiment," Roach answered. "The Duzmier wanted to test human resilience."

"So they chopped off their arms and set them loose like wild animals?"

"There was more to it than that." Roach coughed uncomfortably. "The Duzmier also removed their vocal chords. The point was to see if

the humans" –he said this as if he wasn't one of us– "could interact and build a society despite the handicaps. Quite ambitious, don't you think?"

I wanted to throw up. I wanted to gut-punch Roach and scratch his eyes out, but my duty was first and foremost to these astronauts, so I remained composed.

"We found humans to be quite adaptable. Once they got over the initial shock, they formed this herd."

"And the Duzmier make them run?"

"No, it's something the humans did on their own. Group therapy, I imagine." Without a trace of irony, Roach added, "Too bad they can't tell us why."

A group of ten wandered to the lake. They splashed through the reeds, wading to where the water was waist deep, bent over, and began drinking. One of the women knelt on the grass and angled her head. Another woman stood beside her and, balancing on her left leg, lifted the right and used her toes to groom the other's hair.

"What is most remarkable is how they learned to use their feet as hands and cooperate with one another. All without the use of spoken language."

The queasiness deepened. Roach sensed my distress and handed me a canteen. I accepted it reluctantly, thinking it would carry that pervasive, musty stink. But it smelled sweet and tasted refreshingly cool.

"The tall one," Roach pointed to an especially rangy astronaut, "is Number M-15."

He bore the tattoos of red lightning bolts across his chest. I said, "Flight Officer Commander McNeil. Use his name, not a number. Get closer."

"No. Don't be fooled. They are very dangerous."

"The fence around the compound, that's meant to keep them out?"

"For the first two years they acted docile," Roach explained. "I was walking among them when they attacked. They kicked me to the ground and M-15–Commander McNeil–jumped on top of me and bit me here." Roach slipped one shoulder out of his jacket to expose a crescent-shaped scar on his upper arm. He shrugged back into the coat. "Another time the hover cart malfunctioned and I had to hike back to the compound.

They chased me and I escaped only by locking myself in the building. I built the fence to keep them from sneaking in to wreck the place and kill me." Roach rested his hand on the butt of his pistol.

"And the Duzmier allow it?"

"They consider it part of the experiment. I'm not allowed to harm the humans, except in dire self-defense. And I mean *dire*." He raised his left hand and revealed a missing finger. "The Duzmier yanked it off as punishment for letting the prisoners get the better of me."

I would've yanked off more than his pinky. Feeling lightheaded and still queasy, I took another sip from the canteen to ease my troubled stomach.

"Look," Roach announced. Four of the astronauts clustered together, three men and one of the black women. One man began licking her breasts. Another nuzzled her from behind, while the third man began sucking the first man. Fully aroused, he sat on the ground and lay on his back. The woman straddled him. One of the other men lay between the first man's open legs and used his feet to guide the penis into her.

"This is unusual," Roach said. "They normally hide when they have sex. Watcher drones record them anyway." He pointed, enthusiastic. "They help each other with everything. It's a remarkable exercise in a cooperative culture."

Bile rose in my throat and I drank more water to wash it down. My priority was to help these astronauts. Then, if the opportunity presented itself, I would get revenge on Roach.

"What happens when the women get pregnant?"

"Offspring is the next milestone of the project, but alas, it eludes us. The Duzmier want to see how they will raise a normal child. But the prisoners figured out what the Duzmier were hoping for, so they did everything to frustrate them. If pregnant, the women try to induce a miscarriage. Two failed. One committed suicide by drowning herself and the other jumped off a cliff."

Roach said this so clinically I wanted to smash my fist into his face, but I was nauseous and clutched at my harness to remain steady. My mouth began to feel numb.

Something clunked against the belly of the hover cart. Something else zinged past my ear. Roach yelped and grabbed his head. When he

pulled his hand away, blood stained his fingers. McNeil and twenty of the others had snuck behind us. The armless astronauts clutched rocks with their toes and kicked toward us, flinging the rocks with impressive velocity and accuracy.

Roach hollered a command at the robot and we climbed out of range. Below us, the astronauts bounded up and down in a victory dance.

"See how cunning they are!" Roach explained. "They only screwed in front of us as a distraction."

My mind wobbled, and my hands and feet grew cold. The images of what I'd seen spun through my head in a dizzying kaleidoscope. I remembered one of the art assemblages from the main building. The one that resembled stocks. "You capture them, don't you?" I accused, rage bubbling in me but unable to find traction. "To rape them. You got those women pregnant!"

"They aren't the only ones trapped in this hell hole," Roach said. His eyes darted to the canteen.

The sweet taste from the water turned sour. *I had been poisoned.* I gagged and heaved but could vomit nothing. I tried beating Roach with the canteen but he wrenched it easily from my hand.

"You quisling bastard," I scrambled for his pistol. "I'm going to-" My thoughts fragmented. I pawed at his holster, but my hands and fingers seemed made of rubber. He swam in and out of focus as I asked, "And there's even more to this, isn't there?"

His voice drawled and faded. "These prisoners are not to be repatriated. The experiment continues."

His silhouette melted a gray haze and my thoughts—my memories, all sensations, everything that was me—smeared into the fog. I dissolved into nothingness.

Alternating darkness and light swung over my face, like I was whirling on a merry-go-round.

Pain seared one shoulder, then another.

My mouth was forced open, followed by pain inside my throat.

I floated upward toward consciousness...

And when I was fully aware and awake, I was running.

NEEDLES

JOSHUA VIOLA
& DEAN WYANT

NEEDLES

JOSHUA VIOLA & DEAN WYANT

Natalie slipped the needle into her arm. The relief was instant. The high, sickening, but everything she wanted. She released the tie-off and sat back on the sofa, awaiting the full kick-in. Her head rolled to one side and she observed Denver's lights beyond her apartment window. The colors coalesced into a single, unidentifiable shape. Natalie took a deep breath and drifted away.

Hours passed and she awoke. The world around her was cold, quiet and normal. Everything she hated. Natalie plucked the syringe from her arm and glanced at the needle that had so recently rested within her veins. It was the only thing capable of bringing comfort to her chaos. She pinched the edge of the needle, wiped away the blood, and placed it next to a small baggie and some condoms on the end table.

She'd see her friend again soon.

Again came sooner than even Natalie expected. She followed routine: syringe, high, sleep and then back to reality. But this time, after waking far later than usual, a heavy pain growled in the pit of her stomach and sent chills through her bones. She knew what was happening. She'd experienced it many times before. And with each withdrawal, her body only wanted more. She reached for the baggie.

Empty.

Natalie staggered to the kitchen and reached for the refrigerator, barely managing to pull it open. Small vials chimed inside a container in the door. She yanked a vial from the box, made her way to a nearby drawer and found *them*. Hands shaking, she pulled a syringe from its sleeve and filled it with liquid from the vial. She hoped she had the measurement correct, but her eyes wouldn't focus.

It'll have to do.

She sat at the kitchen table and stuck the small needle into her bare thigh. Naltrexone made its way into her system. Again, she felt better. And again, when she pulled the syringe away, she glanced at her friend.

He'd always been there for her, was always available when she needed him. Natalie appreciated that. Her syringes provided more affection than any man she'd ever known–and she'd come to know many in her line of work. But like all of Natalie's friends, they would, eventually, betray her. Someday, they'd leave her alone, to die.

Natalie looked at the clock above the kitchen sink and sighed. She was late for work.

He promised Natalie he'd get her high if they could go back to her place. Maybe have a drink. Maybe more. She needed to get high. It'd been hours since her last fix and she couldn't hold off much longer, so she agreed. Besides, he wasn't so bad. She'd fucked a lot worse for a lot less. And this one was a businessman, she was sure. Even more than that: a gentleman.

Natalie invited him inside. He dressed like he had money, and lots of it. He wore a three-piece Dormeuil suit and spoke with an accent she couldn't quite make out. And, unlike most of her Johns, he smelled nice.

"Have you ever done this before?" Natalie asked.

"Not like this," the man said, a slight smirk rising at the corner of his lips.

Natalie unbuttoned his collar and whispered into his ear, "I know just the thing to get us started."

She reached into his breast pocket and pulled from it a small baggie.

Natalie gathered her kit, cooked the shit on the same handy, blackened spoon as always, tied off, coaxed up a vein, and slid in the needle with practiced ease.

After the drugs entered their bloodstreams, they kissed. He didn't rush it. He took his time and embraced her as if he actually cared for the woman he'd just met. His moves were soft and precise. Natalie didn't have to fake it. For the first time in years, she was aroused.

But once he was inside her, everything changed. The passion was gone. His actions were robotic. Natalie opened her eyes and looked directly into his. Something strange dwelled within them. Something terrifying. She saw a darkness blacker than night.

The sex was agonizing and the high was starting to fade. He was big—too big—and had no desire to use it like the gentleman she thought he was. After a few more motions, she'd had enough. Natalie tried to pull away, but the man resisted and pressed his body deeper within hers.

"It's too late to back out now," he said.

When Natalie tried to speak, the man shoved his tongue into her mouth, silencing the protest. His tongue was sharp. She tasted blood.

Natalie had no choice but to endure. His athletic frame was far stronger than hers, and if she resisted, he might become violent. She pushed her fears aside for the moment and, with much hesitation, allowed him to continue.

It won't be much longer, Natalie told herself.

Beads of sweat gathered on his forehead. The drops grew heavy and fell upon Natalie with each thrust. When he neared climax, he moved with more intensity. Sweat pooled where their flesh met. Natalie counted the seconds, waiting for it to be over. When he finally finished, it felt as if a million pinpricks exploded inside her.

Natalie cried out in pain.

When Natalie awoke the next morning, the man was gone. She never learned his name. And after recalling the night's events, she hoped she never would. Natalie rolled over to check the clock on the nightstand, but her body objected. Soreness spread through her pelvic region and prevented her from moving too quickly.

That asshole.

Natalie fell back into her pillow and stared at the ceiling, gently massaging her abdomen. After a few moments, she tried again, this time with success. But when she turned to see the clock, numerous stacks of cash obscured her view. One hundred dollar bills, fifty dollar bills, twenty dollar bills... all neatly bundled. There were more stacks on the bed, the floor and the dresser. More money than Natalie had ever seen.

What the hell?

Maybe he felt bad for what he'd done? He should have, Natalie thought. Or maybe it was a down payment for future engagements? She wasn't sure. What she was sure of, though, was that she needed the money. Her drug of choice wasn't cheap and she'd need more soon. With that realization, Natalie almost forgave the man for his crudeness. Almost.

Natalie reached to examine one of the stacks of money when a pain spread through her abdomen. The pain was something different than before. It was something new.

Weeks and months passed. Natalie tried and tried again to fight her desires and dependencies. She knew she had to. She was responsible for more than just herself. She was pregnant. But her friends demanded attention. And the small fortune the man left on her bedside only made it easier to fall back into their arms.

After another failed attempt at sobriety, Natalie couldn't resist any longer. It wasn't just the thought of denying her precious friends; it was

the need to relieve the terrible illness plaguing her body in their absence. Or maybe it was the morning sickness? Perhaps both; she wasn't sure.

Natalie stuck the needle into her arm. The relief was, as always, instant. It all felt so familiar, except for the jabbing kicks coming from her midsection.

"It's okay," she said and rubbed her belly. "All better now."

She plucked the syringe from her vein and, like every other time, glanced back. But this time, when she pulled her friend away, the needle was–

Gone!

Natalie's eyes grew wide with fear. Was the high playing with her? She blinked hard and refocused, staring back at the object in her hands.

She saw the syringe, but no needle was affixed to it.

Like a deep itch, Natalie felt a tug–a slow pull coming from within herself–guiding the needle through her body to–

The baby!

She dropped the syringe and screamed.

Natalie mustered the last of her strength and drove to the hospital, clutching her belly the entire way. She didn't have much time. The needle would be nearing the baby soon, if it hadn't already. She pressed all of her weight onto the gas pedal. Neither red lights nor screeching tires would stop her.

The driver door opened and Natalie fell from the vehicle into a dimly lit parking lot. She pulled herself up and fought the panic rising inside long enough to make it to the hospital entrance. She collided with one of the automatic doors as it slid open. Blood trickled from her arm and speckled the white floor with each of her staggered steps.

"Someone help! My baby!" Natalie screamed.

A woman nibbling on a sandwich at the reception desk glanced over her computer monitor. Others waiting in the emergency room held tight against their own wounds.

A young man with a bloody bandage wrapping his forehead snickered, "Get in line, lady."

He pointed to a row of seats holding soon-to-be patients with varying injuries. Natalie ignored him and approached the desk.

"What's the nature of your emergency, ma'am?" the receptionist said between bites.

Natalie tried to collect her words. She tried to find a way to make sense of the situation.

"I-I-the needle–"

The receptionist swallowed the last of her meal and handed Natalie a clipboard with some paperwork.

"Fill this out and have your ID and insurance card ready."

Natalie scowled. Her life was in danger.

Her baby's life was in danger!

She nearly crashed more than once on her way to the hospital, and this woman–this bitch–didn't give a shit. Natalie slapped the clipboard away. Paper fluttered to the floor.

"I need help, goddammit!"

"Ma'am, I'm going to need you to calm down," the receptionist said with an irritated glare.

"Calm down? I need a fucking doctor!"

The receptionist picked up a phone receiver and punched-in a series of numbers. The announcement echoed across the hospital walls:

Code Gray to lobby. Code Gray.

A security guard rushed into the foyer. The woman at the desk pointed in Natalie's direction. The guard closed-in.

"What's the problem, ma'am?" the guard asked.

Thin trails of blood flowed from puncture marks on Natalie's arm beyond her wrist to the edge of her fingertips.

Natalie stumbled. Her vision blurred. She was starting to fade.

"My-my baby! The needle–"

The guard clutched Natalie's shoulders to keep her from falling. A nurse entered and joined them, his stethoscope at the ready.

"Ma'am, were you using?"

Natalie could feel the high falling fast. She sobbed. The nurse placed one end of his stethoscope against her chest and listened through the other. The touch surprised Natalie. It was cold. Cold enough to pull her focus back to say:

"It's inside me!"

Natalie struggled to open her eyes. The room was bright and smelled like Lysol. Muffled beeps and other electronic noises filled the air.

A voice cut through the haze. "Can you tell us your name, hon?"

The voice startled her. Natalie tried to speak, but her throat was dry. She swallowed and said, "Natalie."

"And your last name?"

"Veno."

Natalie tried to focus on the blurry figure huddling above her.

"Where am I?" she asked.

"Date of birth, Natalie?"

The words rattled through her brain for a few moments before the question made sense. "July fifth. Where the hell am I?"

"Year?"

"Just tell me where the fuck I am!"

Natalie's vision returned. She saw a middle-aged woman staring back at her through thick glasses.

"Saint Luke's. You drove yourself. Do you remember any of that?"

Natalie paused and collected her thoughts.

The nurse pushed her glasses up the bridge of her nose. "You're lucky to be alive, you know? You and the baby."

Natalie was quiet.

"You're going to have to stay here for a few days. Someone from Social Services will be speaking with you soon."

Natalie brushed her inner arm and remembered–

The needle!

"Did you find it? Did you get it out?"

The nurse looked puzzled. "Find what?"

"The needle!" Natalie said.

A call came through from the front desk: *Incoming Code Blue*

The nurse was instantly distracted. "Hold tight, sweetie. Doctor Copple will be here in just a second."

The nurse made her way to the exit.

Natalie's eyes were wide with fear. "No, please, don't leave."

But the nurse was already gone.

Natalie looked up and saw a plastic IV bag hanging from a pole next to her bed. She watched as lifesaving fluids traveled down a tube and entered her body.

A tingling sensation came from where the IV was inserted into her hand. Natalie squeezed her fingers together to shake away the feeling. The liquid inside the bag depleted. Her fist went wet and fluid poured from the IV tube onto the floor.

"Oh my God!" Natalie screamed.

She felt the tug return and watched the shape of the detached IV needle make its way up her arm beneath the surface of her skin. Natalie pinched at it in a feeble attempt to slow its movement, but no matter how much pressure she applied, the needle continued its path through her veins.

Natalie cried out and tore the tape securing the IV away. She ran from the room, throwing people, trays and gurneys from her. She ignored the staff's pleas to come back.

Whatever this was, they wouldn't be able to help. Natalie needed to find another way to stop it.

She rushed from the building and made her way to the parking lot. It was still dark outside. No more than a few hours had passed. Natalie found her car in the same spot she'd left it. The driver side door was still open and the keys, miraculously, still in the ignition.

When Natalie got home, she sifted through a collection of phone numbers scratched onto napkins, sticky notes and receipts, all stuffed into a kitchen drawer holding her syringes. Her suppliers would know what was happening. They'd have to. Odds were they'd sold to others who dealt with the very same thing.

Natalie made some calls, left some messages and chatted with others. Most laughed so hard they nearly dropped their phones. Others simply assumed she was high. And nearly all of the calls ended with her contacts attempting to land another sale.

Goddammit!

Natalie threw her phone at the wall and curled into a fetal position on the sofa. She massaged her arm and felt for any sign of the needles' location.

Nothing.

But they were there, somewhere. They'd gathered up and taken residence inside of her. The thought was terrifying, but none more so than the thought that, despite the needles hiding within, she seemed to be okay. And so did the baby.

Shouldn't I be dead? She thought.

But she wasn't. And neither was her child.

Frustrated, Natalie retrieved her laptop. She opened Google and stared at the screen.

She typed a series of keywords.

Needles inside

Needle left in body

How to retrieve needles from body

The search results brought nothing, save for a few articles on tattoo mishaps and some short horror fiction.

Fuck.

She was at a dead-end. There were no other options. She had no other alternative. She did what she'd always done to cope: she used. And each time she shot up, the needle stayed behind. Natalie's terror never abated, but she couldn't resist. The larger her bump got, the more she got high.

The day finally came.

Natalie was about to get high when it started. The contractions felt exactly as she assumed they would–sharp and piercing, like needles stretching their reach through her body. But they were not needles. They were the rhythms of childbirth.

"Oh my God, the baby's coming! The baby's coming!" Natalie screeched and rushed to the bathroom.

She couldn't go back to the hospital. That was out of the question. After the nurses' inability to understand and diagnose her situation, Natalie knew she'd be nothing more to them than another junkie with a bad addiction.

She tossed her syringe kit on the sink, filled the bathtub with warm water and, when her contractions diminished for a moment, slipped in.

Shit!

Natalie looked to the sink and saw her friends staring back at her. She needed them. They'd help with the pain. But when she moved to retrieve the syringes, her body recoiled. The discomfort was too much. She'd have to do without them.

Natalie dipped her naked body back into the water.

A large window above the tub doused the room in city light. Natalie heard cars traveling several stories below. She focused on the sounds. They were relaxing, tranquil and distracting. Everything she needed. Nothing like a high–not even close–but good enough, for now.

Natalie recalled things she'd seen on TV and in the movies about childbirth. It was simple, she thought. Just have to breathe. She took fast, balanced breaths. Though the breathing helped put her mind at ease, it would do nothing against the next wave of contractions.

Natalie screamed. She felt something large and uncomfortable–*abnormal*–move inside her.

The baby?

Couldn't have been the baby. Natalie felt it move so many times before. She knew what the child felt like and this was different.

The movement came again and Natalie knew something was wrong. Perhaps an organ ruptured? Had the needles finally done damage? There was no other answer. Natalie wrapped her arms around her midsection and fought against the rising pain. Her belly expanded further, poking above the water line. Natalie cried out.

"You've gotta come out!"

The dome of the baby's head pressed against the surface of her skin. Natalie pushed. The baby fought the thrusts and forced its body upward, toward Natalie's navel.

And then something punctured her flesh. Barbs emerged through Natalie's belly, bisecting her in a single, vertical row. She stared in terror as her abdomen split with a geyser of blood. Her pain was replaced by shock and numbness.

The crown of her child's head revealed itself through the bloody opening. The baby slowly unfolded within the void of Natalie's midsection. The thing that was a child didn't look human. Loud cries and gasps for air drowned out the sounds of sloshing water. But the cries were not that of the child. They were Natalie's. Though she sobbed, she did not move. She could not move. She was frozen with fear.

Gouts of blood and offal fell from the child and mixed with the bathwater. Natalie vomited, adding to the mixture. The thing that was a child began to creep. Natalie felt pressure on her spine as the creature crawled from her midriff. With each of its movements, she fought to keep her head above water.

Natalie stretched her legs and wildly clenched and unclenched her toes until she flipped the drain lever. The water level fell fast.

The thing that was a child slowly moved its way up Natalie. Its barbed feet escaped the confines of her exposed innards. It made its way to her chest, stopped atop her heart, and rested its head beneath Natalie's chin. She waited for the child to fall still.

There wasn't much time. Natalie was dying. She gazed at the thing, sitting in a bath of its mother's blood, and watched it breathe. Its ribcage shuddered. Its head twitched. And Natalie was repulsed.

What the fuck? What the fuck?

When the water completely drained, Natalie tried to sit up. She placed her arms at her side and pushed. Her hands slipped and she collapsed. The creature writhed for a moment. When it stopped moving, she tried again, this time with success, and propped herself into a sitting position.

The movements startled the creature. It lifted its head, eyes shut tight, and snarled. Natalie gasped for breath. Her body quivered with terror and fear, nearly convulsing. The child opened its mouth. Natalie saw rows upon rows of pointed, metallic teeth. They glistened in the light.

The needles!

With no time to react, the thing that was a child lunged forward and drove its teeth into Natalie's head. They pierced her skull. The child fed on the nourishment oozing from its mother's brain.

Something moved beyond the bathroom door. A shadow fell over the bathtub. A figure entered and watched the thing that was a child consume its first meal. Natalie twitched a few times before falling still. Her blood gurgled into the drain.

When the creature finished, the figure emerged–a man–and reached for the child. He lifted it into the light. The baby's eyes slowly opened. They were dark, blacker than night. The man cradled the creature into his arms and made his way to the exit.

A sharp light caught his attention at the sink near the doorway. He stopped and saw them–Natalie's friends. Her syringes. He reached for them, placed them inside the breast pocket of his Dormeuil suit and left Natalie alone, her labors done.

THE
PROJECTIONIST

JASON HELLER

THE PROJECTIONIST

JASON HELLER

My twelfth birthday was still a fresh memory the
day Grandma called me into her office to tell
me Mom died. It was a Sunday afternoon. The
matinee was about to begin.

Grandma managed a little two-screen movie theater
at the end of a dusty strip mall, circled by spider-webbed
asphalt with weeds sprouting out of the cracks. That's
how I picture Florida still: as the parched, hairy hide of
some mummified giant.

Mom sent me to live with Grandma that summer.
Always a wanderer, Mom had decided to hitchhike to
New England for a couple months. "Just to feel a little
freedom," she'd said. That was a time when people did
things like that. Feeling free. Hitchhiking hundreds of
miles all alone, despite looking barely older than a teen-
aged girl. Or managing two-screen movie theaters in a
crumbling strip mall, before the multiplexes took over.

Grandma sat at her cluttered desk that day, the curls
of her auburn perm unable to hide the threads of silver
at the roots. She'd given birth to Mom when she was
forty. Mom had given birth to me when she was fourteen.
Grandma always seemed to hold that against me, as if I
were some invader who crawled out of her daughter with
the sole purpose of spoiling both their lives.

Grandma's voice sounded distant when she spoke
about Mom. She was laying out an ad for the local newspaper using an X-Acto knife and rubber cement. Little

slivers of paper held the titles of the theater's summer offerings: *E.T. the Extra-Terrestrial, Conan the Barbarian, Blade Runner, The Road Warrior, The Thing, Tron, Poltergeist, Pink Floyd: The Wall.* Grandma never watched movies. She'd never even liked movies. She shuffled those slivers around on her desk as if they might coalesce into some new meaning. Her eyes didn't move from them as she spoke.

I remember those movie titles, but I've never remembered exactly what she said to me. Something about how Mom's body was discovered the day before. In the woods by the side of a stretch of interstate in Georgia.

Mom only made it as far as Georgia. Somehow that seemed more sad to me than the fact that she had died.

Then, as if it were of equal importance, Grandma told me that a new projectionist started working at the theater. She mostly left me alone at her house during the weeknights, when she had to run the theater. But on the weekends she took me to the theater for the matinees. She didn't have to hire a babysitter, and she got a free weekend employee: me.

I'd never met the old projectionist, so a new projectionist didn't matter to me. As if anything about the theater mattered. How could Grandma sit there, calmly laying out an ad? Then I realized I felt just as calm. My heart wanted to hurl itself through my breastbone, through the thin layer of meat and skin that shielded it, and into the theater's cold, dead, air-conditioned void. But my heart couldn't move. It was paralyzed, held in place, frozen like a prop in a still frame of a strip of film.

It wasn't until I locked myself in the single dingy stall of the men's room that the idea of crying came to me.

A week went by before I met the new projectionist. It was the Saturday after I'd heard Mom died. Crying gave way to a comforting numbness. The only thing that made my gut clench was the question that loomed over me like the noonday Florida sun: How? How had Mom died? An accident? Murder? Something unimaginable?

The problem was, I could imagine. I was only twelve, but I'd seen far more R-rated movies than most kids my age. Grandma didn't really care which films I snuck into while I wandered through the theater each weekend. The concession counter ran down the middle of the place, separating the R-movie from the PG-or-G-movie like a barrier. The membrane between the two halves of a brain. The wall between an innocent world and one less forgiving.

I was cleaning up the dumped buckets of popcorn in the aisles of that week's R-rated movie–*Blade Runner*, which I'd already seen three times, to the point where its shadows and neon had begun to haunt me–when I heard a voice. It echoed from everywhere and nowhere, across the empty, darkened theater.

"The movie is over," said the voice. A man's. It sounded ancient and caked with dust, just like Florida. "You need to leave now."

I stood there, my sneakers sticking to the congealed soda on the floor, peering into the darkness. My veins throbbed. There were no ushers at the theater. With only two screens, Grandma didn't think she needed them. Also, she couldn't afford to hire any staff besides a ticket-taker and a concession clerk. And, of course, a projectionist.

Finally I sensed where the voice was coming from. The projection window. A tiny square of black, high on the back wall, near the ceiling, like the window of a prison.

"I work here," I said, clearing my throat. I wanted to yell, but it came out little more than a croak. The acoustics of the theater amplified my meekness.

A pause. "You're the manager's grandson."

"I'm Joshua."

Another pause. "Names don't matter. They're lies. Disguises. Roles people play." Before I could ponder what that was supposed to mean, he added, "You should finish cleaning. The next matinee is starting soon."

I had another idea. My apprehension stuck like a pill in my throat, I managed to say, "I'm coming up."

"Up?" The projectionist sounded perplexed. "Here?"

"Yes. There." I'd never been in the projection booth before. I'd always wondered what it looked like, how the projector operated, what kind of magic it might hold.

His laugh was throaty yet sad. "Ah. So you're determined. A protagonist. All right, Joshua. I'm assuming you know where the stairs are. Does your grandmother allow you up here?"

"She doesn't care what I do." I was already walking toward the swinging doors that led to the lobby.

Outside them, next to Grandma's office, was the door marked "Employees Only." I opened it quietly and started climbing the spiral staircase that led to the projectionist's booth. It corkscrewed upward into nothingness.

Halfway up, dust filling my nose, I realized the projectionist hadn't told me his name.

Deceiving Grandma came easily to me. She'd deceived me first, I figured. I wanted to know more about Mom, but I knew pressing Grandma for an answer would only vex her. Or more likely, it would make her shrug and feed me more evasions.

I'd never even been told what happened to Grandpa all those years ago. All I knew was that he'd served in World War II, and that he fought in the Pacific, and that he'd died when I was still a baby. Grandma never talked about it, or about him. I'd seen a photo of him once, young and handsome in a uniform, his face already etched with weariness. He reminded me of Mom. I asked Grandma about it, and I never saw the photo again.

Uncertainties, ambiguities, untruths: My life was constructed of them. As I neared the top of the spiral staircase, I wondered if that might be why I was going to the projectionist's booth. If I saw drama in every place, in everyone. I'd seen so many movies, there in Grandma's theater. Like most families in my neighborhood, we couldn't afford a VCR. But I felt as though movies had already become commonplace to me, even

with all their spaceships and androids and aliens, and that life itself held far more mystique.

A sliver of light shone through the dark from a crack in the door. It was slightly open. I placed my palm against it and pushed.

At first I didn't see the projectionist. All I could see was the machine.

The projector engulfed the entire booth. It wasn't a large space, as far as I could tell. The machine filled it like a nest of serpents that had overgrown its terrarium. Instead of snakes, though, tubes and pistons and pneumatic cylinders twisted their way around the central mass of the apparatus, which wheezed and trembled like the torso or thorax of some impossible beast.

Lights flickered from various apertures, random in shape, size, and placement. Here was a star. There was a crescent. One even looked like an eye. The openings dilated and constricted independently of each other, swirling around the projector's dark bulk, flashing occasionally through the small window in the wall that faced the screen of the theater. Half submerged in its black, jagged surface, organs of bulbous chrome contorted and writhed like they were trying to release some tremendous pressure held deep within.

The whole machine was so immense, I couldn't take it in with a single glance. Its silhouette bulged, and its image pressed against my retina, refusing to be neatly interpreted. My lungs seized as if unwilling to share the same air as it. I forced myself to take a deep breath. I smelled grease, rust, ozone. The air held a scorched and coppery tang, like batteries thrown into a campfire.

I'd never seen a projector before, outside the tiny ones that were occasionally wheeled into class to show educational films. I had nothing to compare it to. I couldn't tell how old or new the machine was, or even where the celluloid itself might be threaded through.

"Joshua," came the projectionist's voice. It no longer echoed, disembodied, across the chasm of the theater. Now it was intimate, a thing of breath and hisses, still somewhere just beyond my senses. Florida was already moist, but a new and inhuman humidity suffused the room, as if

the projectionist's exhalations had condensed on the walls. They looked slick, like wet skin. "What is your father's name?"

"My... I don't know." My answer was an honest one. Mom never married, and whomever had gotten her pregnant in high school never claimed me. As far as I knew, I'd never met him. He was just another mystery. "Why do you ask? Where are you?"

He must have been standing slightly behind me all along, because I didn't hear a thing until he laid a hand on my shoulder. The clamminess of his fingers seeped instantly through the thin fabric of my T-shirt. The fact that I didn't flinch made me feel either brave or numb. I wasn't sure which. I wasn't sure there was a difference.

Before I could think of what to do next, he stepped forward, his back to me. His hair couldn't have been curlier if it had been the result of some cartoon electrocution. Its color almost wasn't a color at all, but some indeterminate hue between sepia and silver that subtly changed shade every time I blinked.

I blinked a lot. He stank. My eyes watered at the sudden thrust of his scent, a mix of the acrid battery odor from before and another, muskier chemistry. He wore a black shirt and brown corduroy pants. When he turned to face me, I could see that the bow tie and ruffles of a tuxedo were silkscreened on his shirt, although the printing was fading and flaking off.

His face was thin and gaunt. Long shadows hung below his brows and cheekbones. Despite the humidity, his skin was as dry and flaky as the tuxedo design on his shirt. Colorless stubble marked the sharp slash of his jaw. On top of that, the smeared remnants of a drawn-on, pencil-thin moustache traced his upper lip, vestiges of some prehistoric suaveness.

He smiled.

His teeth were like glass. Transparent and glittery, as if his mouth had been stuffed with a ballroom chandelier. I could see right through them.

"I'm right here," he said finally, his crystalline smile evaporating. He tipped his head toward the heaving, pulsing mechanism behind him. "Have you met him yet?"

"My father? No. What does that have to do with–"

"Not your father. *Him*. The projector." He gestured toward the machine, an ancient locomotive turned inside out, a giant squid built out of the viscera of a Model T.

My bones locked into a static panic.

The projectionist didn't seem to notice. He took a step toward the nearest steaming tubule, rolled his sleeve up to his shoulder, and placed his fingertips gently against its slick, shuddering shell. An opening appeared, spiraled like a sphincter. The dim illumination in the room began flickering spasmodically.

"You want to know how he works, don't you?"

Then he pushed in his arm.

The scenes replay a dozen times.

A hundred times.

Maybe more.

Mom, on a highway. Standing there with a backpack slung over her shoulder. Trees are all around. A truck goes by. Three men are in it. Mom waves at them, but the men don't see her.

Grandpa, on a beach. Muscular, suntanned, stripped to the waist. Men in helmets hand him a rifle. He cradles it in his arm, elbow to wrist. He loads it with bullets then shoots them into the sky.

A man, in a chair. A girl stands in front of him. His hair shines as his head bobs in understanding. The man sobs. The girl sobs. Their faces look similar, blurring, cut from one cloth, almost the same.

Rewind.

Repeat.

Rewind.

Repeat.

Rewind.

Repeat.

The projectionist slumped beside me, leaning against the machine.

His shirt was in shreds. His arm had been swallowed by the projector, along with a leg and a hip. Slits had opened up in the machine's carapace like tiny knife wounds.

The projectionist's skin was being fed into them.

Long strips of his flaking epidermis unwound from his flesh. They made a tearing sound as they came detached from the fat and meat beneath. The slits then sucked them in. As those strips of skin quivered in the naked air, stretched taut and thin, they took on the translucency of yellowed cellophane. Swirls and whorls of sparse hair and puckered pores threw small, soft shadows along the ceiling.

As his skin unspooled and disappeared into the machine, they threaded their way just under its shell like a serpent squirming under loose earth. An aperture, ovular and unblinking, had focused itself on the tiny window at the far end of the projectionist's booth. The skin passed over it, throwing images onto the screen in the theater below. The images I'd been seeing. A dozen times. A hundred times. Maybe more.

The projectionist spoke. "Is it good?"

I forced my tongue to work. "Good?"

"The movie. I can't see it. Only you can."

I had no answer for him. The flickering of fiction, I kept telling myself it was fiction, held me rapt.

"This is it, you know. The greatest story ever told. The last picture show." He was talking in film titles now. I wasn't sure what that was supposed to signify. I listened. "This projector is the final specimen of its kind, and I'm the last projectionist who knows how to operate it." His eyes rolled back in his head and his body shuddered. The machine unpeeled a strip of skin across his chest, dragging a nipple into the air and drawing it toward a flickering slit as if it sat on a conveyer belt.

He gurgled far in the back of his throat, an animal noise, then regained his voice. "Soon there will be no need for us. The many-headed hydra has come. There will be no craft, no art, no autonomy. A man will

sit in an office and push a button, and the films will come. People won't come to our church anymore at all. They will receive sermons in their homes, in their hands."

The skin of his lips lifted off, and plasma oozed like melted celluloid from where his moustache had been.

"The movie... Is it the truth?" Part of me hoped he wouldn't be able to answer.

"It is the only truth," he said, his lips dripping plastic, his voice crackling out of his throat like a scratchy old phonograph. "Our truth. We are cameras, you and I."

Bile roiled in my belly. My insides seemed to eat themselves. Through the pain, a vast aloneness pressed down on me like a revelation. I was an alien marooned on Earth, an android discovering she isn't human, a man losing his mind to worms that weren't worms. "What do I have to do with it?"

"It is up to you," he said as his eyelids flitted into one of the machine's slits like acetate butterflies, "to learn how to operate it. The projector."

How long had I been in the projection booth? Minutes? Hours? Years? I looked over my shoulder to see time accordioning behind me, a jumble of frames stretching back into the distant darkness. Ahead was only the projectionist. Ahead was only the projector.

In each frame was me. I was flattened, positioned in still life, a stop-motion snapshot, a cross-section, a core sample, a slide on a microscope.

I reached a hand toward the nearest lens. It blinked and shivered at the top of a telescopic stalk, leaking milky oil, clouded by some cataract of obsolescence. My fingers brushed against it, and it pivoted toward me like a plant grasping for the sun.

I think of Grandma, downstairs, in her office, pushing pieces of paper. She never watched movies. She'd never even liked movies. She just sat there, a collection of dust, waiting for the multiplex to come.

Slowly at first, with the fluttering rustle of insect's wings, my skin began to unravel.

The scenes replay a dozen times.

A hundred times.

Maybe more.

Mom, on a highway. Standing there with a backpack slung over her shoulder. Trees are all around. A truck has stopped. Three men get out of it. Mom talks to them, but she's glancing at the trees.

Grandpa, on a beach. Emaciated, sunburned, stripped to the waist. Men in helmets hand him a hunk of meat. It looks like a leg, thigh to knee. He picks out small, white worms then eats it raw.

A man, in a chair. A girl squats in front of him. His belt buckle clinks as the leather slithers out of its loops. The man grunts. The girl grunts. Their faces look similar, cut from one flesh, merging, almost the same.

Rewind.

Repeat.

Rewind.

Repeat.

Rewind.

Repeat.

THE
WOLF'S
PAW

JEANNE C. STEIN

THE WOLF'S PAW

JEANNE C. STEIN

David is getting antsy.

Makes me smile since it's usually me doing the squirming.

"What's the matter? We've only been here an hour. You got someplace better to be?"

I turn my face away so he can't see the smile. I *know* he has someplace better to be. I saw her in the doorway when I picked him up at his condo.

"Don't be a smart ass, Anna. Tell me again what we're doing here?"

"Easy money. Five thousand dollars, remember? Snatch and grab."

"Snatch what? Where is the prick?"

A movement from the bushes on the opposite side of the road. David doesn't see it. But I do. Vampire eyes. We've been watching the guy's front door. There's no back door out of the apartment.

Still. I catch a scent.

I reach for the door handle. "I've got to pee."

David reaches for an empty coffee cup.

"Very funny. I'll be right back."

He mutters something under his breath but I'm already behind the car and bolting to follow the sound of the rustling bushes to our right. Vampire senses jump to the fore. Eyes pierce the darkness, turning night to day.

Ears hear every insect crawling, skittering or buzzing out of my path. Nose catches the scent of the creature moving away from me.

Human. Familiar.

But something else.

Feral. Fur.

What the...?

David doesn't know that I got close to the guy we're after this afternoon. Got close enough to breathe in his scent, close enough to make the grab myself before I was interrupted by a pain in the ass who stopped me on the sidewalk to ask for directions. By the time I got rid of him, the skip had disappeared.

But it's the same scent I detect now under the musk of fur and testosterone.

I move noiselessly through the bushes. Close the distance between us. He's just ahead of me. But he's moving faster than a man would be and is crouched low to the ground. It doesn't take much of a jump to determine what I'm chasing.

I let vampire have her head. Fighting werewolves is not my favorite pastime. They can be nasty creatures. If I'd known that's what I was chasing, I'd never have involved David. Can't worry about that now.

Where's the guy going? We're in Balboa Park. It's not quite dusk on a hot summer evening and I can't make out where he's headed. Until he takes a sharp turn and waits for traffic on the Prado to clear. Then he lopes across the road and straight into the dog park–the only area open to off-leash pets.

Curious. What's he doing? Looking for a chance to get lucky?

I call vampire back and proceed after him, fully human. The park is not yet as crowded as it's going to be in an hour or so when the home-from-work crowd brings their pets for a romp. But there are a half-dozen dogs sniffing and scuffling, their owners chatting nearby.

The wolf pauses, watching. He's bigger than most of the dogs but no one pays any attention. I enter the park and start toward him.

The wolf turns and meets my eyes. He lifts his nose. He recognizes vampire. But then he turns away, casually ignoring me, resuming his perusal of the animals as if searching for just the right one.

He makes his choice with a snarl and faster than I would have thought possible, he lunges.

Toward a child, playing off by herself to the right of the group of adults.

I reach her first, scoop her up and thrust her into the arms of a startled woman.

Wolf gathers himself to lunge at me.

If I call up vampire in front of all these people, it won't be pretty. Instead, I pull the .38 from the waistband of my jeans, aim and fire.

I catch the wolf in midair, but I haven't accounted for his speed and the bullet slams into his leg, blowing off a paw and breaking bone with a sickening crack. He lands with a howl, whirls on three good legs and stumbles off the way he came.

I want to go after him but my way is impeded by a group of frantic onlookers, all reaching out hands to thank me, all asking the same questions at once.

What was that?

Who are you?

Are you a cop?

By the time I finally get free, and make it back to David, he's standing by the car, our skip, naked and bloody.

David has his cell at his ear. When he sees me, he clicks off. "Where the fuck have you been?"

I point to the skip. "What happened to him?"

David has fastened a tourniquet around the guy's arm, just below the elbow. A stump at the end of his wrist drips blood. "Somebody blew this guy's hand off. He isn't saying who. I got him as he tried to sneak his way back into the apartment. The paramedics are on the way."

The guy and I–wolf and vampire–stare into each other's eyes. I wonder if we're thinking the same thing... my, what big secrets we have.

DANNIKER'S COFFIN

KEITH FERRELL

DANNIKER'S COFFIN

KEITH FERRELL

Not long after his neighbors moved out, Jim Danniker, the coffin maker's son, started thinking of having a fence put up. He had thought of it before, more than once over the years, but this time was different. This time he was serious. This time he would get it done. Danniker was seventy-one now, and time was too limited to waste. He should have done it years ago, but there had nearly always been people in the house, neighbors, and he had no wish to insult them by erecting a fence after they had lived next to him, grown to know him and his ways, proved themselves to be, most of them, good neighbors even without a fence. He hadn't wished to give offense.

Offense! Danniker said the world aloud and laughed. Chain-link–for that is what he thought he would go with–to separate you and your property from that of neighbors you'd lived next to for years would be insulting. An offensive fence. A fence offense.

He wouldn't do that to the Johnsons, who had lived next door for eight years, any more than he would willingly give offense of any sort to anyone, neighbors or strangers.

Now the neighbors were gone, and the house next door was empty. He didn't think it would stay that way for long; for all the decades he had lived next door to it, it had never stayed vacant for long. The longest stretch was four, maybe five months after the Rosemunds moved away, but that was during the worst of the hard times,

and that was the exception. Usually the house sold within a matter of weeks, and Danniker had no reason to think this current vacancy would be any different.

But the times were different–the town was growing in this direction. Already two new lots were being cleared up the road; another year would undoubtedly see at least two more. So he would need to act swiftly, get the fence started and the Danniker property enclosed before the next owner closed the purchase, much less moved in.

This time he would get it done.

This time he was serious.

This time he was determined.

Tomorrow he would prove it.

By midmorning of the next day, after getting the most preliminary and ballpark sense of what it would cost to have a fence built, it was clear that he could not afford even the simplest of fences, even if he restricted the fence to the side of the property facing the neighboring home. Armed with this knowledge, Danniker began putting his determination through a process of revision. He had learned some things, a lot of things really, and not just regarding cost, about fences, and as always when he was equipped with new knowledge or fresh insights, he had to rethink things to make certain all the new pieces fit. Sometimes that meant throwing out some of the old pieces altogether, but most times it meant merely modifying them, shaving off something here, planing down something there until all the pieces fit together seamlessly, the way he had seen his father and grandfather working wood when they made the coffins for which they were so well known.

In their day, he thought. The coffins they were known for *in their day*, a day that was decades gone now, half a century and then some for Danniker's grandfather, thirty-seven years–more than a third of a century, Danniker realized–for his father. In the ground that long, Granddaddy Jeet in a coffin his son had made, while Danniker's father

rested in a store-bought casket, not a coffin at all, and the difference was just one of the things that had changed. A casket was just a box, graceless even when rounded at the corners, same at the head as at the feet, no tapering where the shoulders of the body it contained gave way to the neck and head. Just a box.

But it was a box the funeral home charged plenty for; even the least expensive of them was pricey. Danniker could remember when Granddaddy Jeet charged $20 for a plain coffin–$25 if the deceased weighed more than a quarter-ton, Danniker's father used to joke. Danniker couldn't remember Granddaddy Jeet laughing at much of anything, but he had laughed at that, even as he kept his price at a flat twenty whether it was being built to hold Jack Spratt or Jack Spratt's wife. When the price went up to $25, it was because times had changed and everything else had gone up too. By the time Granddaddy Jeet died, they were charging $50 for a plain coffin, a fair price, and far less than even the least expensive caskets the funeral homes offered.

He had tried to build a coffin for his father, made an effort and more, but it was no good. Danniker didn't have the gift.

Danniker spent most of his childhood in the workshop where his father and grandfather built their coffins, but the trade hadn't taken with Danniker. He didn't have the feel for it, or the touch, or the gift, or whatever it was that made the Dannikers, father and son, such respected coffin makers. Danniker's great-grandfather, Haskell, whom he never knew, had possessed the gift as well. Had, in fact, brought the knowledge of coffin making with him from Europe, and passed that knowledge and, clearly, gift, down to Granddaddy Jeet, who had in turn transmitted it to Danniker's father, but that was where the gift stopped.

It hadn't stopped for wont of trying. Everybody called Danniker's father Upper Jim as a result of his toddler son's calls of "Upper, Daddy! Upper, Daddy!" when he wanted to be swung up to ride upon his shoulders. Those shoulders were where Lower Jim–a nickname that hadn't lasted much past the first year or two of elementary school–rode to the workshop out back, spending his days there starting when he was three. They gave him his first tools of his very own when he was four, showing

him their purpose, placing their big rough hands over his small ones to guide the tools, as though the gift could be transmitted from their fingertips to his.

Danniker had tried then, had made the effort, and made it for years, had been *determined* in his pursuit of the ability, but it eluded him. When he worked a hand plane he was as likely to gouge the wood as to shave it smooth. His angles never matched, there were gaps between the boards when he joined them together, his corners wouldn't hold. He got better as he got older, but never got good enough, not even good enough to do much more than the simplest of prep work on the lumber his father and Granddaddy Jeet transformed into coffins. By the time Danniker was twelve he knew that he would never develop the ability; his father and grandfather had known much earlier, and Danniker knew that too.

But still Danniker had spent the hours after school, and the long days of summer vacations and the shorter ones of holidays, in the workshop building behind the house, helping with those tasks for which he was suited, if not gifted. He organized the lumber for the coffin makers, he cleaned and sharpened his father's tools (Granddaddy Jeet kept the edges on his own tools himself, sharper than either Danniker or even Danniker's father could achieve), he made coffee, he swept up.

For those who wanted more than the plain pine that was the primary product of the elder Dannikers' craft, Jim varnished and buffed the coffins as they were assembled. He took great care with the task, leaving neither bubbles nor brush strokes to mar the finish. Neither Granddaddy Jeet nor Upper Jim ever found any fault with his work, but neither did any of the three pretend that varnishing the coffins was a craft.

Unexpectedly, during his senior year of high school, Danniker discovered that he did possess a gift that could be of service to the family business after all, a gift for organization and numbers, for working with both suppliers and the public. He quickly took over the bookkeeping and taxes, dealing with suppliers and the bereaved, becoming as adept at seeking better deals for lumber and other supplies, and also displaying a genuine talent for welcoming the newly bereaved, putting them at ease, sharing their sorrow even as he gently solicited the most delicate of infor-

mation that might require special consideration in the construction of the coffin. Usually there weren't any, and usually the workshop held one or two coffins that would serve the grieving family just fine. But when there were special requirements–great girth or height being the most common–Danniker collected it effortlessly, without distressing even the most emotionally distraught customers as he took the measure of their needs and recorded the information in a small notebook he carried with him everywhere.

Danniker still carried the notebook. He had made notations in it about the fence he could not afford.

When the deceased was a child or an infant, young Danniker knew how to make his shared grief become a palpable thing, and often the bereaved found themselves speaking comforting words to the young man who was so moved by their loss. Children's coffins were virtually always painted white, and Danniker attended to that task as carefully as he did the darker varnish on adult coffins.

They were a good team, Granddaddy Jeet, Upper and Lower Jims, and nothing was ever said by the older men about the fact that their gift, the real gift upon which the business rested, would die with them. It bothered the youngest Danniker sometimes, the thought that he was the obstacle that brought the family trade to its close, but as the years passed, it became clear the business would not have survived even had the gift for making good coffins been passed on.

When he was a boy–this was during the 1940s, the years of the war and the years just after, when he had still literally been Lower Jim–some of those seeking coffins would still arrive by horse and wagon, though fewer of them each year. Often it was a preacher who came to arrange for the coffin; the preachers had been among the first to have cars, before the war even, many of the local ministers were driving automobiles provided by congregations, the majority of whose members still traveled to and from the churches in farm wagons or buggies. Granddaddy Jeet and Upper Jim had replaced their own horse and wagon with a truck, but not until after the war. By the time Danniker was ten, everyone had a car or truck; by the time he was fifteen, Danniker was doing most of

the driving for the family business. There was still some good business then, when he was fifteen, and still good when he was twenty, steady if declining when he was twenty-five, a decline dramatically steeper, and in fact clearly terminal by the time he was in his thirties. People were still dying, no doubt of that, and people were still being buried, no question of that either, but now that they had cars, and some money, they could drive to town, to one of the funeral homes, and do business there, no matter that the price was higher than anything the Dannikers could even consider charging. But that didn't seem to matter to them. More and more of them died in hospitals rather than at home, and that cost money too.

Some few of the coffins the Dannikers made were used only as vessels, holders, for the bodies of deceased loved ones bound for cremation, Danniker-made coffin and all. It bothered Danniker to think of their handiwork consigned to and consumed by flames, not that the cremated coffins bore the benefit of Danniker's skills. People didn't pay extra for varnishing and buffing and polishing for a coffin that would be ash within a couple of hours of being delivered or picked up. It was plain pine coffins that burned, and Granddaddy Jeet and Upper Jim told Danniker not to worry about it. Once the bereaved took possession of a coffin, it was theirs to do with as they would.

But the majority of the coffins the Dannikers sold were lowered into graves dug behind or beside one of the dozen or so small churches within ten miles of their home and shop, although a fair percentage went to long-established family plots. Granddaddy Jeet and Upper Jim were in a plot like that, out back behind the workshop, all three of the gifted coffin makers–Great-granddaddy Haskell, Granddaddy Jeet, Upper Jim– there in that plot, and their wives as well. Each of their wives had died in childbirth. Danniker spent a few moments every day straightening the family plot, collecting dead leaves or bits of trash that had blown in, pulling weeds, brushing dust from the simple stones that marked his family's place of rest.

There was a low wrought-iron fence, not even knee-high, around the plot, but Danniker hadn't put that fence up. Great-granddaddy

Haskell had done that, same as he had built the house in which his son and grandson and now great-grandson lived. When Great-granddaddy Haskell's wife, LucyAnn, died delivering their son, Danniker had been told often, Haskell Danniker had not allowed himself even a moment for grief, but had set to work immediately, taking his grief with him to his tasks, building a coffin for his wife and then, as the varnish he had applied to the coffin himself dried, he had taken a shovel and dug the first of the graves that would serve the family. Great-granddaddy Haskell put the same amount of care and attention into creating the grave that he did into the crafting of the coffin that would fill it. He had carried the coffin to the grave himself, and lowered it, and with it, within it, his wife, into the ground. If Haskell Danniker spoke any words over LucyAnn's grave, those words and whatever sentiment they held were heard by no one other than the coffin maker himself, and his newborn, as yet unnamed son, whom the coffin maker carried to the graveside, lying there on a blanket while his father filled in the grave as carefully as he had excavated it. According to Upper Jim and Granddaddy Jeet, all Great-granddaddy Haskell ever told them about that day was that the infant stopped crying the moment he was placed on the ground beside the grave, and never cried again, not even once, in all the years since. Within a day or two, Great-granddaddy Haskell had hired one of the Simms sisters, Dolores, from down the road to come in and care for the baby, now named Jerome Turner Danniker–J.T., which at some point became Jeet, though no one, including Granddaddy Jeet himself, had ever been able to tell his grandson how that name came about.

For thirty-two years the low fence surrounded only LucyAnn Danniker's grave. Then Granddaddy Jeet married Helen Campbell, and when the time came for their child to be born, the time came for Helen's grave to be dug as well. Jeet Danniker dug the grave for his bride, same as his father had for LucyAnn, and lowered her into it, and stood next to the grave with Great-granddaddy Haskell, while the new baby, James Campbell Danniker, who would become, in a bit more than a quarter of a century, Upper Jim–lay without crying on a blanket just outside the fence.

Upper Jim married early, at twenty-two, and was both a father and a widower before his twenty-fourth birthday. By this time, the family burial plot held Great-granddaddy Haskell as well, and the fence had to be taken down and then extended to accommodate the latest addition. This work was done, and the new grave dug for the new coffin as the baby, James Haskell Danniker, to be known within five years as Lower Jim, lay on a blanket nearby, and did not cry.

Others were crying, though, throughout the country–as the coffin holding the baby's mother, Joanne Rider Danniker, was lowered into the ground, radios began carrying the news that the Japanese had attacked Pearl Harbor. The Dannikers didn't have a radio, any more than, a decade later, they would have a television, but the news of the attack and the war it launched reached them from neighbors. The next four years brought plenty of business to the house on Steeple Road, some of it the bodies of boys sent home to die, (most of those killed in combat were buried where they fell in Europe or the Pacific), and the bodies of parents dead of heartsickness and grief over their losses. The coffins of soldiers were draped with flags before burial. Danniker always made sure the varnish on the coffin was completely dry, with not even the least bit of tackiness to clutch at the flag when it was time for it to be removed, folded, and presented to the parents.

Danniker himself never became a parent, any more than he ever became a coffin maker. Had Danniker married and fathered a child, he had no doubt that he would have lost his wife to its delivery as well. But since the coffin maker's gift had not been passed on to him, he had no reason to believe that the gift would skip him and pass to another generation, and thus he had no reason even to try. He shed no tears over this decision, any more than he had ever shed so much as a single tear over anything. As with his father and grandfather, tears had been fenced off from him from the moment he lay swaddled on the ground beside the plot into which his mother was being lowered.

Only lately, only as he entered and then moved more deeply into his seventies, did Danniker begin more carefully and thoroughly to ponder the consequences of the decision he had made so many decades ago.

He had been aware of those consequences even during the long seasons of Upper Jim's dying, and not simply because he had been forced to bury his father in a purchased casket rather than a Danniker coffin. There had been a bit of inventory when Upper Jim fell ill, same as through all the years the shop had been in operation: there were always some coffins, never more than eight, never fewer than three, arranged along the outer wall of the workshop, in readiness.

But Upper Jim worked more slowly each month as the disease ate its way through him. The inventory had dwindled faster than Upper Jim could replace it, even with his son helping him as much as he could. It wasn't enough, wasn't good enough, the work Danniker could do to make Upper Jim's work easier, and they both knew it, though neither ever spoke of this.

Nor did Danniker broach the topic of a coffin for his father until it was too late. When there was a single completed coffin left in the workshop, Danniker had gone and stood beside the bed Upper Jim had not left in two weeks, and told him that the last coffin, the final Danniker coffin, would be his. Upper Jim would go to his rest in a coffin he had built himself.

His father had nodded weakly. But his eyes were clear and his touch warm when he pressed his fingers against his son's face.

If Upper Jim had died then, Danniker thought as he had thought for more than thirty years, since the moment ten days before Upper Jim actually died, if he had died at that moment after touching his son's cheek, then all would have been as it should have been. His father would have by now rested in a coffin of his own making for those thirty years, instead of in the casket Danniker had been forced to purchase.

In a way, it was Upper Jim who had forced Danniker to go to the funeral home and buy a casket, because it was Upper Jim who had insisted that the last coffin be put to the use of someone else's body, and he insisted because it was a preacher who had come and asked, had come to his deathbed and spoken of being in *need*.

Danniker had never seen a preacher who wasn't in need. Often it was preachers who came to the house to arrange for coffins for members

of their congregations. Danniker supposed that at one time or another he had met and done business with every preacher within a ten mile radius of the workshop.

The preacher that day–just over a week before Upper Jim died–had come in a new Chevrolet, not top of the line, but not bottom of it either. He wore a good suit, and carried with him both a Bible and a scent of aftershave. He sat beside Upper Jim's bed–his deathbed, and no way the preacher didn't know that–and spoke of a member of his flock, an elderly woman whose husband had died and who didn't have the money to bury him properly. Was there anything that could be done to help her?

And Upper Jim had nodded a long, slow nod, before telling the preacher–and Danniker, too, who stood nearby–that there was one last coffin, the very last of its kind, that he would be happy to provide for the woman, and provide at no charge.

Danniker had started to protest, but his father waved the objections aside, and told him to load the coffin into the truck and deliver it wherever the preacher asked.

Danniker had done that, done every bit of it just the way his father asked, and only when he was back from the delivery, the last delivery he would ever make, did he ask his father what was to be done with *his* body when the time came.

"You go buy me a casket," Upper Jim had said. "Don't you spend too much, don't need nothing fancy, but you go buy one and put me in it and I'll be fine."

Danniker had done that, too, done every bit of that just the way his father asked. Brought the casket home in the back of the truck, almost the same as he had carried so many coffins–but real coffins, not caskets–away from the workshop. He had not shown the casket to Upper Jim, nor had Upper Jim expressed any interest in seeing it. Danniker placed the casket on a wheeled cradle he'd cobbled together, and waited.

When the time came–peacefully at night after a long and agonizing day of gasping for breath and groaning in pain–Danniker had cleaned his father's body, dressed it, placed it in the casket, and wheeled it out to the plot where it stood while he dug the grave in which his father

would rest. Would rest in a casket, there among the others in the plot, all resting in Danniker coffins.

He had shoveled the earth back into the grave carefully, just as he had seen Upper Jim and Granddaddy Jeet do, and smoothed the mound over Upper Jim's grave. At no point during any of this had he wept.

Now, pacing the fenceless eastern perimeter of the property and staring at the neighbors' house, he was stunned to feel something rising in his throat, his eyes; something that could only be tears.

Danniker tried to imagine what would happen when his own time came. He could go into town and buy a casket and bring it home, but then what? Who would place him in the casket?

He could dig his own grave, but then what? Who would place the casket, with Danniker in it, in the ground?

Who would shovel the earth onto the casket, who would cover him, who would smooth the earth into place?

Who would tend the gravesite after he was gone?

Danniker had never made a will—he had no one to leave anything to, and he had not, until now, considered what a problem this created. It was not just the house and workshop and the land. It was the burial plot, but not just that. The tools in the workshop, the tools that had been wielded by Danniker hands to fashion Danniker coffins, Haskell's tools, and Granddaddy Jeet's, and Upper Jim's, their handles and grips worn smooth and familiar by their owners' fingers.

What would become of the tools—of everything?

Would the county claim the property? The state? And what then? An auction perhaps, the tools—the *tools*!—sold to the highest bidder along with everything else?

That could not be allowed.

He began to have an idea about how to prevent it.

He began to think that he had what he needed to solve the problem. His tools.

Danniker's own tools, never really used, never really used *well* at all, not touched nor even looked at in more than thirty years. Danniker wanted to see the tools now. He was beginning to think he might

have a use for them. He was beginning to think the answer to all of his questions lay in the tools and the purpose for which they were meant.

He stepped toward the workshop.

The air inside the shop was cool. There was no mustiness and sur-prisingly little dust. When Danniker switched on the lights, the blades of the tools still gleamed. He saw the tools with new eyes now–eyes that had come close to shedding tears. His eyes were dry now.

Slowly, Danniker stepped over to the long workbench where his father had worked. The bench ran for twenty feet along the shop's north wall. Granddaddy Jeet's identical bench stood snug against the west wall. Had Danniker possessed the coffin maker's gift, he would have had a bench of his own along the east wall, but there had never been any need to build it. Danniker's workspace was a small desk tucked into the northwest corner. He had not sat at the desk in years: without income, without a business, there was no need. There had been enough money after Upper Jim died for Danniker to live quietly on; the house and land were paid for even before Granddaddy Jeet was born; the tax evaluation and property taxes were still small this far out. For the past few years Danniker had drawn Social Security, but he didn't really need it.

What he needed, he thought as he rested his fingertips on his father's workbench, was to know what to do. More than that, to know what needed to be done after he died. Done with all of this.

He leaned forward until his palms were pressed flat against the scarred surface of the workbench. He breathed deeply, could still smell the scent of fresh shavings as his father worked a board at the bench while Danniker worked the numbers at his desk. He let his fingers trace some of the grooves and scars worn in the thick oak surface of the bench.

He turned and looked at the lumber, 200 board feet of fine pine, enough for three, possibly four, coffins, the boards still neatly stacked. They were the last load Danniker had fetched from the sawmill. The mill had gone out of business long before the turn of the millennium–people got their boards at big chain stores now, the same store Danniker had driven to town to visit when he was pricing a fence. He had brought this lumber here at his father's insistence, not long before Upper Jim had been

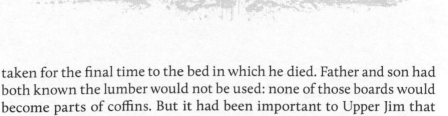

taken for the final time to the bed in which he died. Father and son had both known the lumber would not be used: none of those boards would become parts of coffins. But it had been important to Upper Jim that there be enough wood in the shop, neatly stacked and in readiness for when he was feeling better, feeling up to working again. And so Danniker drove to the sawmill and purchased the wood, and brought it here and stacked it where it still lay.

Danniker moved to the lumber and drew the top board off the stack. He pressed his hands flat against each side, aligned down the board, same as he had seen his father and Granddaddy Jeet do a hundred times. The board was true, unbowed, next to no warp despite the decades. He wondered if boards this true were available at the big stores. It didn't matter; he wouldn't need to find out.

He started to replace the board on the stack of lumber, but hesitated, then carried it to his father's bench, and laid it there. For a moment Danniker didn't move, then took a single step back from the bench. He looked at his father's tools, then looked at the smaller rack of tools, his own tools, that his father had hung to the right of his bench, close to Danniker's desk. Upper Jim had hung the tools there, not in mockery or chastisement, Danniker thought, but in reminder of gifts given far more than of gifts not received. Upper Jim and Granddaddy Jeet had wanted the boy to have these tools, and they would want him to have them now, now that he had, at last, a use for them.

Between the far end of Upper Jim's bench and Granddaddy Jeet's stood a tall set of shelves holding glues and varnishes and paints. Danniker went to the shelves and took down a can of varnish, grabbed from the hook, where it had hung undisturbed since Upper Jim's dying, the church key they used to pry open lids. It took Danniker a while, and finally he went to the tool rack–to *his* tool rack–and fetched a heavy chisel and mallet. The sound of the mallet striking the chisel's haft startled him. No tools had been used here, no noise made, since before Upper Jim's death. It sounded good.

The tools felt good in Danniker's hands, natural in a way that they had never felt when he was younger. They felt like they belonged there, being held by him, doing work at his guidance.

Danniker needed several taps, the chisel's blade wedged beneath the rim of the can, each tap harder than the previous, to get it open. The tools and his control of them felt better, more sure, with each tap.

As he had suspected, the varnish had long since dried out and hardened. A bit of its scent lingered, vaguely alcoholic, but he wasn't sure whether or not the varnish would still burn. That didn't matter–he would go back to town when the time was right and buy new varnish, as well as solvents and similar products. Danniker patted his back pocket where his notebook rested. He would make a list in the notebook and buy what he needed.

He was sure he would use varnish, he thought, not paint, and not just because of what he was reminded of by the scent of the dried varnish. It had always seemed to Danniker that paint covered the qualities of the lumber his father and grandfather had worked with, while varnish actually enhanced and in some ways exposed the wood's nature, its beauty, the pattern of its grain.

Danniker left the lid off the can. At some point, sometime from when his other work was done, he would take the lids off the other cans, no matter that their contents were dried. They still possessed their own gifts, which they would contribute before the job was finished.

He returned his attention to the board he'd brought to the bench, running his fingertips over its surface, along its edges, feeling, already, the presence, real and growing, of the gift he would need, that he had waited for until now. After a moment, he moved to the stack of boards and, after some consideration, drew another one out. He placed it on the bench beside the first, aligning their grains, pressing them together, touching them, looking for what he would need to do before joining them and then adding a third. These two boards and one more, he thought, would form the bottom of the coffin.

The first coffin, at any rate. The gift was growing by the moment but he wasn't going to rush it. Danniker laughed. The gift had waited

until he was seventy-one to make itself available to him–rushing it was clearly not Danniker's choice.

He had enough lumber to build three coffins, maybe four. But three, he thought, would be enough. By the time he finished the third, his skills would have improved. He would have a coffin he could use, that he could place himself inside, and close the lid over himself, and be proud of. He would wait until he finished all three before deciding which one to varnish and buff. He would do that, as well, he was sure, as he ever had, despite the fact that no one, save himself, would ever see his work.

Danniker's coffin would not enter the ground–he would not dig a grave for it, there would be no need.

Some of the coffins built by Upper Jim and Granddaddy Jeet hadn't gone into the earth either, but those hadn't been varnished when the flames touched them.

At some point Danniker would go to the desk he had not sat at in a third of a century, and open the ledger that had lain closed for just as long, and go through its pages to find out just how many Danniker coffins had carried their occupants into flames and not into the ground, and check to see if any of them had been varnished or painted, though he knew that none had.

His would.

Danniker's coffin would shine before it burned.

DEEP
WOODS

AARON MICHAEL RITCHEY

DEEP WOODS

AARON MICHAEL RITCHEY

"Are we really going to kill him?" Sammi, of course, would ask. Cute little brunette Sammi with her cute little upturned nose.

"Of course we are." Kaylie chopped up the line of drugs in the Coyote Ridge High School bathroom. She was tall. She was blonde. She wore red lipstick like she'd cut a lip.

And finally, Judiann, smoking like a fire. Dead calm. Red hair pulled back to her scalp. "No one is gonna miss that freak."

Kaylie snorted a fat line and then winced, blinked, and grabbed the cigarette out of Judiann's hand. "That's right. The woods are deep. He's a hermit. We'll be fine." She snapped her fingers. "Let's see it."

Out of her purse, Judiann's .357 magnum.

"You look so hot holding that," Kaylie husked.

"Damn straight," Judiann said. "We'll get him on his knees. We'll put the gun to the back of his head. And we'll pull the trigger. Executioner style."

Sammi chewed a nail. Sammi and her stupid nose, which ended up like the others, buried in the powder.

A snort.

"You ready?"

"Let's go."

Kaylie's pickup jangled down the dirt road. All three girls, crammed in the cab, Sammi in the middle, in case she tried to bolt. Kaylie driving. Judiann riding shotgun.

Autumn woods shadowed in crimson. Trees blotched and bleeding. Yellow leaves like trash on either side of the road.

"What happened to him?" Sammi asked. Thumbnail back in her mouth. "Why is he all freaky?"

"He was a vet. Came back from Iraq messed up. That's why he gets those fat checks from the government." The cigarette jumped on Judiann's lips as she spoke.

Kaylie reached over Sammi and took the cigarette from Judiann. "It's also why he wears that mask when he goes to the post office to pick up his money." Kaylie took a drag. Breathed out smoke. "Won't be no trouble for us to get the checks. I got the key to his box. The postmaster is a pervert." Red lips curved into a grimace. "A real pervert."

"Whose knees got dirty?" Judiann punctuated her question with a kiss.

"Not no more," Kaylie held a whisper in her eyes. "When we start picking up his money instead of him, well, we won't need short skirts to earn our blow no more."

"You'll blow, Kaylie Ann. You'll always blow." Judiann held a whisper of her own.

Cabin in the woods. Slumped. Wood rotting gray. Sparrows chittering from the trees in the chill. Twilight.

Kaylie, all hips, swayed up to the door. Knocked.

Shuffling inside. The door creaked a slow open. The freak was there, bigger than Kaylie thought, up close, so close she could smell him. Wood smoke, dirty man, filthy gross.

A fringe of hair and balding, gnarled flesh. Pulpy, misshapen brow and cheeks. Wet mouth. But his eyes were pretty, bright blue. They dart-

ed from Kaylie, to the truck, back to Kaylie, back to the truck. Squirrels squabbled.

"Hey, Mr. Voorhees," Kaylie said with a smile. "I'm Kaylie Ann. I know this is kinda weird, but I'm doing a report for school about vets. Maybe we could talk?"

A grunt from the freak. "Maybe."

She looked down. In his hands was a magazine. On the floor, scattered pictures of naked women.

The drugs told Kaylie what to do. She reached down and eased the magazine out of his hands. "Sexy. I look at my brother's magazines all the time." She felt the creepy all over her, but the feelings were muted by the drugs, and her heart was roaring like a waterfall in her chest. She rolled up the magazine into a tight cylinder and put it to her mouth. "So can we do the interview?"

"Maybe."

"I hope so," Kaylie said, tapping the magazine on her lips. Only a couple more minutes. Her friends went into the cabin through the back.

The freak's mouth gaped and oozed. Freak.

Behind him, movement. Judiann with her gun, Sammi to back her up, but Kaylie couldn't see them. The freak was taking up the entire doorway.

He turned and the gunfire deafened.

Blood speckled Kaylie's face. "Christ, Judiann, you could've-"

The freak didn't go down. His ear and half his face were gone, but he was still moving. By the door, he picked up a rusted ax. Handle gray.

"Judiann, shoot him again!" Kaylie backed off. Her feet moving to the truck, her breath like barbed wire in her lungs.

Another blast from the .357. Pieces of meat everywhere. And then he disappeared into the cabin.

A tussle, screaming, roaring. Judiann and Sammi hit the doorway at the same time, both trying to squeeze through.

Kaylie watched as the ax came down on Sammi's head, splitting her face in a line.

Judiann ran out, toward her. But above her footfalls, Kaylie could hear the squeak of the ax being pried from Sammi's skull.

Then the freak was running for them, blood raining from him in a patter on the leaves.

Hands empty. Judiann must've dropped the gun. Stupid. Something was wrong with her hair. Ponytail must've come undone.

Kaylie banged into the truck, threw it in gear. She couldn't wait for Judiann. Kaylie jammed the gas pedal to the floor, but her hands slipped on the wheel. The pickup struck an oak tree. Leaves scattered and acorns pinged the roof.

The door opened. Kaylie yanked out.

Looking up, Kaylie expected the freak. Instead: Judiann.

Her face crushed with rage. "You were going to leave me! You bitch!" Judiann's red hair was coming loose, but not her hair, her scalp. Hanging from her skull. The freak must have chopped her.

"Are you crazy, Judiann? We have to go!"

Judiann sat on Kaylie, bleeding on her, obviously crazy. Crazy in the eyes. "I hated you stealing my cigarettes all the time. I hated you!"

The freak came up, ax high, then a chunk of metal on bone. Eyes rolled back and Judiann sank down to the side. Another squeak of ax leaving bone.

Kaylie looked into the freak's mangled face. All of her fear gone.

This is how legends start, she thought with stupid calm. *Deep in the woods, three girls killed by a maniac with an ax. No one will ever know the truth.*

It was a relief. It felt unfair.

Her turn.

Chunk.

DIAMOND WIDOW

DUSTIN CARPENTER

DIAMOND WIDOW

DUSTIN CARPENTER

He stops and watches for a moment, sweat collecting on his brow. The air is thick and swampy, stirred with the congesting stink of cheap cologne and body odor. He pushes through the crowd before he asphyxiates, keeping his eyes locked on the mark.

The song changes, the bass thuds, the crowd pumps, the DJ rolls his arm in a circle. A group of girls down front howl and raise their drinks, libations sloshing from the confines of their hi-ball tumblers.

Staring beyond the spectacle before him, he stalks with the precision of an experienced predator. He's been casing *her* for a month, dropping faces to sit near her in the VIP area, Ulysses S. Grant sailing away from his pocket faster than a hooker in a naval port of call.

But it will all be worth it. These stones look rare, and even though she tells people she knows about jewelry, she knows fuck-all about diamonds compared to him. It's his bread and fucking butter.

Every weekend she's there in the VIP room, covered in diamonds, with an assortment of interested gentlemen. Tonight she's adorned in no fewer than twenty baby blue stones–twenty fucking rocks that set off a Pavlovian stiffie for anyone in his field. He might as well be a slobbering dog.

She tells people she works for a jewelry store in the Creek, where the snobs and assholes live. She's designing her own sets. This is delicate work he's doing, and he

plans on walking away with at least five rocks. Then, he'll vanish. He's done it a hundred times.

Tonight the mark is alone.

Eyes on his goal, he sweeps through the club, attitude cool, projecting his image. Tonight, he's a stock broker–he even pulled the Porsche out of storage.

He stops at the velvet rope and eyeballs the bouncer, who could probably clean the floor with him. With the money he's tossing away, it wouldn't be in the bouncer's best interest to lay a finger on his lapels. Armani suits and altercations don't go together.

His inner-pocket contains his wallet. Smooth as the ropes blocking him from the lounge, he fishes it out and shuffles two Benjamins and a Grant toward the bouncer, tells him to keep the extra. The bouncer nods and lets him through without incident. A chestnut-haired bundle of daddy-issues, wearing just enough to shame her family, seats him at a table near the railing. It's a little too close to the speaker array for his comfort.

Now, the mark is talking to a short man who looks like someone took Tom Cruise and smashed his face into the curb a couple of times. He's one of those alpha male types. Little Tommy is staring at her tits and she doesn't even notice.

Maybe she does–maybe she likes the attention.

The waitress sets a drink down in front of him; three fingers of aged gin walked in front of a bottle of tonic for good measure.

"Twenty-seven dollars," she yells over the music.

Twenty-seven fucking dollars? he thinks. *Goddamn rip-off.* He smirks and glances up at the waitress, points at his target. "What's she having?"

She glances back. "Anything top-shelf," she says with a wink.

Squinting, he watches the mark as he assesses his strategy. "Something in a martini glass. Something nice." He hands the waitress three twenties. "Keep the rest."

He knows he's got to get the target away from the alpha male, and by the looks of things, all interest in Jerry Maguire is waning. A drink will

send her his way–he knows it will. He examines the diamonds hanging around her neck, studded in her ears, decorating her fingers.

Blue fucking diamonds.

Not aquamarine, not topaz, or zircon or sapphire. They're diamonds. His mouth watering, he takes a sip and waits.

The waitress saunters up, hands her the drink, and points back to him. He smiles, nods. Raises his glass just the slightest bit.

Target engaged.

The mark is one cold-hearted bitch. She doesn't even say anything to little Tommy, just walks on over with drink in hand. She stops at the edge of the table and takes a sip. "Orange cranberry martini?" Holding his gaze with hers, she splashes the rest of her drink across the floor. "I'm not that kind of girl."

He sits back a little. *That cocktail hussy must have pocketed at least fifty.* "It got you over here, didn't it?" He holds his hand toward the empty seat. "I'll order some champagne."

She stares at him. "What's the occasion?"

"I told the waitress to bring you something nice. We can do a little better than that." He nods to her glass. "Let me buy you a real drink."

She tugs at her skirt and slides into the booth, leaning forward on her elbows, draping a five-stone necklace across the top of her cleavage. "What do they call you?"

"Logan," he lies.

"And how does Logan afford champagne?"

As rehearsed: "Logan is a stock broker," he tells her. He lays it on extra thick. "And what does one call you?"

"How about one calls me Ella," she replies with a suspicious smile.

"And how did Ella come across so many fine diamonds?"

"Some were gifts," she says simply. "And the rest I made."

"You made?"

"I work in jewelry," she replies. "I make all sorts of things. Things that require diamonds." With a shrug, she holds up her right hand to display the setting on her ring finger. "This was my ex-husband," she

says. "Men like to give me gifts." Pointing at various diamonds she says, "Gentleman caller, gentleman caller, live-in boyfriend, boy toy."

He nods.

"Does that intimidate you?" she asks.

"Should it?"

"These are unique. Special." She leans farther forward, a coy smile across her pouty lips. "Rare." Closer. "One-of-a-kind."

He locks his sight right on her kisser. Her perfume is overpowering. "Just like the woman who wears them." *Your move.*

Coming closer still, she sets her lips on his, and swirls her tongue around his mouth.

Bullseye.

He pulses the engine a few times as he slows to a stop. He's got two of her diamonds in his pocket–an earring and a raw stone he pried off one of her rings with a little cunning.

Ella rubs her hand down the armrest on the door. "Jesus Christ, I love Corinthian leather," she moans.

Corinthian? Ricardo Montalban is doing back-flips in his grave. "It's just a plain car seat unless an attractive young lady, such as yourself, is present to admire it."

"You are too much," she says. She teases him–goes in for a kiss, and once their lips brush, she shies away a little bit. The smile on her lips... she's his. "How about dinner tomorrow?"

Shit! "Sounds good. What are you thinking?"

She hums. "You pick the place. Pick me up at seven."

It's not going to happen. She'll notice she's missing some rocks, and she'll be pissed. Hell, missing diamonds like this will land him on the police radar. "I know the perfect little restaurant. You won't be disappointed."

She unbuckles her seatbelt and straddles the console, pressing her body against his. After a sloppy kiss, she says, "I don't think I'm done

with you just yet." A wicked grin on her lips, she grips the shifter and hammers it like it's his tool.

He raises an eyebrow. "Oh, really?"

"How about you drive us over to the Creek? I've always wanted a man to have me on a blanket of diamonds."

Suddenly, she's speaking his language.

"I know the safe combo," she whispers into his ear.

"Isn't that illegal?" he asks with a smirk.

"Very."

He slams down on the accelerator and spins the tires, Ella still grinding her hips against him. The Porsche rockets down the street, engine screaming into the dark night.

She hits several buttons on the security system and pulls him in by the collar, nearly toppling them both over. She laughs, shushes him. *Who would be here to hear it?*

"Let me show you the basement," she says. "It's where I do most of my work."

That wicked grin, again. Briefly, he wishes this were real. She's the sort of girl who could be fun, who could get him into a lot of trouble. But he has his eyes on the prize, and it's getting closer by the minute.

They go through a small workroom. He quickly inspects each station: benches with table-mounted magnifying glasses and tweezers, Petri dishes, chairs pushed in. Everything is put away. Not a single diamond in sight.

She pulls against the handle of a metal door, and with some heft, it slides open, revealing a thin stairway down to a dark room.

Ella turns to him. Kisses him. "I'll show you the new ring I'm making. It's platinum." She looks him over top to bottom with a grin, with hunger in her eyes, and leads him down the stairs.

A draft blows over his arm, and he's chilled to the core.

The room has high ceilings and walls made of brick. It feels like a cathedral, a cavern of his creator. The room smells of smoke and polish-

ing rouge with a hint of dank. There are workbenches down here, these more lovingly used. There's a metal furnace in the corner, sitting unlit for the night. It stinks of hot, as if it hasn't completely cooled after a long day. Tools of the trade hang from a pegboard on the wall.

Four large machines sit in a row, ten feet off the wall. He inspects one of them. "What are these? Kilns of some sort?"

She takes his hand and tugs him farther into the room. "We use those to make diamonds."

His breath catches, his blood runs cold. *Are they artificial?* "Diamond furnaces? Are yours–"

"Oh, God no. My diamonds are all natural. I wouldn't dream of wearing anything else." She pulls him up for the umpteenth kiss since they've entered the building.

There's a moment of relief, but he won't know for sure until he can have a closer look at the stones. "Diamonds really are a girl's best friend."

"You have no idea," she says. "I want to show you something."

They stop before a large cylindrical machine that takes up a considerable amount of space. Whatever this machine is, it runs hot. It's connected to a metal ventilation hose and has its own Ansul system. It sits in a pit, which he guesses is around ten feet deep, its bottom lip lining up with the floor. The machine is open, the top section at eye level, and shuts with a large lever. There's a hand crank on one side, and an instrument panel attached to the front.

"This seems like a lot of machine to make such a small ring," he mutters.

"It doesn't make rings," she says, pulling him in and shoving her tongue down his throat. "You should let me make you a ring."

He raises an eyebrow. "What do you have in mind?"

"For someone your size, I'm guessing..." She lays her lips on him again, gives him a forceful kiss he won't have time to forget. "Mmmm. Four carats."

The swing of her hand is quick and unexpected; the pipe hits him square on the face. His ears ring, his mind goes blank, and the simple motion of bringing his hand to his cheek saps all of his energy. He aches

everywhere. His head shakes and spasms, and for a moment, he's nothing more than a six-foot-tall bobblehead.

A line of blood runs down the side of his face and laps over his fingers. He tries to speak, but can only manage a short moan.

Ella shoves her hand in his pocket. "I'll be taking these back," she says calmly. With little effort, she fishes the two pilfered diamonds from his pocket and sets them aside. She tosses the pipe away and examines the side of his face, looking as if she might be concerned. "Don't worry," she says quietly into his ear. "I'll make you a good ring."

She shoves him hard. He stumbles back and falls into the machine, hitting his head on the lip of the column on his way down. The last thing he sees is the cool smile spread across her face, her hand resting on the lever. The lid comes down and latches shut, leaving him in total darkness, suffocating on the smell of hot metal. He hardly has time to register it before the searing pain rips through his body. In the fraction of an instant before he is subjected to two-million pounds of pressure and enough heat to instantly melt the face off his skull, he thinks: *you fucking bitch.*

"This is a nice set," Ella's boss says, plucking the loupe from his eye socket. "The diamond is nearly flawless. I love the shape, the color. The setting is exquisite."

Ella nods. "Thank you."

"I'd like to feature this in the display case," he says. "What do you call it?"

"The Logan."

He glances over at her and nods. "I like it. It'll bring in quite a bit of money."

"I've already paid for the materials. It's my favorite piece, and I'm not ready to part ways with it."

"That's too bad. The commission you'd make on that..." He sighs. "When can you make me something like it? Something I can sell?"

She shrugs.

"You're too modest for the amount of talent you have." He hands the ring back to her. "I have never seen anyone make a band quite like yours. I'd like you to design me a set to sell by the end of the month." With a wink and a smile, he palms her ass in passing, giving it the slightest squeeze before walking away.

She glares at him, red-hot anger flickering behind her eyes. "Don't worry," she says. "I'll make you a *real* nice ring."

THE
CAMERA

JOSHUA VIOLA

THE CAMERA

JOSHUA VIOLA

A lone cloud blocked the sun and cast a thin shadow over the trail. Goosebumps spread across Patricia's arms. She rubbed her exposed shoulders–she needed more than a tank top, at least for the morning. She took a T-shirt from her backpack and pulled it on.

She yawned, wishing for nothing more than to be back home and in her bed after a long shower. No: a *bath*. She wanted to soak forever in a hot bath. Her yawn became a sigh.

"Tired already?" Mick said. He was ahead of her on the trail and turned to stare. Patricia saw the same disappointment and annoyance on Mick's face she knew so well from outings with her father.

"I'm okay," Patricia said, hoping Mick couldn't tell how little she meant the words.

"Sure you are," Mick said, making no effort at all to hide how little he believed her. "Suck it up. You're the one who wanted this trip."

"I know," Patricia said. "I just hadn't expected it to be this cold. We always go hiking in July."

"It's *late* September, Trish," Mick snapped, "and you knew that when you stuck us with this weekend. And we couldn't go this July because of my job. You think I don't know that? You think I've forgotten how many times you've mentioned it?"

"Mick, I–"

"Just don't, Trish," he said. "Don't. You picked the date, so suck it up. We're here, and we've got two more days of this. So don't."

Patricia didn't move, and was not surprised when Mick turned and strode off, quickly disappearing around a bend in the trail.

Suck it up, Mick said.

Same advice Patricia's daddy gave her so many times. Didn't sound any better coming from her fiancée than it had coming from her father.

Suck it up.

Patricia drew a deep breath, then another, shouldered her pack and adjusted its straps, then set out after Mick, moving fast so she could catch up, although she didn't know why.

She was panting when she caught sight of him again, still a distance ahead of her on the trail. He was leaning against a tree, watching her. That was a good sign, she thought, and an unexpected one. She hadn't expected to see him again so soon. Much less to find him waiting for her. Her father had never done that much for her. When she couldn't keep up with Daddy on a hike, the bastard simply left her behind. Maybe Mick was less like Daddy than Patricia assumed.

She tried to calm her breathing, not let Mick see how winded she was. It didn't work–the closer she got to him, the more clearly she could see his sneer. Daddy's sneer.

"You're out of shape," Mick said as she neared him. "And the weight you've gained doesn't help, does it, Fatty Patty?"

Patricia didn't know why she ever told Mick about the nickname. The weight her father mocked so mercilessly was long since gone before Patricia met Mick. Not before Daddy died, though. She was still Fatty Patty to her daddy when he went.

Patricia was aware of the extra weight. *If only you knew,* she thought.

Mick stood straight, raised and flexed his bare arms.

"Okay, okay. I get it, Superman. Back to the gym when we get home," Patricia said.

"Don't make promises you won't keep," Mick said.

"Like you?" Patricia said, harshly, and regretted her words immediately.

"I'm here," Mick said. "*You* wanted me here, remember? So here I am. Keep up."

He swung his backpack onto his shoulders and set out again, just as fast as before.

"Goddammit, Mick," Patricia said, but not loud enough for him to hear.

She took only a minute to catch as much of her breath as she could before starting after him.

It took more than an hour for Patricia to reach Mick, and only because he'd found something on the trail.

"'Bout damn time!" Mick said when she reached him. "Thought I'd have to wait all day. Check it out." He pointed to a cluster of bushes not far off the trail. A wisp of bright red adorned the top of a small shrub.

"What is it?" Patricia said.

"Fun flag!" Mick said and stepped into the bushes, reaching out to tug the red fabric free from the branches and hold it high.

A bra.

"Jesus, Mick, don't touch it! You don't know who or how long–"

"Oh, it's fresh," Mick said. He made a show of sniffing the bra and pressing its lace against his cheek. "Not off long is my guess. And they must be *this* big. Judging by these cups. Real ones, something a man can grab onto."

"You're disgusting," Patricia said.

"Just being honest," Mick said. "Isn't that what you always say you want? *Honesty*?" He made the word sound like something foul and obscene. "And, honestly, Trish, this thing would swallow yours whole, with plenty of room to spare. Then again, keep gaining weight, Fatty Patty, and maybe you could grow into it."

Asshole.

Patricia was sure her father was the biggest asshole she'd ever known. Until she met Mick. A few months into their relationship, after Mick cheated on her the first time (and blamed her for it), she realized her

daddy, though cold and unfit for fatherhood, was trying to teach her something. His ways were harsh–*too harsh*, Patricia thought–but his lessons served a purpose.

"Wise up, Patty," he'd say, "or this world will chew you up, spit you out and leave you to rot."

His words were like chisel to stone–sharp and powerful.

Patricia's stomach lurched, but she was not about to vomit in front of Mick. She'd gotten good at hiding her vomiting from him, and she fought down the wave of nausea.

"Come on," Mick said, stepping deeper into the woods. "And try to keep up for once, will you?"

"Where–"

"On the hunt!" Mick said. "On the scent! Where there's a bra, there's got to be panties, and where there's panties there's got to be–"

Patricia didn't hear the rest–the roaring in her ears was too loud. But she had a pretty good idea of what he said, the same word she'd heard her daddy use more than once.

Squeezing her eyes tight against tears and memories, Patricia stood still in the forest for a long moment before following Mick.

This time she didn't lose sight of him. Mick was moving slowly, examining bushes and undergrowth like some parody of a primitive hunter on the trail of something. He wasn't very good at it, not the way Patricia's father had been. She'd gone hunting with Daddy two or three times when she was a kid, and could still remember the way he spotted and followed tracks in rough country. He'd been no more pleasant on hunting trips than hikes, but hunting he'd moved slower, and Patricia had been able to keep up. The challenge was keeping up quietly.

Keep it down, Fatty Patty! Daddy hissed at her. *You want to spook every animal in the state?*

Daddy never let her hunt, even though he promised it a lot. She could go along, but she never got to hold the gun. Only at the range he took

her to sometimes. He was no more patient with her there than in the woods, but Patricia showed him. She was a good shot, a natural, better with a pistol than a rifle, but not bad with a long gun.

Deep in the woods, Mick turned toward Patricia. He pressed a finger to his grinning lips–*keep it down, Fatty Patty*–and winked a leering eye as he knelt to pick up something. He raised his find high–another wisp of red fabric.

Mick mouthed: *panties*, and pressed them to his face.

Patricia bent at the waist and vomited without making any noise.

Mick draped the bra around his neck, and carried the panties like a flag as he moved forward, well ahead of Patricia. She wished she could stop following him, but she couldn't help herself. She had followed him too far already, and not just into the forest.

The woods thinned ahead, and Mick stopped, and then lifted a fist, thumb up. He turned and nodded at Patricia, his leer broader and even more disgusting. He waved for her to join him, and again she couldn't help herself.

Even before she reached Mick, Patricia could hear them. Hear *her* anyway, a woman shrieking, moaning, shouting obscenities, crying out, and not from pain. Not from pleasure either, Patricia thought as her stomach roiled. Nobody made *that* much noise outside of a porno film. Unless they were faking it. Patricia knew a lot about faking it.

She stepped beside Mick, who was looking down into a little glade. He was breathing heavily, and each inhale and exhale was like the blade of a saw drawn across Patricia's flesh.

"Look at 'em go!" he whispered, pointing down the slope of the hill.

Patricia didn't look. "Let's go, Mick," she said, not whispering.

"You want to spook 'em?" Mick hissed.

He grabbed Patricia by the scruff of her neck and forced her to look. A dark haired woman was vigorously riding a man, her screams and shrieks becoming even louder–and even harder to take seriously–with each gyration.

Mick was taking it seriously, though, Patricia could tell, and for an instant she thought she would vomit again.

Instead, she twisted free of his grip, and spun away from him.

Just as a ranger emerged from the woods.

Patricia caught her breath.

The ranger was old. Latino, she knew–like her daddy. He was white-haired, and the park ranger's uniform he wore was threadbare and much-patched. He limped as he stomped toward them, each firm footstep jingling. Patricia didn't look at his feet to see what made the jingles. She couldn't take her eyes from his face.

He looked like Daddy.

He looked like Daddy would if Daddy was that old.

If Daddy hadn't gone the day he turned fifty.

When I was twelve.

"You two like what you're seeing?" the ranger asked, his voice more like Daddy's than not.

"What the fuck?" Mick said, turning at the sound of the ranger's voice. "What the–"

"Fuck," the ranger said, his tone still flat. His eyes were flat, too, Patricia thought, not a spark of life in them.

"You like using them dirty words, boy? Ought to shame you. You ought to be more polite in front of a girl, even one like this."

"Who–" Mick said.

"Why don't you just shush up now?" the ranger said. "Way you might say it is *shut the fuck up*, boy. Now, smile for the camera."

The ranger unslung a camera–an expensive one, Patricia thought, a big SLR with a long lens, out of place with the man's shabby uniform, the old rifle slung over his right shoulder, the battered handle of a pistol resting in the scratched and worn holster on his right hip.

"What?" Mick said.

"I told you to shut up while I get some pictures for my records. Got to keep good records, keep these woods safe."

He snapped two pictures of Mick, and then turned the lens like a gun barrel toward Patricia.

"Smile for the camera, Fatty Patty," he said, and took two more pictures.

"How–"

Patricia felt her knees beginning to buckle, but then Mick's arm was around her waist, holding her up and moving her a bit behind him, protectively, she thought, like a father might do, like her own father never had.

"Now I got your pictures, you two get moving," the ranger said. "Get on with it! I gotta take care of them down there."

The ranger moved to the glade, the jingling sound loud. Patricia looked down. The ranger's boots were as new and expensive as his camera, beautifully polished black leather.

He was wearing spurs.

"Come *on*, Trish," Mick said even before the ranger was fully past them. "Didn't you hear him? Come *on!*"

Mick took Patricia's hand, hard, and jerked her into motion, pulling her along behind him through the thick underbrush. Patricia wanted to say he was hurting her–he was hurting her–and they were going the wrong way, deeper into the forest instead of back toward the trail, but before she could speak there was the sound of a rifle shot, and then the ranger's voice shouting at the couple in the glade.

"Don't you move! Either one of you, don't you move an inch until I tell you to smile for the camera."

Patricia held tight to Mick's hand, following him, wherever he was heading.

"Holy shit!" Patricia yelped. "What happened?"

"I don't know. Hurry up," Mick said.

A few minutes later Patricia thought she heard screams, the woman screaming again–and not faking it this time. Patricia thought she heard a man screaming too. Mick moved faster and Patricia did her best to keep up.

The screams from behind didn't stop until two more shots were fired, after which the only sounds Patricia heard were her own breathing and Mick's, and the noises they made as they moved through the forest.

Too much noise, Patricia thought. *We're going to spook every animal in the state.*

Patricia didn't know how long they'd been moving, only that the sun had traveled much of the way across the sky. She had no idea where they were, only that they were nowhere near the trail. They were lost, but she didn't want to say that to Mick.

"There's a place up ahead we can catch our breath," Mick said. "He won't find us there."

"You–you know where we are?" Patricia said.

"I always know where we are, Trish," Mick said. "Always have, good times and bad. More bad than good lately, but you know that, too."

"We'll be okay," Patricia said. "We'll get out of this and we'll be okay again, we will, we have to be."

"We're already away from him," Mick said. "He's not a problem for us anymore. Or at least he won't be soon."

"I think he killed that couple. That old man–"

But Mick wasn't paying attention to her. They emerged into a small clearing with a single aspen at its center.

The ranger's camera was dangling from one of the tree's branches.

"Well look at *that*, Trish," Mick said.

Patricia remained at the edge of the clearing while Mick trotted to the aspen and retrieved the camera.

"Don't you think that's a little weird, Mick?" Patricia said and glanced around the clearing. "Let's go."

Mick made a show of bringing it to life and stared at the screen.

"Wow!" Mick said. "Holy shit! Come over here, Trish, you've got to see this."

"No. I don't want–"

"*Now!*" Mick said.

Patricia walked to Mick and stood beside him near the aspen.

"Closer," Mick said. "You've gotta see this shit."

Patricia didn't move, and Mick grabbed her and pulled her next to him. "Look at it." he said.

Mick thumbed through the pictures slowly, jerking Patricia's arm angrily every time she tried to look away.

"Gorgeous, isn't she?" Mick said as he thumbed through a sequence of nude photos of the girl in the clearing. "And what a great figure, not a bit of Fatty Patty to her at all."

"You asshole," Patricia said. "What is this?"

"Keep watching."

The images of the woman gave way to a series of her riding the man in the glade, then both of them looking straight into the camera, startled and fearful expressions replacing the ecstasy, real or feigned, their features had worn just an image or two before.

"Now check this out," Mick said, advancing the camera roll.

The image showed the girl, naked, on her knees. She had deep scratches and marks across most of her body. Tears streamed down her face.

"The spurs were a nice touch," Mick said.

"What do you mean?" Patricia said.

"Look."

Mick advanced to the next photo.

Patricia fought down a scream.

The next image showed the girl draped lifelessly atop a pile of leaves, caked in blood.

Mick hit the advance button again. Another photo came into view. It revealed the boyfriend, naked as well, twisted and disfigured, his body marked by deep cuts and scratches and–a bullet hole in his forehead.

Mick hit advance.

The final image showed their empty eyes staring up at the photographer. The perfectly polished tip of one boot was clearly visible in the picture, resting on the girl's blood-streaked belly.

"Real nice," Mick said.

Patricia began to back away.

"Just stay where you are, Patricia," came a voice from behind her.

A woman's voice.

Patricia turned to see the woman from the glade, from the images, step from the forest. There wasn't a mark on her.

She was dressed in denim shorts and a halter-top, sturdy hiking boots and thick socks.

She was holding a pistol–the ranger's pistol–aiming it directly at Patricia.

"Nice job, babe," Mick said to her.

"I didn't think I'd ever get that shit washed off," she said, stepping close to Mick.

"I'll scrub you clean once we're out of here," Mick said.

"Let's make it soon," the woman said. "Let's get this done and get gone."

"Almost there. The others taken care of?"

"What do you think?" the woman said. "You just fucking *saw* Bobby in the camera. And nobody's ever going to be finding Darrell. *Or* those damned spurs. Nearly cut my hand on them dragging him into the woods."

"Lucky guys," Mick said with a chuckle. "Last thing they got to see was you naked."

"Yeah, well if *you* ever want to see me naked again, let's get this over with."

"Almost there," Mick said once more. "Just another picture to take. Of you, Trish. A selfie, in fact, once I get my prints off this thing."

Mick plucked the red panties from his pocket and began wiping the camera clean.

"Nice touch," the woman said.

"I'll buy you some new ones when we're back in town. Not that you'll be wearing them much."

The woman laughed deep in her throat.

Patricia forced herself to take a long, slow breath. It didn't help. "The two of you–"

"Are pretty fucking happy," Mick said as he meticulously wiped the camera clean. "Have been for a while. For as long as we've been putting this whole thing together."

"This?"

"Haven't you figured it out *yet*, Fatty Patty?" Mick said. "You really are slow, aren't you?"

"You killed those two–the boy and the... ranger?"

"Gloria killed them," Mick said.

"And without a stitch of clothes on, too," Gloria said with another deep chuckle.

Patricia didn't think she'd ever heard anything as horrible as that laugh.

"And you're next, but even *you* should have figured that out by now." Covering his own fingertips with the panties, Mick held the camera out to Patricia. "Time for one last photo."

Patricia moved her hands protectively over her belly.

"Mick. I'm pregnant!"

Mick grinned and made his eyes wide.

"Mick, I–"

"You think that matters?" he said. "I saw the First Response box in the trash weeks ago. I've known for a while, Patricia."

He shook the strap, setting the camera in motion like a pendulum. "Take it!"

Patricia reached out a trembling hand to the camera strap.

The instant she had it in her grasp, she jerked hard, swinging the camera above her as fiercely as she could and then pivoting to drive the camera's full weight and momentum into the side of Gloria's head.

Gloria crumpled fast to her knees, the pistol slipping from her fingers.

Patricia lunged for the gun and had it up and cocked before Mick could move.

"You bastard," she said. "You fucking bastard."

On her knees, Gloria whimpered and moaned. Her temple was bloody, her eyes unfocused. Patricia watched with something like pleasure as the woman raised a hand to her head and then quickly pulled away red fingers.

"Mickey! Mickey, she hurt me!"

"Shut up," Patricia said, "you want to spook every animal in the state?"

"Patricia, easy," Mick said softly.

"You shut up too–*Mickey*," Patricia said.

"She broke my head, Mickey," Gloria whined. "That bitch broke my fucking head."

"It'll be all right, babe," Mick said.

"No," said Patricia. "It won't."

Patricia stepped back a bit before pulling the trigger. She didn't want any of Gloria's blood or brains anywhere near her.

Mick shuddered as Patricia turned her attention–and the pistol–to him.

"Patricia," he said, his voice weak, "please, please–"

"Please what?" Patricia said. "Please don't kill me?"

"You can't. Think of the baby, Trish. Our baby, Patricia, *ours.*"

"No," Patricia said. "Not ours."

Mick looked surprised. "What? What do you mean?"

Patricia smirked, "Not. Ours."

"Then whose?"

"David's," Patricia said, pleased to finally reveal the truth.

Mick took a moment. "Who?"

"David. From work."

"Oh Jesus, that chubby asshole with the braces?"

"Not an asshole, Mick. Believe it or not, there are people in this world capable of being different than you."

Mick scoffed. "When?"

"Fourth of July picnic."

"I'm–"

"You're what?" Patricia said. "A worthless piece of shit, you and that bitch? You hate me that much that you planned to kill me? And not just me, but that poor, dumb kid who probably thought he was getting the lay of his life in the woods?"

"He wasn't anybody, he didn't matter, just a kid Gloria found. Nobody's gonna miss him."

"And the ranger? The old man, who was he?"

"Old man?" Mick said. "What old man? What the fuck are you talking about?"

"The *ranger*, you asshole. You know he looked just like my daddy."

"Your dad?" Mick said. "What the fuck are you talking about? He was just some dumbfuck nigger willing to dress up in a uniform and throw a scare into you for a hundred bucks."

Patricia paused for a moment. She thought of the last words her father said to her just before he died.

Keep an eye out, Fatty Patty.

A chill washed over her.

Daddy?

"I see now," she said with a glare in her eyes.

She held the pistol steady, hoping Mick would piss his pants. When he didn't, she had an idea.

Patricia was still holding the camera strap. Carefully, not giving Mick any hint of a chance to do anything anymore stupid than he already had, she worked her fingers along the strap, brought the camera up and thumbed it back to life.

"This is one tough camera to take a beating like that and still work," Patricia said. "Then again, it *was* Gloria who took the beating, wasn't it? And maybe her head wasn't as hard as it sounded."

Patricia laughed, honestly, and not deep in her throat at all.

"Patricia, please," Mick said.

She waited until a dark stain began to spread across his crotch.

"Smile for the camera, asshole," Patricia said, and squeezed the trigger in a single, steady motion, just like her father taught her all those years ago.

LOST
BALLS

Sean Eads

LOST BALLS

SEAN EADS

M arty, Jim and I had been golfing buddies since
college. All three of us were weekend hackers
whose knowledge of the PGA rules wasn't precise when it came to matters of drops and penalties. I
just liked swinging the clubs a little and drinking a few
beers, hitting playfully on cute cart girls (what my wife
Rachel didn't know wouldn't hurt her), and managing a
par here and there.

I hadn't played Five Pines before, but the course was
all Jim and Marty could talk about after they participated
in a tournament sponsored by their work. They wanted
to play there again right away, this time with me. But
I balked after learning that the green fee was over one
hundred dollars *without* a cart.

I said, "Forget it. We could play six rounds at a muni
for that price. Count me out."

"You won't believe this course, Brad. It's *worth* the
price."

I doubted that. Better golfers, golfers who *cared*,
might appreciate the intricacies and beauty of a really
expensive golf course. But when you're going to go out
there and shoot forty over par, it's adding insult to injury
to pay a lot of money for the privilege.

I relented when Marty got a coupon that discounted
our round to $90 per person, with a cart plus lunch. We
had an early afternoon tee time and everything was going
great. Jim and Marty shared a cart while I drove my own.

I couldn't quit smiling. Five Pines *was* beautiful, and despite being difficult as hell–lots of sand traps, ponds and creeks to clear, inconvenient trees and uneven lies–I was playing one of the best games of my life. It wasn't anything to write home about, but breaking 100 on this course was noteworthy for anyone, especially a hacker like me.

Marty and Jim weren't doing as well, and they were pissed. Marty in particular was having one of the worst rounds I'd ever seen. By the seventh hole, he'd lost six balls and started borrowing from Jim. You knew he was upset because Jim kept offering him weed and Marty wouldn't smoke. Usually those two got high as shit together during a round. Jim *was* high as shit by the fifth hole, and as usual it was helping his game.

"Man, you'll play a lot better once you have some of this spinach," Jim said, refilling his pipe on the ninth hole.

It was a lengthy par 3, and Marty was already on the tee box, taking aggressive practice swings as we waited for the group ahead of us to finish putting. "I've got to figure this out. Something's wrong with my hip rotation today."

Jim and I traded smirks. Marty liked to talk about his golf game in technical terms, usually repeating whatever information he picked up from the last YouTube video he watched. Jim offered me his pipe. I didn't usually smoke weed, but I felt so great just then that I wanted to top it off with a buzz. I took a few hits and handed it back.

"You guys were right. Five Pines is the best course I've ever played. Every hole is something else."

"Yeah, it's a *real* Arcadia," Marty said, making another practice swing. The green had cleared and he teed up his ball.

I was getting out of the cart when he swung, so I didn't see the result. Marty's sudden outburst gave me an idea.

"Oh, you fucker! You goddamn piece of *shit!*"

"It went left into the woods," Jim said.

"I fucking *saw* where it went, okay?" Marty brushed past us and jammed his club into his bag.

I looked toward those woods. The ball might be in there or it might have caromed into the creek that crisscrossed the course. Five Pines was

really stretched out, a total bitch to walk, with its winding paths through the forests and long wooden bridges to cross. The design was so alien to the efficient, mundane municipal courses I called home.

Jim drove his ball over to the right, which was safe because the course opened up. I put my ball on the green, hole high, for a long birdie putt.

"Fucker," Marty said.

I smiled. "I think I like this course. I could play it every weekend."

"Better get a second job," Jim said, getting behind the wheel. He and Marty drove off while I put my 5-iron in my bag. Before I drove after them, I took a second to look around at all the beauty and listen to the chirping birds. I took a deep breath and felt a sort of *Zen*. I just wanted to shout for joy and listen to the echo.

Marty and Jim were arguing when I pulled up behind them. Marty had taken his putter and several clubs out of his bag and was marching into the woods.

"Come on, man," Jim said. "You won't find your ball in there. Just take a drop."

"Hell no. I've lost too many already. I'm going to find it and play it."

"Don't sweat it, Marty. I've got plenty of balls you can use. No point wasting your time—"

"*Shut up.*"

"Wow, he's pissed off," I said, watching Marty weave in and out of the trees. I drove my cart farther up, following the path to the top of the green. There I parked, took out my putter, and studied my putt while I waited for Marty and Jim to join me.

Jim went ahead and played his ball, making a good chip. Another couple of minutes passed with no sign from Marty. We called for him and got no response. More minutes passed. I looked up the length of the fairway to the tee box. The foursome of old guys playing behind us had caught up and were standing there in identical poses, arms crossed at the chest.

"Come on, Marty," I said. "We've got to hurry this up."

After a moment, his voice filtered over to us: "I found it! It's under the bridge."

Jim and I looked at each other. "Well, pick it up and bring it over here and just putt."

"No, I can play it."

"Trust me, Marty, you *can't* play it."

"There's no water down here. I can chip out and then lob it up."

We couldn't see him, but the plan he detailed was so absurd I didn't need a visual. I looked up the fairway again. The old guys were clearly pissed. My face got hot.

"Just putt out," I said. "Those guys are going to hit into us if we don't speed this up."

"Sounds good to me."

Jim made his putt. I was nervous and anxious and ended up four-putting. I didn't care about my score at this point. Marty still hadn't shown.

We got into our carts and drove the path about twenty seconds before coming to the bridge. I expected a creek, but the bridge actually crossed a small, dry gulch about nine feet deep. The sides were steep but climbable. No sane person would have tried to play out of that, but that wasn't on my mind just then.

Where the hell was Marty?

We leaned over the railing and called down to him. He didn't answer.

"What the hell?" Jim said.

I peered down but the space between the planks revealed little. "You don't think he had a heart attack or something, do you?"

Jim and I looked at each other and a silent agreement passed between us. I was reasonably fit. Jim was carrying too much extra weight and had bad knees. It was up to me to go down there and check.

I used my 8-iron as a hiking pole. Still, I skidded my way down and was lucky not to break a bone. At the bottom, I felt an intense chill, as if I'd actually descended several thousand feet in a few seconds. For a moment I forgot where I was. There was nothing to obstruct it, but the sunlight didn't seem to reach me down here. The sky that had been a gorgeous blue looked strikingly overcast as I gazed up at Jim.

"What is it?" he said.

"Nothing–Marty's not down here."

I didn't sound sure, even though I could see *everything* under that bridge. But somehow there seemed to be a massive blind spot right in front of me. I took a few steps forward. I could have walked under the bridge without stooping, but it *looked* cramped. It also looked like a great place for wolf spiders to nest and fall on your head like rain.

The foursome behind us had pulled up to our carts. They were asking Jim what the hell was happening. I started to climb up when I heard a hard *pinging* noise, like a golf ball knocking against a rock. I turned and that's just what I saw. There was a golf ball lying right where I'd been standing. I went over and picked it up only to drop it immediately. The ball was covered in slime, like spit when a dog's been chewing on a toy. The white casing was mauled and cracked.

That ball wasn't here before.

"Hey Brad, you find anything?"

"No," I said, bending to snatch the mangled ball and put it in my pocket. I looked to the bridge again. Was something there, staring back at me? Something I somehow couldn't see?

I high-tailed it up the gulch, almost slipping a couple of times in my haste. Now the foursome behind us and the foursome behind *them* were gathered to hear about Marty's disappearance. They joined us in the search. We dialed Marty's cell phone and it rang behind us–in his bag. Then we called the clubhouse and the staff came out. It was the damnedest thing. In fact, every single person who took part in the hunt that afternoon at some point muttered: "Well, this is the damnedest thing I've ever seen."

Eventually the police got involved, after we went through the process of filing a missing persons report. Doing so felt ridiculous, but the simple fact was we ended up leaving Five Pines that day without finding a trace of Marty. At first the police seemed to agree with the staff that his disappearance was a prank. Hadn't he been playing poorly? Maybe he decided to quit and run off to the clubhouse for a beer. But no one reported seeing him. The big deal, of course, was that his car was still in the parking lot the next morning. So the cops scoured the woods for

him too, and we were all convinced he must have had a heart attack or something and was just waiting to be found.

Jim and I helped in the search that second day, until it got too dark to do much of anything. I'd call out for Marty, all the while feeling my right pocket for the cracked golf ball I found in the gulch. I wasn't about to show it to anyone. Christ, what could it even mean? I was sure it hadn't been there when I reached the bottom, just as I was certain I *heard* the sound of a ball hitting a rock and then *hocus pocus,* there it was. Could Marty have thrown it at me? There *might* have been other places around the bridge where he could hide. Perhaps he'd intended a practical joke and was too scared to come out because of how fast the situation escalated.

But how had he mutilated the ball?

The police broke out their flashlights and called in a couple of blood-hounds to continue the search.

I looked at Jim and said, "If you need to get out of here, I'll stay. Rachel won't mind. Frankly, last night she sounded like she'd be fine if I was the one who'd disappeared."

Reluctantly, he said, "I don't want to, but I better. Amy's upset. It's like she thinks I'm in danger by coming back here."

Amy was Jim's wife. Of the three of us, only Jim and I were married. Marty wasn't even dating, and neither of us had a clue about who to notify regarding his disappearance, other than his boss. Yesterday, we'd both delayed calling our wives because we didn't know where to begin explaining the situation. We were both way overdue and Marty still hadn't shown up, so we had to tell them the truth. They couldn't comprehend it any more than we could. Unlike Amy, Rachel didn't sound worried. She practically called me a liar and hung up on me. We'd been fighting lately over the usual stuff–money, free time, the future (which meant having children). She hated me playing golf precisely because of the cash and weekends I spent on the game. (I wasn't about to tell her how much the Five Pines round cost me). Our marriage had been building to a crisis for some time now, but I never thought the implosion point would be Marty disappearing into thin air.

So Jim left and I joined the police for what seemed to be a last ditch effort. We focused on the area around the 9th hole, including the bridge and the dry gulch. While they focused on the woods, I walked alone back and forth across the bridge, listening to my footsteps on the planks. The bridge was about thirty feet long and only a little wider than a golf cart.

"Brad."

I stopped in the middle of the bridge, hearing the whisper.

"Down here."

I looked straight down and the beam of my police-issued flashlight glinted off Marty's eyes. It was like his face was *right there.* I gasped and then he was gone, like a creature terrified by light.

I bent down, pressing my face to the planks. "Marty? *Marty?"*

His voice answered, but the words were indistinct and somehow distant. Regardless, he had to be right below me.

I ran to the end of the bridge and started down the gulch. I was going too fast to worry about falling, and of course I did fall, tumbling most of the way to the bottom. I lost hold of the flashlight and found it a few feet away from me, its beam jousting along the ground.

Hands shaking, I picked it up and pivoted toward the bridge. "Marty?"

A cold breeze answered from the dark and I put my free hand over my mouth and nose as I got a whiff of the stench. I started to backpedal when Marty called to me again.

"Here, Brad. Help me."

I scanned everywhere with the light. I couldn't see him. Coughing, I shouted back, "Hang on. I'm going to climb up and get help."

A white flash crossed the light's beam. I ducked and heard something buzz past my left ear. I turned and found a golf ball on the ground. It was shiny and wet like the one I'd found before. I bent down and prodded it with the edge of the flashlight. The ball was also cracked and mauled.

As I stood up, another ball shot toward me. Then another. Some rolled on the ground and others came at me like gunshots. I was struck several times in the chest and cried out for help. My voice felt heavy, like it couldn't possibly climb out of the gulch and be heard. Meanwhile the assault continued until I was reduced to shielding myself in a fetal

position. I found myself buried in balls, so many it looked like a freak hailstorm. I staggered to my feet and pushed through them, calling again and again for help, each syllable a futility. There was no strength left in my voice and none in my body as I tried to claw my way up the wall, managing a few feet before falling back on my ass.

"Brad, it's me. Come help."

That cold breeze blew again from underneath the bridge. I raked the darkness with the flashlight's beam and this time I saw Marty standing there. His shirt was torn, and he had dirt or dried blood on his forehead. Marty beckoned to me, and I stumbled toward him. As I did, the flashlight's beam flickered and died. The air grew colder with every step. But I thought if I could just grab Marty and pull him out from under the bridge, everything would be okay.

As I reached him, however, I found that Marty wasn't there. Everything was dark. I turned to run but the gulch was gone too. There was just encompassing blackness, and a stench so vile I doubled over to dry heave.

"Hungry."

This word, spoken in growled English, was followed by a cry both piteous and mocking. "Marty?" I shouted, smacking the flashlight with the butt of my hand. Suddenly the beam burst forth and I caught a glimpse of something green and wet, squat and roped with muscle. It seemed to be wearing a tunic of dark moss; or perhaps it was naked and that moss was its body hair. The thing snarled as the light struck its face, and it swung a disproportionately long arm at me, striking me to the dirt. I held on to the flashlight and gripped it like the hilt of a sword, yelling, "Stay back!"

I labored to get up. The creature was *heavy*. Its stomping feet sent vibrations along the ground and through my bones. A clawed hand lashed at me through the light and then disappeared into the dark. By now I had pissed myself and was praying aloud to God through chattering teeth. Pointing the flashlight straight up, I sought the bridge. It should have been right over me, but it wasn't.

Where the hell am I?

"Hungry."

There was a scream. At first I thought it might have come from my mouth. Then Marty staggered toward me out of the dark. His face was battered and bruised, but it was his hands that captured all my attention. They were crossed over his crotch as if he sought to protect his modesty. But he wasn't naked, despite all the rips and tears in his filthy clothes. He fell into my arms.

"Brad," he said, his voice a gargle. As his legs gave out, I was barely able to lower him to the ground.

Ahead of me I heard only silence. I trained the flashlight's beam and it disappeared into the dark.

Had the creature retreated? Was it watching me?

"Jesus Christ, Marty. What's happening?"

Marty tried to move his lips. I heard two words– *"Eat soon."*

The words came from the surrounding darkness. I clutched Marty closer to me.

Now Marty did speak. "I'm sorry, Brad. It's so hungry and I was so scared."

Marty's head thrashed to the left and right. He started crying.

"Tell me. What the hell is happening?"

"It lives under the bridge. It's always lived under bridges."

"What, like a *troll*?"

Marty laughed, hoarse and nasty. "It's like a spider, and bridges are its web. But this bridge has upset it. Every day golf balls fly into the gulch and roll under its bridge. It's... frustrated. It's hungry and angry."

"Marty–"

"No one ever comes down for their balls. Until me. I saw it and I was so mad about the idea of losing another one that I determined to play it from down there. Then the... the troll... took me. Under the bridge. Somewhere."

His eyes went wide, his body racked by a violent shiver.

"It's very hungry. Brad, I'm sorry. I made a deal with it. It's just like in 'The Three Billy Goats Gruff.' You remember the story, don't you?"

"Vaguely."

This answer seemed to relieve him. "Then you'll understand the bargain. I told it not to take mine because yours would be larger. It's very greedy and very hungry and eager, and I knew you guys would come looking for me."

He was just talking gibberish and I shook my head. "You told it not to take your *what*? I don't understand–"

And then I did understand.

I reached into my pocket for the mangled golf ball and imagined the annoyance of ball upon ball landing under the bridge, frustrating the troll, tempting it to come out and try its tongue and teeth on hard shells when it wanted warm, succulent flesh. It must have come to loathe the golfers who never came down to be victimized.

I heard the troll's lumbering footsteps and swung the light defensively toward it. The beam found a long, curved knife.

"You fucking bastard. You–"

I stared at the blade and realized I had something to prove.

Paradoxically, you might say, I unbuckled my belt, unbuttoning my pants and dropping them and my underwear to my knees. Marty nodded, as if I had just decided to accept my fate. Instead, I lifted my penis, pointed the flashlight to my groin and held it there. "Now see if *his* are bigger."

"What are you doing?" Marty yelled, sobbing. "No–*no!*"

I leaned toward the outline of the troll and said, "He's a liar. His are larger than mine. Take *them*."

Marty wasn't about to be as accommodating with his nudity. The troll solved this problem for him. It was quick with the blade, which slashed open the front of his pants and drew a deep gash across his thighs. I held the light steadily to his groin and prayed. I'd never seen Marty naked, but Rachel was always saying I had little nuts. Back when our relationship was good, she'd treated this like an endearing trait. Soured, she brought it up to mock my masculinity.

Say what you want about Marty, but he had big balls. His testicles would have been at home on a bull's body. Marty screamed as the troll claimed them with even greater viciousness, perhaps because it now

realized Marty's bargain would have cheated it of the better meal. It hunched over Marty's groin and ate with relish. But it wasn't distracted enough to let me go. I had to make a bargain of my own; and once I convinced it of my sincerity, and it convinced me of the consequences of not following through, the troll released me. I hiked up my pants and ran, dropping the flashlight and not bothering to try retrieving it. I seemed to run for miles, and then, suddenly, I was back in the gulch and plowed right into a policewoman's arms.

She was speaking to me. I couldn't hear her over the sound of the dogs. They were sitting on the ridge, barking and howling.

"Why didn't you answer me the first time I called for you? Why were you hiding under the bridge, and why did you leave your flashlight?"

I turned. The flashlight lay on the ground, just a few feet from the bridge.

"I–got spooked. This is all so crazy."

The officer gave me a curious, but not suspicious, look and went to pick up the flashlight. She walked under the bridge herself, gave it a final inspection, and returned to me.

"Look at all these lost balls," she said, kicking a few out of the way.

I shuddered and said, "Yeah."

The dogs continued barking.

"Christ, what's got into them? We could barely get them onto the bridge. Did you see anything?"

I shook my head. She looked back at the pile of balls.

"This is just the damnedest thing I've ever seen," she said.

The policewoman studied the area a moment longer then cleared her throat and said, "I'm sorry, but it's getting late. Won't do much good searching in the dark."

I nodded.

"We'll start at dawn," she placed a hand on my shoulder. "And we *will* find him."

I nodded again. We climbed up the gulch and returned to the parking lot with the rest of the search force. I endured a few more questions, to which I surely gave numb answers, and then I drove home.

Rachel actually showed me some decency when I arrived. She'd made me dinner and asked a lot of concerned questions about Marty. Quite a change from yesterday. She hardly knew him. To her, he was just a man I played golf with, and therefore an enemy.

I couldn't eat despite my hunger. I had the image of the feasting troll in my head. I went upstairs and took a shower, and my hands kept fondling my balls like someone obsessed with detecting testicular cancer. They were there and they'd be safe as long as I held up my end of the bargain.

But how the hell was I going to trick Jim into going under that bridge?

BATHROOM BREAK

J.V. KYLE

BATHROOM BREAK

J.V. KYLE

You think you've got it bad? You haven't got it bad. *I've* got it bad.

But I've always been the kind of guy who learns from his mistakes, even the ones I never admit to anyone but myself. Especially those.

Once I learn my lessons, I steer clear of making the same mistakes twice, and do my best to help others avoid them as well.

So let me give you some advice upfront, and then I'll tell you how I learned the lessons, which will tell *you* whether or not my advice has any place in your life.

Number One:

Don't fuck a co-worker, and not just because HR could have your ass for it no matter how high up the company food chain you feed.

Number Two:

If you're going to fuck a co-worker, don't fuck her at the office, and not just because there's a chance of being caught.

Number Three (which could also be number Two-A):

If you're going to fuck a co-worker, don't fuck her at the office Christmas party, especially if your wife is there.

Number Four (special case):

If you're not going to fuck a co-worker at your office Christmas party, don't try to break things off with her instead, no matter how pissed off you are or how determined you are to make clear that the whole thing was just a fling.

There may be one more piece of advice, but I'll let you decide once I've put things into perspective. Which is:

I wasn't in any mood for the Christmas party anyway, and most of my bad mood had to do with Joanne, my wife, deciding at the last minute she was going to accompany me. That was bad news across the board, but mostly because Linda–*the* co-worker, you know what I mean–was going to be there. Why wouldn't she? It was the company party and she worked for the company. She and I had been a thing for six months or so–and a very hot thing for the first three or four of those months. Once things got started–the night of the company's summer cookout; something about company affairs seem to jumpstart, well, company affairs, if you know what I mean. We had trouble keeping our hands off each other. We were always looking for places to do it, and we found more than a few. Quite more than a few.

It was good–it was better than good. Part of it was just that simple: Linda and I were good together, physically, we fit, we meshed, our tastes were similar (and, frankly, not all of our tastes were all that ordinary: I had known I had a few kinks, but she showed me things about myself that I never suspected), were hot and in need, and we scratched each other's itches.

And we both had them; itches I mean. Things hadn't been good between me and Joanne for years. We kept on, we stayed together, but it was more from inertia than any sort of deathless love or, even, commitment. We hadn't had sex in ages; we slept in separate beds. We didn't even wear our wedding rings on our fingers anymore, the result of an argument that led to Joanne flinging hers at me and mine at her. The next day neither of us could remember what the argument was about, but neither of us put our rings back on either. The day after that, though, Joanne surprised me by producing two thin gold chains, one for her and one for me, so we could wear our rings without wearing our rings. She wasn't ready to call it quits yet and neither was I, I guess. *Inertia.*

Linda was the first person at the office to notice that my ring finger was bare. We were in the break room, grabbing coffee before a planning session. Nothing planned; we just came into the break room at the same

time. I got to the coffee station before her, and ended up pouring for both of us. Linda's hand brushed mine and that's when she said, "Good thing it's summer. That will tan up pretty quickly."

"What will?" I said.

"Where your ring... was," she said.

We started meeting in the break room a couple of times a week. At first it was still almost by accident, but that changed quickly. Two weeks after that first encounter, we had become as regular as a vegan on a high fiber diet: coffee every morning at eleven. Sometimes she poured, sometimes I did.

Three weeks after our first cup, we had our first lunch. We were both late getting back to the office, but it was just talk that day. A long, honest talk: me about my problems with Joanne; Linda, the lingering effects of her divorce, now six months old. We had a lot in common.

The first time we kissed—just a kiss, but a heavy one—was a month later, after our very first evening meal together. We'd picked a quiet Italian place, well out of the way, and it was just perfect. The wine flowed and so did our conversation, deeper and more honest than any we'd had before. Afterward, I walked Linda to her car and it just happened, either me taking her into my arms or she coming into them or a little of both. Whatever. It happened, that kiss, and while neither of us was ready for it to go any farther that night, I think both of us knew it was going to go farther soon.

Soon turned out to be the company picnic. Not during the picnic itself, but not thirty minutes after things started to break up. The picnic was held at the largest shelter in the city's largest park, and Linda and I had some luck with the weather, which was awful and got worse as night fell. Big, dark clouds, heavy thunder, lightning coming frighteningly close. Nobody stayed late, Linda included. I volunteered to finish the cleanup and haul the trash out. I didn't mind—everybody got soaked running for their cars while I was dry under the roof of the shelter, and happy to be going about mindless cleanup tasks instead of driving home to Joanne. We were barely speaking that summer, but we were still together. *Inertia.*

I'd finished bagging the trash and was seated on one of the picnic tables, waiting for a break in the rain, when a car pulled up and stopped in the parking area up the hill from the shelter.

Linda's car.

She walked down the hill toward me, slowly despite the rain. I could hardly see her, it was coming down so hard. But every second or two there would be a flash of lightning and there she was, a step closer. She was unbuttoning her clothes and with each lightning flash, each step closer, I could see more of her. Each flash of lightning was larger and more brilliant than the previous one. Each flash revealed more of Linda.

She dropped her sodden clothes on the concrete floor of the shelter and mine joined them. We didn't speak. We came together and it was as furious and frenzied and violent as the storm that unleashed its brightest lightning and loudest thunder as if right on cue.

We didn't speak afterward, either. Linda pulled on her wet clothes and I pulled on mine. We kissed and she returned to her car and drove away. I waited a few minutes, carried the trash bags to my car, tossed them in the dumpster on the way home, tried not to let myself think of anything, and especially tried not to let myself think of how stunning it had been. I'd never experienced anything like what happened with Linda, and I knew I wanted to be with her again. Soon.

Joanne didn't say a word when I came in, not even a comment about how soaked I was. I showered and went to bed and dreamed of Linda.

We were careful, we were cautious, but we were also pretty constant for the next few weeks. Couldn't get enough of each other. Motels, the back seat of my car parked on hidden lover's lanes, once in the back row of a movie theater where we were the only patrons, a couple of times at the office after everyone was gone (Rule Two; I know, believe me). It bothered me, a little, that we never went to Linda's place, but she was weird about that. She said she wanted to "be sure of some things" before she took me home. I didn't think anything of it. I didn't want any more out of this than we had, and going to her place would somehow raise the stakes, make it more than what it was. My place either, for that matter.

Joanne went on occasional overnight trips that I never mentioned to Linda even though I felt oddly guilty about keeping it to myself.

So I was caught off-guard early in the fall when Linda invited me home with her. "I know what I need to know now," she said. "Come over tonight."

I told her I would, but I had second thoughts. It wasn't that I was tired of what we had together–not sure I could ever get tired of that–but, actually, things were starting to thaw a little between me and Joanne. We were talking again, just trivialities and chitchat. Nothing serious, but still talking more than we had in months. Linda exerted a powerful pull on me–but so did inertia.

Still, I ended up going to Linda's and if she had been wild and uninhibited in the other places we'd fucked, she raised things to a whole new level at her place, in her bed. Turned it to eleven, if you know what I mean.

I did my best to keep up–and I did pretty good if I say so myself–but part of me was distracted by her... décor. On the outside it was a nice little suburban ranch house, nothing special, but the inside...

Walls painted dark red, windows covered with velvet drapes drawn tight, black sheets on her bed. No one who saw Linda in the conservative clothes she wore to work would have guessed that she was so sexually voracious once those clothes were off. But I had known that about her for months and never would have guessed she was a closet Goth too. Weird.

But once she was in my arms and I in hers that night I didn't notice the surroundings anymore. Only Linda.

More Linda than I'd ever known, even during our most passionate trysts. Maybe more than all of our previous trysts combined. She was relentless, insatiable, demanding, inexhaustible, violent. I matched her as best I could, but I had part of my brain–the analytical part–on high alert to make sure she left no marks on me that might be noticed by Joanne or someone at the office. I managed to keep my skin intact and got away after midnight, drained and, at the same time, dissatisfied. But my dissatisfaction, which grew rapidly, was with myself.

I didn't go back to her house. I made excuses for not meeting her there, and our times together returned to their traditional venues, motels

and secluded spots, and over the course of the fall those locations began to remind me more and more of that old song, "Third Rate Romance, Low Rent Rendezvous." I began to make excuses for not getting together with her.

She wasn't happy about that, but she took her anger out on me in her own special way–sex between us became even more frenzied, even more violent. I loved it, but it scared me, too, and I began looking for ways to end it between us.

Joanne and I spent Thanksgiving with her family, and I was surprised to find how much I enjoyed it, enjoyed being there, enjoyed being with my... wife. Maybe I was getting older or maybe I was just worn out, but inertia won the tug of war, and after the Thanksgiving holiday I let Linda know it was over.

She took it quietly; so quietly that I couldn't tell *how* she was taking it. She just nodded and walked away.

We didn't speak when we encountered each other in the hallway or the break room at work; we didn't pour each other's coffee. It was over, and while there were aspects–mostly involving no clothes–of my time with Linda that I missed, and knew I would miss for the rest of my life, mostly what I felt was a sense of relief. I had gotten through it, I had gotten over it, and I had gotten away with it.

I didn't mind. I wouldn't, I realized as the winter deepened, mind if we never spoke again. She was a memory, a vibrant and almost over-whelming one, but no more than that. Vibrant and overwhelming take a hell of a lot more energy than inertia, and as the year glided toward its close, it was inertia that I wanted.

And maybe it was something more than inertia. Joanne and I did better and better, small improvements almost every day, every one of them welcome–until Joanne announced she wanted to go to the company Christmas party with me.

There wasn't any way out of it, of course. And she looked so happy when she told me, beaming actually, that I couldn't refuse her. But the prospect of being with my wife in the same room as Linda was nowhere

near my idea of a good thing. I didn't think Joanne suspected anything. I'd been careful both at work and at home to give away nothing.

So far. That's what I was thinking as Joanne and I drove to the office for the Christmas party. I had gotten away with it so far—the real test would be this party, and Linda's reaction to seeing me with my *wife*. I probably should have warned Linda. Looking back, I definitely should have warned Linda. But I didn't have the nerve.

The party had been going for half an hour by the time Joanne and I got there. The center of the party was the second floor lobby, our company's main anteroom, spacious and open, even with the big Christmas tree facing the elevators.

HR had made it very clear that no alcohol would be served or consumed on company property, but the sales force had a solution for that—they'd hosted a pre-party at a nearby bar, invited the top HR people, and got them so drunk before the office party that we could have set up a still in the president's office and nobody from HR would have been the wiser.

I didn't see Linda at first. Between taking care of our overcoats, saying hellos to co-workers and their spouses, introducing Joanne to those she didn't know, getting us both a drink, I was too busy to look for her. Not that I wanted to see her. I began to hope she hadn't come. But even as I went about the little tasks and pleasantries involved in settling into a party, I knew she was there. I could feel her looking at me.

When I did finally see her, she was staring at me. At *us*. At me and my wife. Linda's eyes, even across the crowded, jovial party, were fierce, angry, blazing, and aimed at me. My stomach dropped and my heart rate rose as I stood, bathed in that hate-filled gaze, wondering how much she had had to drink, how clouded her judgment would be, and what she was going to do. I could feel everything beginning to slip away.

But what she did, it turned out, was leave the party. Shooting one last deadly look at me, Linda spun and stalked to the exit, jostling and bumping anyone in her way. I caught a glimpse of her as she pulled on her coat and left. She didn't look back.

Once Linda was gone, I began to relax into party-mode. I actually started having a good time. I ruffled my hair, loosened my Christmas tie,

undid my collar button, had another drink. And without Linda there, I began to appreciate Joanne's company. She was having a good time, too, hearing stories about me–some of them embarrassing, but none of them scandalous; I never had any reason to believe anyone at the office knew about Linda and me, and the party seemed to confirm that.

Plenty of nice things were said about me too, and Joanne let me know she was proud of me and my stature in the company. She squeezed my arm a couple of times and unexpectedly, almost shockingly, at one point leaned close and kissed my cheek, her fingertips stroking the back of my neck as she did, a tickling finger tugging at the chain on which my wedding ring hung. She dragged a teasing fingernail across the nape of my neck, and then flicked an earlobe with it. When I looked at Joanne, she winked.

Like I said, once Linda left, I started having a good time. I actually began to suspect that tonight Joanne and I might end up having a *very* good time. Inertia can be warming, too, I was discovering, and I really liked the feeling.

It lasted almost twenty-three minutes.

That's how much time elapsed between the moment Linda left the party and the moment she texted me.

I felt my phone vibrate and didn't think too much about it. I was having fun–I'd check my messages later.

But the phone vibrated again, and a moment after that, a third time. Joanne had stepped out to the restroom, so I found a fairly quiet corner and thumbed my phone to life.

My stomach fell farther and faster than before. The messages were from Linda:

4th floor Ladies Rm 5 mins or u'll be srry

And the second:

4 mins or I tell J and everyone evrthing

And the third:

3 mins or I come back to the prty

I put my phone away and moved as quickly as I could to the exit at the back side of the building. It was deserted there and I was able to

head up the stairs–I didn't want to risk the elevator, and I sure as shit didn't want to *wait* for it. Fortunately, I only had to go up two floors–I didn't want to be out of breath when I confronted Linda. I had some things to say to her.

The fourth floor was deserted, and I hurried to the women's restroom. I took a deep breath before I entered. I would say what I had to say and get back to the party before anybody–especially Joanne–missed me. Maybe I could even get back before Joanne. I was hoping there was a line at the ladies' loo on the second floor as I pushed open the door to the fourth, ready to say what I should have said weeks before and what I had to say, forcefully, now.

But when I saw Linda, I was struck speechless.

She was seated on the counter between two sinks. Her slacks and panties were on the floor, her blouse unbuttoned, her breasts exposed. She opened her legs and said, "Fuck me. That's the price of my silence. Fuck me now."

I took a step toward her, responding as powerfully to her as I always had.

"Hurry," she said. "You don't want to be late getting back to that bitch, do you?"

Her words, her tone, the look in her eyes all came together and stopped me. I thought of Joanne's touch on my neck. I thought of Joanne winking at me.

"No," I said.

Linda's eyes grew wider, wilder. I had never seen her like this, not even that night in her bedroom.

"Now!" she said, nearly screaming. "Now, you bastard!" I heard a peal of something like distant thunder, but it was probably only the roaring of blood in my ears.

"No," I said again, more forcefully, and took a step backward.

But I didn't step back far or fast enough.

Linda came off the counter with her hands raised, fingers curled into claws aimed at my face, my eyes, my neck. She crossed the distance

between us in an instant, growling deep in her throat as she launched herself at me.

I raised my hands to defend myself, and stopped thinking of anything but getting free of her. Free of her in every way. Free of her forever.

I couldn't hear her growl or her curses or her scream over the thunder.

She didn't put a mark on me; I saw when I checked my reflection in the mirror before heading back to the party. But she had come close, wrapping her fingers around my neck, tugging at my collar hard enough to pop a button from my shirt, clutching at me, trying to choke me.

No harm done, I thought as I stared at my reflection. No marks on my throat, no scratches on my cheeks. I didn't even look particularly flushed. The thunder was gone from my ears. No harm done.

To me, at any rate.

The other—I would deal with that later. The analytical part of my mind, the part that made me so good at my job and earned all of those compliments that made Joanne so proud, was already at work on the problem. It was a big problem, even though she had not been a large woman. But I would solve it—later. Now, I had to get back to the party.

Things had moved into even higher gear downstairs, and my return to the festivities was masked by a riotous level of laughter and off-key carol singing. No one saw me come back in. I let myself be swallowed by the reverie and the crowd, a blur of happy faces all blending into each other. I didn't even see Joanne—or she me—for a couple of minutes.

But when I did see her, the way she was looking at me—with fresh eyes, eyes filled with love and what I hoped was desire—told me I had done the right thing. I hadn't had much choice, there had been no time to think, no time to do anything but react—

And so I had.

Half the room away from me, Joanne raised her glass in a toast, drained it, and then, never looking away from me, lowered the empty glass. Her hands went to her neck and she slowly, seductively lifted the chain and unfastened it, took her wedding ring from it and very slowly returned it to its place on her finger.

She winked at me and nodded again. *Your turn*, her gaze said.

I raised my own hands and felt for the chain.

My stomach fell.

I heard a peal of thunder.

The chain wasn't there.

I took a step toward Joanne, working as fast as I could to come up with an explanation that would at least sail close to being convincing. One started to take shape but I didn't need it.

Before I reached Joanne there was another peal of thunder, but it wasn't loud enough to drown out the screams that erupted from the lobby.

The crowd turned as one in the direction of the screams, which grew louder, as did the thunder.

The revelers–though they were surely no longer that by any stretch of the imagination–parted, some screaming, some vomiting, and I saw her, coming toward me.

She was still naked except for her open blouse.

Her eyes were no longer wild–they had no life in them at all.

Her head was tilted at a terrible, unnatural angle, just as it had been when I snapped her neck.

Her arms were outstretched but her hands were not claws. They were held palms up, bearing a gift.

The gold chain Joanne had given me for my ring.

"Yours," Linda said in a harsh, horrible croak, barely audible above the sound of the heavy thunder that began breaking over the winter night.

MARGINAL
HA'NTS

EDWARD BRYANT

MARGINAL HA'NTS

EDWARD BRYANT

S o here I am, trying to go to sleep in my new bedroom on the second floor of my new house on Wildwood, and I hear the squeak of trodden floorboards outside my door. No one should be walking that hallway since I'm the only one in the house. This place is new to me, but it was built in 1912, so it's known the tread of many feet.

I've always loved vintage homes with histories and traditions, but I can't say I'm fond of intrusions. So I sit up, completely wakeful as the footfalls stop precisely on the far side of the bedroom door. I stare hard at the floor. Dim yellow radiance pools there. I've evidently forgotten to switch off the hall light at the top of the stairwell.

Something moves in the pooled light. Something occludes the darkness. I'm guessing that something is standing right outside my door, probably shifting its weight from one foot to the other.

I cannot abide this. I need my sleep. So I swing my legs out from under the stacked comforters and lever myself upright. Evidently I am not as awake as I first thought, and I stagger a bit as I cross to the door.

For a moment I hesitate with my hand on the cold brass knob. At my feet the light brightens and darkens and there is a single hardwood shriek.

I yank the door open. No one is there. I step forward and look each way. Nothing.

I don't bother walking down the hall to switch off the light. I quietly shut the door and turn back to bed.

There's a sound. It's a low moan. Another. A sharp exhalation of breath. The light of a classic Midwestern full moon dimly illuminates my bed. I can see the covers undulating, writhing as if they barely conceal bodies beneath. The sounds suggest the urgent passion of coupled lovers.

Great. I'd just laundered my sheets this afternoon.

But when I jerk the bedclothes back, there's no one there. And the impassioned sounds cease.

"Get a life," I can't stop myself from saying, "or whatever."

Nothing wakes me the rest of the night. At least the dawn doesn't creep through the wooden slats shading my east-facing window. The morning light doesn't pounce. The ambient illumination simply and slowly brightens the room. I realize I'm staring at the face of the alarm clock on the bed stand. It stares me down and I blink first. My head feels like someone splitting firewood with a hatchet. Coffee is in order. Also acetaminophen. Maybe a .357 Magnum round.

The room lightens gradually. I've been told cloud cover rarely departs the airspace above the neighborhood. Or maybe it's just the sky over Wildwood Street. *Why is that?* I had asked Marty, my Realtor.

She just shrugged.

My shower goes uneventfully, other than the water temperatures oscillating randomly between cool and tepid. I'd had a new forty gallon tank installed, so there's no easy technological explanation for this anomaly.

Once I make it to the kitchen and find the cord for the coffee maker, there's another annoyance.

I've only got a limited number of ground coffees from which to choose, but while I'm facing the cabinet and pondering my choices, something flashes across the open doorway to the dining room. Dark and fast, it's a shadowy blur in my peripheral vision. I ignore the first pass. The second and third times, I turn my head to try to secure a better look. Nope. Just the suggestion of a blur across my vision. The effect reverses direction. Now there's the audible suggestion of cloven air.

"Forget it," I say to whatever entity is behind me as I return to coffee preparations. Lingonberry machado, I finally decide.

Sitting at the kitchen table, I watch as daylight gradually defines the yard. A flight of birds alights on the picket fence and begins to serenade me. It's like a Disney animated feature, except the chorus is not bluebirds. My fence is dotted with crows.

That does it. I pick up my phone and dial my Realtor. She answers on the first ring. "Marty Bryce Real Estate," she chirps more tonally than the crows outside. "Have I got the perfect home for you!"

"Well, I thought you had," I say. "This is your new client down on Wildwood."

"Wow!" she says with excitement in her voice. "You just spent your first night there. Was it divine? It's such a beautiful home."

"Well, I want to speak about that with you."

"Oh, no," Marty Bryce says with less evident enthusiasm. "There isn't a problem, is there?" Her voice sounds like she knows there is.

"How long was this house on the market?" I ask. "A bit of a while, wasn't it?"

She hesitates momentarily. "Not really that long. Just over..." Her voice drops off.

"How long?" I say again.

Silence. "Four years. I picked up the listing after the original Realtor retired."

"Ah," I say. "That's a fair bit of time."

"Good things take time," she says. "You know how difficult the market can be."

"When you showed the house, were there signs of anything strange?"

"Such as?" she counters.

"Anomalies," I say. "Strange sights. Odd sounds. Things no one ordinarily expects to go bump in the night."

"You mean, um, ghosts? Spirits, all that?" Her voice suggests she doesn't really want to talk about such things.

"That's basically it," I say gently. "What my sainted old Aunt Siobhan used to call 'ha'nts.'" I sip my cooling coffee. "The remnants of dead folks."

My Realtor, when she speaks in turn, sounds a bit unhappy. "There are no ghosts," she says. "No such thing. And even if there were, this state's realty disclosure laws do not cover such things as alleged supernatural hauntings. This state is not California."

"The previous owners," I say. "What happened to them?"

Marty says, "I really don't know." She sounds distracted. "I'm afraid I'm overdue for a showing. I have to go. Can we talk later?"

I don't even have to answer her because she clearly is already gone. I close up my phone on dead air.

Bap.

The sound is a new one since I've been in the house.

Bap. The bounce of a rubber ball.

I turn to look back through the kitchen doorway toward the staircase.

Bap.

Bap.

The ball bounces off the last step and rolls into the kitchen. It's a child's plaything, a rubber ball cheerfully striped red and blue. It rolls to a halt just short of my bare toes.

I stare. I have no balls in my house. That's what my departed wife used to say, usually with a smile. An old joke, no better now than then.

The spate of recent apparitions also is an old joke. Though I've never directly experienced this sort of spiritual activity until now, certainly my sainted Auntie Von had given me plenty of preparation with her seemingly inexhaustible supply of colorful talks and occasionally racy anecdotes from a swath ranging from the bayou country to northern Minnesota–from houngan voodoo priests to the frigid wendigos of the winter woods. Now *there* were some real players. Genuine ha'nts. The phenomena in this house on Wildwood are just a bit sketchy. Even marginal when it comes to scariness.

I could show them a thing or two. Yes I could.

Slowly, I lower my coffee mug. From where had *that* come?

I am certainly not a force of evil. I'm just a middle-aged white guy with a dead-end job at the Mutton Power Group (pronounce Mutton the French way, natch) out on Illinois Road. Not many friends. Terrible

with relationships. No doubt some would call *me* marginal, living a colorless life.

I suppose I should be glad for the attention I got last night. Better than getting no attention at all, I suspect my friends would say, if I told them, which I won't.

That's when I decide to call in to work and announce that I, like half the others in my department, have suddenly come down with the flu and will be sparing the company my contagion for a day or two.

Now with time on my hands, the first thing I determine to do is take a walk around the neighborhood. Maybe I'll meet a neighbor or two. I go up to my bedroom and slip on jeans, sneakers, and an over-sized tee depicting two gators and an Orthodox Jew walking into a bar.

A problem only surfaces when I actually try to leave the house. As I approach the front door, the deadbolt slams shut like a shot. I hesitate momentarily, reaching out to slide the bolt free. No problem. It slides instantly.

"See you later, guys," I say aloud to the invisible, intangible host. No answer. Cool air rushes in from outside as I exit.

The late October sun can't really pierce the cloud cover over Wildwood, but the morning is still comfortably warm on my arms. Then the fine hairs on my wrists abruptly prickle and I look up.

The young woman waits at the demarcation where my stone path meets the sidewalk. She stands as tall as I, smiling from a face defined by angles. Her cheekbones could slice a man's soul. Her eyes and sleek long hair are a black that could swallow the light should the sun ever break through.

"I am Nadja," she chimes and smiles. The gleam of those white teeth obviates any real need for the sun. "I believe you are my new neighbor. Welcome!"

The crows in the trees caw. Nadja's voice is far sweeter.

I acknowledge her greeting with a nod and my own smile. "Charon Keene. I moved in yesterday."

"Are you enjoying the house? It's so wonderfully vintage."

"Maybe too much so." I hesitate. "I think I've moved into a charming but perhaps haunted house."

Nadja shrugs and her smile widens to a grin. "Not surprising, but this *is* Wildwood."

I must look quizzical.

"There's a shadow over the entire street," Nadja continues. "Always has been. People seem to move here when they're, well, between places. After a while, something happens, something life-changing, and they move on." That smile again. "A lot of uncertainty. Like that old movie. Between two worlds."

I shrug. "I just hope I can start getting some sleep tonight."

Nadja flashes her gleaming smile. "Well, if you can't, please come over to my place for tonight's party. Consider yourself formally and warmly invited."

I can't help myself. "The time?"

"Any time."

"I should bring?"

"Just yourself. And friends, if you wish."

"Costume?"

"Mm." She cocks her head. "Whatever evokes the real you."

"That may take some thought."

She nods and turns back toward her own house. It's compact; smaller than mine. I thank her for the invitation and head out on my walk.

If I turn right, I'll end up at Broadway. That intersection to the north is bracketed by two shadowy antique stores and a neighborhood bar. Turn left and I'm headed for terra incognita. I don't know yet what's down there. So I turn left and start walking.

A hundred yards and I'm in the most immersive stretch of Wildwood. Unlike the rest of the city with its stern German Lutheran rectilinear geometry, Wildwood flouts the urban grid by curving seductively. I've seen similarly charming streets in the likes of Paris and lower Manhattan. One can see neither beginning point nor end. I could be walking in a huge circle. Or on a Moebius strip.

The crows seem to be following me, fluttering in raggedy bands from tree to fence to eave. Their black eyes track me with eerie diligence. I tire before reaching the presumed lowest arc of Wildwood, so I turn and head back toward my home. My black reflection, sculpted in crows, follows me.

Once home, the night of vanished sleep and lost dreams catches up to me suddenly, so I trudge upstairs and flop down on the flowered comforters I haven't yet taken the time to make up. I pass gratefully into sleep.

I feel myself falling deep, I think. None of my new household ha'nts can disturb me this time.

It all seems so familiar. I walk through a vanilla world. All is pale, colorless. It is, I think, a diorama of my life passing before my eyes.

First there's my childhood, tepid but not loveless. My parents certainly care, but aren't quite sure what to do with me. My Aunt Siobhan tells me stories that add color and even heat, but she tells me I must find my own path. I have a few friends, but they are kids who gravitate toward me because all the rest find them just a little too weird.

I see a brief parade of adulthood. It's pretty dull. There's a whole procession of jobs that I take because I know I can perform them. I certainly do not love them.

Then I meet the young woman who seems to care about me. But not much. Pale hair, pale eyes. We do come to care for each other. A little. Eventually we marry. It's expected of us.

My parents grow older and die. So does Auntie Von, which is a real shame. She, I really miss. Then my wife passes on from an utterly unexpected toxic sepsis in childbirth. The baby, our daughter, dies with her. The shock is greater than I would have expected.

This whole white world might as well be yogurt or custard, or perhaps flan, for all the slight resistance as I pass through it. As I walk onward, I realize it's increasingly harder to breathe. What I am sucking into my lungs is nothing less than the world itself. It enters me and stays there. No air, no oxygen, no life. I asphyxiate.

The world outside me dims, my eyes bulge, my lungs sear as I struggle. Then—a sudden release. What expels from my mouth and nose sprays a

bright, shocking crimson, the color of arterial blood. Or strawberry jam. The feeling is sharp and astringent, burning me up from the inside. The red drips down and covers the lens of my vision, and then I awaken...

Into darkness.

What I see when I open my eyes is just the black of fallen night with the glow of sullen red sparks pulsating in the periphery of everything around me.

I hear the knocking of small fists at my door–and then that goes away. I lie quiet on my bed as orientation settles in. I could go back to sleep. Or I could get up. I remember the invitation for the party next door. Will it have started? Any time, I recall the young woman, Nadja, saying.

Any time could be right now.

It takes no energy at all to arise. *Costume?* I think. I've hung only a few clothes in the bedroom closet. Still, I pick out black slacks, a gray dress shirt, and a dark jacket. I don't bother with shoes.

I like the feel of rough treads on my soles as I descend to the first floor. The cries of excited children filter through the front door. Through the window I catch flashes of exotic costumes in the street.

At the door I barely touch the knob–and hear the cat cry out. This is wrong. Just as this morning, there are no balls in my house–in similar fashion, there is no pussy. But again I hear a feline appeal. It sounds hungry. Turning toward the kitchen, I hear a third yowl. It seems to come from beyond the door to the basement stairs.

When I open that narrow wooden door, it creaks inward to–what else?–utter blackness. There's no cat to be seen. But I do hear, once again, one somewhere below. It sounds in pain now. I flip the switch by the jamb and a low-wattage bulb flickers on far below. It casts skeletal shadows along the shaky painted pipe railing.

"Kitty?" I call. Something stirs in the darkness beneath. So of course I start down, trailing fingers along the cold metal rail.

"Cat? How'd you sneak in?" No answer, obviously.

As I step from the bottom stair to the broken concrete cellar floor, the kitchen door slams shut with the sound of a thunder crack. The

echo fills the basement end to end. "More tricks," I say. "Swell. Have your fun, guys."

Turning, I take the steps up two at a time. My bare soles register the rough splinters. With no expectation of the door cooperating, I twist the knob and it opens suddenly and surprisingly.

A bland little man in a suit, bowtie, and spectacles confronts me. Wally Cox from *Mister Peepers*? I'd seen him on the vintage TV channel. How long had this spirit infested the house on Wildwood? He smiles and his mouth opens far wider than it has any right to. His features wildly distend and he sneezes explosively into my face. His breath is foul.

I recoil instinctively, stepping back, only to find no support at all. My arms windmill helplessly and I tumble backward.

On my back, head first, I toboggan down the wooden steps like a luge in the winter Olympics. I cannot control the plunge. The hard leading edge of each riser washboards along my spine. The fingernails of my right hand rip loose as I claw at the brick beside me.

Muscles tense hopelessly as I try to brace for the inevitable impact. The back of my skull smacks into the concrete floor and my shoulders skid across the breaks in the cement. I remember the four-by-four vertical wooden support–and then my head fetches up against it, jamming my neck to the side. Mass times velocity. It's all simple physics. I feel something in my neck snap. Actually it crunches–*then* snaps all the way.

That's when the pain flares, as if I've grabbed a lit burner on the stove.

Upstairs the little man, the Thing at the Top of the Stairs, snaps off the light and gently closes the door.

I lie in darkness as pain simmers, peaks, dies out. That's something, at least. I wonder when someone will find me. When I try to test my limbs, nothing happens. It won't matter when someone will find me. I think I'm dead.

As soon as I realize this, everything changes. I *can* move now. I *can* get up, and I do. Now there is a soothing blue spectral light around me and I can see.

Upright, I take a deep breath though I certainly do not need to. It feels a bit odd to step over myself as my one-time mortal body lies there

in a most awkward and disheveled fashion with limbs splayed out with total lack of dignity.

It looks acutely uncomfortable. Well, it *was*. Now I have so much energy, I'm quite amazed. Auntie Von had given me some forewarning. "Ha'nts have energy," she'd said. "They lay down the infirmities and indignities of mortal life. They can let go of a miserable past–but only if they wish to. They can grasp a glorious future–again if they wish to. But too many lack the true vision. Don't you be one of them, boy. Use your get up and go. I think you're a late bloomer, but bloom you will." That's why I love Auntie Von. She had true faith.

And I remember what my unusual neighbor Nadja had said earlier today–about the folks who pass through their homes on Wildwood–and those who do not. For all the marginal ha'nts, the underachievers who hang around indefinitely to provide lukewarm hauntings and tepid terrors, there have to be a few who can and will go for greatness...

Like me. Finally I feel some real hope. I can achieve. For the first time in my memory, I envision real accomplishment.

I need not be marginal. Whatever I am now, I can use it as a springboard to–what? What *do* I want? Careful, there. Don't slip into megalomania. But I can't ignore how good I feel; how hopeful.

I believe I'll be slating my Realtor for a courtesy visit. I smile at the thought.

Pausing there on dark cellar stairs, the inspiration crystalizes into startling clarity. How hard can it be to become the best haunt ever? And I do think I have the raw talent.

Boo? Screw that. I can create the Mormon Tabernacle Choir of scariness. I can do it. And I'll bet I can inspire that in my fellows. I wonder if ghosts have adult extension classes? If they don't, I will teach them.

My enthusiasm builds. The doofus spirits in this house on Wildwood? I will whip them into shape as a portfolio. The passionate and unfulfilled entities in my bed last night? I mentally invite them to return to rumple my sheets and moan while awaiting my enthusiastic participation. I reach out to the Thing at the Top of the Stairs and request him to return to his post in the kitchen.

The cat howls from the inside of one of the basement's brick-and-block walls. Hold on, kitty, I communicate. Sour milk is on its way.

Images flood my mind as I climb to the top step. This will be fun. I firm the substance of my new form and knock.

The Thing at the Top of the Stairs opens the door to the kitchen. It's the little man in the drab '50s TV suit once again. No imagination. Me, I now present him with a flayed man, my doubly bared muscles flexing and ripping. Tendons twang apart like snapped guitar strings. Blood bursts forth like a Technicolor geyser onto the kitchen's worn tile floor.

When I scream, my mouth gapes so wide, it tears at the corners. More blood, leavened with saliva and a few rotting teeth, spews forth. I add my snot to the spray. I love the smell of it.

I think even the Thing at the Top of the Stairs is appalled. He takes a half step back.

"I have such wonders to show you," I say to him. Maybe I'm overdoing it.

So I'll practice. But my creative exercise feels *so* good.

I summon the other spirits from around the house. They are such a dull and uninspired lot. But that will change. *They* can change. I swear it.

At last I have found my calling.

Come on, I tell them all. *Think about costumes.*

We're going to a party!

DELICIOSO

WARREN HAMMOND

DELICIOSO

Warren Hammond

S tuart leaned against the bar and studied the crowd,
wondering exactly which one of these *chicas* he
was going to kill.

Maybe the hot thing with the push-up bra. Maybe
the wallflower with the starving-puppy gaze. Or how
about that dye-job with the loud laugh sitting in a circle
of chatterboxes? Oh, he'd shut her up good, gag that big
mouth of hers. Wipe the lipstick off first. Scour it off
with a sponge, the green scrubber side.

No. Not her. Too hard to separate from the herd.
No matter whether it was Mexico or Indiana, women
were herd animals.

He grabbed his sweat-stained Hawaiian shirt by the
top button and fanned some air conditioning inside.
Jesus, Juárez in July was like standing over a barbecue pit.

"Puedo ayudar?"

Stuart turned to face the bartender, a kid with gel-
slicked hair and one of those barely whiskered moustaches.

"Cerveza," said Stuart.

The kid fished out a bottle of Sol from an ice bath,
set it on the bar, and popped the cap. Stuart took a deep,
refreshing swig before pulling the money clip from his
pocket and handing over two American singles. He
took another draw, sat on his stool, and looked into the
mirror behind the tequila bottles. The reflection gave
him a decent view of the place.

A woman sat on the stool next to his. Narrow wrists. Short nails. A single ring on one thumb.

He couldn't help but smile. Back home, he was invisible. A suburban forty-something living among all the other suburban forty-somethings, all of them just a bunch of office whores. Yes, sir. Right away, sir. All of them counting the days to Friday–casual day, as if losing the tie was a reason for celebration.

But here it was different. Here he was a star. He didn't need looks, or an expensive car, or big money. Didn't need anything but white skin and an American accent.

She raised a finger to the bartender. "Tequila. *Plata.*"

He took another swig of his beer and watched her in the mirror. Black hair pulled back and cinched in a satiny lemon-colored band. She wore a sleeveless T, a necklace hanging over the collar, a simple chain with one of those cheap wood pendants showing the colorful image of some female saint.

And most importantly, his new bar mate was wearing lipstick. He made sure of that.

The bartender poured her a glass, and she fished in a faux-leather purse with hot pink piping. After a few seconds of digging, she let out a *humph*, and then a sigh, and then another *humph*.

It was too easy below the border. It really was. Stuart pulled out his money clip and paid the bartender.

"*Gracias.* Thank you. I don't use this purse often and I thought I had–"

"No need to explain. Your English is very good."

This time she thanked him with a smile and a playful toss of her hair. "I used to work in Oklahoma. Meat packing."

"Deported?"

"No. But they raided a nearby meatpacker and my company got scared. They let everybody go who didn't have papers."

"That's too bad," he lied. As far as he was concerned, illegal was illegal.

She nodded and took a small sip then put down the glass, the rim smudged with lipstick. Something in the deep reds. Maybe Forever Rose or Sun-Kissed Berry.

"What about you?" She patted his shoulder. "Where are you from?"

"Wyoming." He'd never been there, but he liked the idea of Wyoming. All that open country. He spun a yarn for her, no more than a bunch of threads pulled from movies, TV, and random conversations, but he spun it just the same. And she smiled and nodded and pulled in every inch of that yarn, wrapping it around herself with lots of well-timed ohs and reallys, wrapping it round and round like a fly sacrificing itself to the spider.

He tensed inside, a good kind of tense as anticipation mounted. Tight stomach. Tight throat. He watched her lips, the way they stretched taut with a smile, the way they wrinkled and puckered when she sipped her third tequila. He was into his third beer, but stopped after a sip. He wouldn't drink anymore. What he felt welling inside was an infinitely more powerful high.

She finished her glass and waved for another before dropping her hand to his knee. Warm tingles ran up his thigh, and he leaned in to smell her hair, honey and lavender.

The bartender poured and more bills leapt out of Stuart's pocket.

"Each tequila tastes better than the last," she said.

"I don't like tequila."

"You probably never had good tequila. Here, have a sip." She held up the glass.

He refused with a shake of his head.

She dipped her index finger into her glass and twirled it about before pulling it free and sticking her finger in her mouth. "Mmm. *Delicioso*."

He got lost in her lips, so red and glossy, her moistened finger slowly pulling free. Her finger went back to her glass, but his eyes didn't move off lips that lengthened into a smile.

And then her finger was in his mouth, his taste buds firing on the hot sting of alcohol and the salty flavor of sweat.

He felt a stir in his pants and, like always, the sudden shame that accompanied it. Who the hell did this bitch think she was? He snatched her wrist and jerked her finger out of his mouth. Her eyes widened in surprise, and he heard a gasp.

Oh, no you don't, Stuart. Don't screw this up. He searched for a way to salvage the situation, to calm those nervously searching eyes.

"You better be careful," he said with as much playfulness as he could muster. "I bite, you know." He pulled her hand close and pretended to take a chomp before letting go.

"You bite?"

With a fake growl, he leaned in and acted like he was going to bite her shoulder, repeating the move twice before succeeding in getting her to play along.

"I bite. Like an alligator, I bite."

They walked up the stairs, flight after flight, five stories with no elevator, sweat breaking on his forehead and around his elbow, where her arm was looped through his. Their skin slid back and forth like it was greased. He unhooked his arm, pulled keys from his pocket, and worked open the triple locks.

He turned the knob, and they stepped into his rooftop apartment, his pleasure pad, his house of pain.

His sanctuary.

He rented the place year round, but only used it for a long weekend here or there, a couple longer vacations when he could get away from work.

She started to laugh for no apparent reason and threw her arms over his shoulders, giggles of tequila breath assaulting his face. Drunk bitch was getting damn annoying, but he wouldn't have to put up with it much longer. Soon he would be in control of her. Complete control.

He led her to a sofa, sat her down on the end by the toolbox. A thrill ran up his spine at the thought of the tools inside that box. Lemon zester. Carrot peeler. Kitchen scissors. And the knives. So many knives.

A loud boom sounded outside. She reacted with an excited clap of her hands. "I forgot it's the Fourth of July. The fireworks are starting."

"Yes," he said. "You can see across the river to El Paso from that window over there. Why don't you watch while I get us a drink?"

She rocked and swayed her way to the window. Dumb whore had no idea what was in store for her. He practically skipped to the kitchen, heart beating like that incessant Latin percussion that made all the music down here sound the same. He nabbed a bottle of red wine and a pair of glasses and sneaked a peek at the door before pulling a baggie full of sedatives from the drawer. He made quick work of smashing one of the pills with the handle of a spatula.

The booms were getting more frequent, bangs and snaps, pops and sizzles. He heard her call from the other room. "Hurry up, you're missing it!"

He uncorked the bottle and poured, wound up spilling a few drops, he was so eager. He held her glass below counter level and swept in the crushed roofie. A quick stir with the spatula handle and the flakes floating on top disappeared.

Back to the living room. His eyes went to the window, but she wasn't there, the glass tinting red, then blue, then green with successive pops.

He looked to the bathroom, but the door was open and the light was off, his revved up heart starting to sputter. The toolbox. It was open. Oh hell, where did she go?

He barely had time to finish the thought when a sharp pain entered his back. The wine glasses fell from his hands, burgundy liquid raining down. His back felt wet, blood seeping into his pants. He looked down, the bloody tip of his butcher knife protruding from his chest. He watched the tip disappear, nerves screaming at the blade as it dragged slowly, painfully back out.

Weak, he dropped to his knees, then fell to the floor, blood and wine wicking into the wool rug. He felt her hands on him, turning him over. She reached for the wound in his chest, dipped a finger into the river of blood, and showed it to him before she put the finger in her mouth.

He fought to focus his pain-blurred eyes. Lips the color of blood pursed around her finger, the finger sliding free. "*Delicioso.*"

He kept his eyes on her lips, even as she took the knife back up and lifted it for a swing at his throat.

Her lips screwed into a snarl. "I bite too."

THE
LIBRARIAN

JOSHUA VIOLA

THE LIBRARIAN

JOSHUA VIOLA

F irst day on the job at the library and already things were weird enough that Emma was ready to risk it all by asking a stupid question.

Or what might be a stupid question–she wasn't sure.

She waited until she was certain the tall man, who looked like a walking corpse, was gone.

"He brought books back, but didn't check anything out?" she said to Wallace Reed, the librarian.

"He turns in on Monday, checks out on Tuesday," the librarian said. The old man was bent over a cart, sorting the books for their return to the shelves.

"But he didn't even glance at the new releases," Emma said. New books went on a special shelf at the front of the small library, and had been the first thing Mr. Reed had shown her when she reported to work that morning.

"They don't matter to him," the librarian said. "When he comes in tomorrow, he'll be checking these out again."

"The same ones?"

Wallace Reed ran his fingers along the spines of the books in the cart. "These very ones. Out every Tuesday and back every Monday."

"Why doesn't he just renew them? Or buy them on Amazon or something?" Emma asked.

"Not his way," the elderly man said. "Now, come along and I'll show you my shelving system." He pushed the cart slowly, one of its wheels squeaking, as Emma

followed. She offered to help but he waved her away. "Watch and learn. This is my system and there's not another like it in the world."

Emma could believe that–the library's organization matched no system–Dewey Decimal, Library of Congress, even straight alphabetical, she had ever seen. That mattered less to Emma than the books they were shelving.

"If he checks out the same books every week, why not just leave them behind the counter instead of putting them back on the shelf?" Emma said.

The librarian sighed as though being questioned by a child. "You never know who might be looking for the same book. It'd be a disservice to keep them hidden. Plus, we aren't very busy–kids these days prefer phones to books. It gives us something to do. And it'll help you get used to the layout of this place," he said.

"But–"

"No buts–pay attention and learn. I began developing my process when I opened the library sixty years ago. If you pay attention, it will make sense to you soon enough. If you don't–misplaced titles, misshelved books, *chaos*! And you'll be looking for another job. Without, I might add, a recommendation from me."

Emma got the message. She needed the job. Her scholarship covered tuition and her dorm room, but there was little left for anything else. Wallace Reed's library was too perfect of a job to lose–close to campus, flexible hours, and surprisingly good pay, well above minimum wage. She kept her questions to herself and tried to make sense of the shelving system.

She felt sure Mr. Reed had a system in mind, or *had* one when he started the library, but Emma couldn't figure it out. Fiction next to nonfiction, history beside poetry, religious texts all over the place. No science books, she noticed, no contemporary politics. She decided she would have to memorize the placement of the books on the shelves if she was to have any hope at all of re-shelving things correctly.

Emma followed Mr. Reed's every step and studied his every move. He returned a book to a shelf littered with old tomes. One of them caught her attention. She removed the book and examined it.

Demonology.

It'd been a few years since Emma's Goth days. She'd outgrown the eyeliner and The Cure albums, but her infatuation with devilish things remained.

"Come now, Emma. Far more to see," Mr. Reed said.

She gave the book an affectionate pat and placed it back on the shelf.

There were only two other patrons that first day on the job, and Emma subtly shadowed them, making mental notes of the spots from which they withdrew their books, hoping she would remember those locations when they were returned.

The library's circulation system was as eccentric as its organization. There was no computer; the books bore no barcodes or catalog numbers. Rather, there were long drawers of 3x5 cards with notations–book title and customer number, date out and date in–in what she assumed was Wallace Reed's handwriting. His script was neat, but contained flourishes and curlicues, like something out of another century–and not the 20th.

Emma got through the first day without asking any more questions, determined to find or figure or just bull her way through anything that came at her. There wasn't much–only the two other customers, and then the dusting and straightening of shelves that Mr. Reed assured her to be one of her constant responsibilities. It would have been boring work, but Emma took it as an opportunity to further familiarize herself with the library.

By the time she left at three–Mondays she had a four o'clock class and a seminar at seven in the evening–Emma felt certain she had pleased the librarian with her diligence. He smiled absent-mindedly at her as she wished him a good night.

The tall man came in Tuesday morning at eleven. Emma had been looking for him since she got to work, casting glances at the window whose view included the slate walkway that led up to the library. When she saw him approaching, Emma quickly moved to a range of shelves near the entrance, ready to watch the man make his selections.

Emma was careful to be unobtrusive with her surveillance, but she needn't have bothered—he paid no attention to her, but strode purposefully to each of the six shelves where the books he sought resided. Emma made it back to the circulation desk just in time to be waiting patiently when he arrived.

"Ready to check out?" she said in her sweetest voice when he deposited the six volumes on the desk. He said nothing. "All right," Emma said. "Your card, please?"

He already had his library card out and tilted it so she could read the member number. Emma reached for the card, but the man held tight. She bent her neck to read the numbers.

"One-thirty-six," she said, "let's see." Emma turned to a cabinet holding member circulation cards, thumbed through until she reached 136, a little less than a third of the way into the drawer, then began riffling to find the final card in the man's file.

It took a while, and Emma was convinced 136's circulation cards would extend into another drawer.

Finally, she saw a card marked 137, tipped it up to mark the place, and withdrew the final entry in the run of 136 cards. It bore, in Reed's unmistakable handwriting, the six titles that were before her, with an out date seven days ago—last Tuesday—and return date of yesterday.

Emma took a pen and worked her way through the same titles, squinting at the faded lettering on the books' spines. Some of the letters were still bright gilt, but others had been completely rubbed away. That didn't matter. The titles were already on the circulation card. Emma wondered what would happen if she simply wrote "DITTO" six times

and added today's date. She knew what would happen–*chaos!* She could hear Wallace Reed saying the word, and saying it angrily.

Chaos–and then she'd be fired.

When she finished filling out the information, she smiled again and said, "Thank you. Enjoy your books."

But the man simply picked up the books, took a moment to rearrange them–Emma had taken the trouble to sort them as she checked them out, placing the larger volumes on the bottom of the stack–and left.

Emma watched through the window until the tall man turned the corner onto the sidewalk and vanished from her line of sight. She carried his circulation card to the drawer and replaced it, tucking 137 into its proper place as well. Before she closed the drawer, Emma riffled backwards through 136's cards. There were hundreds of them, dating back more than half a century–he hadn't looked *that* old–and each of them bore the same six titles.

The selection of books made no sense, not for books that were checked out and, presumably, read over and over again: a romance novel from the 1890s, a history of Armenian folkways, a statistical survey of dams in the Midwest in 1948, a survey of minor Elizabethan dramatists, a book on saddlery and tack, and a guide promising to tell how to have a perfect wedding in 1951.

What could such a variety of books have in common, other than being checked out, endlessly, by the same person every week for more than fifty years?

Maybe she would ask him. That was something to think about, and it wasn't like she didn't have time. After all, he was due to return on Monday.

Emma had the library to herself the following Monday–Mr. Reed was away on business for the day, but made a small ceremony of telling Emma how pleased he was with her work, and how confident he was she could run things in his absence.

There was only one patron that day, 136, and once more Emma's attempt to engage him in conversation failed. He placed the books on the return counter, and turned to go, ignoring Emma when she said, "Wouldn't you prefer to renew these now? Save you a trip tomorrow."

She sighed, checked the books in, rearranged them in an order that made them easier to work with, and returned them to the shelves in their proper places.

The following day the man returned precisely at eleven for his Tuesday visit. He efficiently made his way through the ranks of shelves to find his books, and brought them to the desk where Emma already had his circulation card out and ready. She could be efficient herself, and annotated his card in barely a minute, taking time to reorganize the six books by size. She thought she heard 136 sigh as he took the books from her, reordered them to his preferred ranking. He looked from the books to Emma and then back at the books.

"Is there anything else? Another book, maybe? Something different perhaps?" she said to him, but he simply looked from the books to Emma and back at the books, his eyes repeating the circuit twice before he turned and left.

Mr. Reed emerged from his office as soon as 136 departed. "Did I hear you speaking with him?" he said, a tone of reprimand in his words.

"Just being pleasant," Emma said.

"Don't trouble yourself, not with that one," the librarian said. "He'll never answer you, and I don't want him disturbed."

"But–"

"No buts, Emma. You're a fine employee, and I would hate to lose you, but you are not to speak to patron 136 again. I can assure you he won't speak to you."

"Yes, Mr. Reed," Emma said.

The librarian's features grew gentle, and he smiled. "Please, Emma," he said. "Call me Wallace. And I didn't mean to sound so stern. It's just

that I know our customers better than you do, and I know him best of all. Leave him be with his six books, check them out and check them in, and all will be well."

"Yes, Mr. Reed," Emma said.

He wagged a friendly finger at her. "Wallace."

"Wallace," Emma said with a nod.

By the time winter set in, Emma was running the library almost entirely by herself. Mr. Reed–*Wallace*–was out more often, and when he was in the library, he usually remained in his office all day, emerging only to wish her a good morning when she arrived and a good evening when she departed. Sometimes he came out to exchange a pleasantry or brief bit of conversation with a guest, but he never emerged when 136 was in the library.

Emma didn't mind. She liked having the place to herself. She had grown comfortable with the organizational system, had gotten to know many of the customers, and came to think of 136 as her own special project. She was determined to get him to talk and employed various conversational strategies in attempts to engage him–but only when Wallace Reed wasn't present.

None of them worked.

When the librarian was in the building, even with his office door closed tight–Emma knew Wallace often napped in his office, and she suspected that he had a bottle in there that he nipped at from time to time–Emma said nothing to patron 136. But she made a show, sometimes an almost flirtatious one, of rearranging his books and watching as he placed them in his preferred–obsessive–order. He never even came close to speaking.

Emma could wait.

The Tuesday before Christmas, Wallace told her he had to be out for a while. "Just a little errand, it won't take long," he said. "And who knows? It might have something to do with you!"

Emma suspected the librarian was going out get her a Christmas present. She had one of her own for him: a small, silver bookmark.

Not long after Wallace left, 136 came in. Emma glanced at the clock: eleven on the dot. She got his card from the file–the sixth card she'd made out for him since she came to work there–and was already entering the information when he brought his books to the desk.

"Big Christmas plans?" she asked, expecting no reply and receiving none. "Remember, we'll be closed this Thursday and Friday, and for the weekend, but you don't come in on those days anyway, do you?"

She finished with his card, and before he could take his books, Emma grabbed them.

"I want to show you something," she said, and began re-sorting them. "Now look," Emma said when she was done and the books were neatly stacked, largest on the bottom, smallest on top.

136 reached for the books, but Emma pushed his hand away. His skin was surprisingly warm. "If you don't want to carry them this way, that's your business," she said, "even though it would be a lot easier. But that's not what I wanted to show you."

She took the books and turned them so their spines showed. "See? The letters that are left make a name: ADAM R LEECH. How about that!"

Emma thought she saw a hint of a smile cross his lips, and a tease of glint dance through his eyes. He tilted his head, and then shook it gently. He took the books from her and rearranged them, then turned the spines to face Emma. His eyes lingered on the books before slowly adjusting his gaze to meet hers. She looked at the spines and began to sound it out just as Wallace Reed, carrying a brightly wrapped package, entered the library.

"NO!" Wallace screamed. "Emma–NO!"

But she had begun to read and, having finally won some sort of reaction from 136, wasn't about to stop.

"Adramelech?" she said tentatively, then with more confidence, "Adramelech!"

The lights in the library flickered, went out, came on, went out again, and then blazed more brightly than Emma had ever seen them burn.

But the lights did not burn as brightly as 136's eyes, which burned crimson. An aura surrounded him as he stood taller, as his shoulders broadened, as bright red wings ripped through his clothing and unfurled. He turned and in a deep and sepulchral voice addressed Wallace:

"Adramelech!" he said. "My *name*, unsaid and unheard by me in all the years since you imprisoned me here. Imprisoned me with only those six insipid, stupid, stultifying, dull books for companionship. I loathe their every page, their every word," the creature said. "You can never know how much."

Emma wasn't even tempted to look away, didn't take so much as half a step back. She assumed patron 136 had some secrets, but this was beyond anything she could have imagined.

"And what was it you claimed from me when you imprisoned me?" Adramelech–the more she heard it, the more Emma liked the name–said. "What was it? Oh yes. Immortal life. Your immortal life."

"Yes," Wallace said, his voice tiny. Emma felt for him, but it wasn't right to lock somebody up with the same six books for eternity, or even fifty years. Especially those six books. Whatever it was Wallace had coming to him, Emma figured he probably deserved it–and only hoped whatever it was didn't get any blood on her present.

"Yes!" Adramelech roared. "Immortal life–for so long as my name is not said in my presence!"

"But–" Wallace began.

"No buts!" Adramelech bayed. He raised a hand and pointed a long, taloned finger at Wallace Reed.

Who vanished!

Emma didn't move. She wasn't afraid–far from it, in fact. She was mesmerized. The power 136–a *demon*!–wielded captivated her.

Then she thought of Wallace. Mr. Reed hadn't always been the nicest to Emma. Sometimes he was outright mean, but she *would* miss him. Emma gazed at the spot where he had stood moments ago and was happy to see her present appeared to be unharmed. Whatever it was, it would be like having a little bit of Wallace Reed with her.

Adramelech turned to her. "I trust you can keep a confidence?" he said. "And this will remain between us?"

"Who am I going to tell?" Emma said. She batted her eyes at him, but subtly.

"Good." He furled his wings and turned.

"Wait!" Emma said.

"Yes?"

"My job–I mean, I was wondering, with Wallace gone–where *did* he go?"

"Mr. Reed has a new position. In *my* library. More than that, you need not know, trust me."

"What's not to trust?" Emma said.

The creature moved to leave.

"What about *this* library? I mean, I really like the job, and–"

Adramelech stopped. "It's yours," he said.

"Mine?"

"Consider it a gift from one who has enjoyed seeing you twice a week for these many months. The library is yours," the demon said.

He touched her hand–now, oddly, his touch was cool–and turned away.

"I won't see you again?" Emma said, disappointed. She had become more than a little accustomed to his visits, and imagined the visits would be even more interesting now that she knew who he really was.

"Perhaps, perhaps not," Adramelech said. "More likely perhaps than not. I may wish to peruse your shelves from time to time. If you wouldn't mind."

"Not at all!" Emma said. "I'll keep your card... warm."

"Then I shall see you again, you may be assured. But I wonder if I might impose upon you a favor before I return?"

"Name it," Emma said.

"Take these six books out of circulation. They've more than served their purpose."

Emma made a show of fetching the inkpad and rubber stamp and, in the moments before Adramelech departed, she emblazoned each volume, in the order the patron preferred, with the word:

WITHDRAWN

GURGLE.
GURGLE.

MARIO ACEVEDO

GURGLE. GURGLE.

MARIO ACEVEDO

B obby Martinez unlocked the front door to his uncle's home. Bobby's best friend, Güero Salazar, followed him in.

Güero wore his North High School hoodie. He dropped his backpack on the floor and gaped. "Holy shit, *vato*, this place is awesome."

Soft light shimmered through a floor-to-ceiling aquarium that lined one wall. A gigantic flat screen television hung from the opposite wall. Custom blown glass light fixtures dangled from the twelve-foot ceiling. The artwork and leather and chrome furniture made the front room look like the lobby of a super-fancy hotel.

Güero shuffled in a small circle, still gaping in wonder. "Your *tio* owns this house, right?"

"Yeah."

"The same Moises from back when?" Güero pointed to a photo on the credenza. "Is this really your uncle? The same chubby guy we called *Sapo*?" Güero inflated his cheeks and bugged out his eyes to imitate a toad.

"Yeah, the same guy." Bobby studied the photo. Even he was amazed by the change. The image showed a dark haired man arm-in-arm with a hottie brunette on a foggy beach, tousled hair windswept over their smiling faces. Around the eyes, the hair, maybe Bobby could see the resemblance. But this version of Moises was slender and tall and looked way *mas macho* than the dumpy *Sapo* he grew up with.

"So what happened?" Güero asked.

"He went into the Air Force and got sent to Iraq. And then–"

"The Air Force? He was a pilot?"

"*Pendejo*, he was no pilot."

"Then what did he go to Iraq for?"

"I dunno. He was a clerk, or some other shit. Anyway, he came back looking like that." Bobby gestured to the photo and then spread both arms to encompass the house. "And he came back loaded."

"I remember what was here, *ese*," Güero said. "Some rundown house. That was what, a hundred years old?" He plunked his skinny *nalgas* on a couch. "*Gente* bitch about how the *gringo* hipsters are ruining the neighborhood, but I gotta admit," he slapped the leather upholstery, "these new digs kick ass." He toed off his shoes and propped his stockinged feet on an ottoman. "Man, you get a babe in here and before you know it, second base."

Güero was right about that. Bobby perched himself on a stool along the brushed steel bar counter. He palmed his cell phone and scrolled through the address book. The problem was he wasn't on good enough terms with any girls to invite one on short notice. Guys with no car didn't have much luck scoring with the *rucas*.

"Where did *Sapo*–" Güero began.

Bobby interrupted. "Better not let him catch you calling him that."

"Okay, Moises then, how did he score the money? By winning the lottery? A lawsuit?"

Bobby shrugged. "*No se.* When his enlistment was up, he came home all fit and good-looking. He bought my *abuela's* home, tore it down, and built this."

"Drugs, maybe?" Güero offered.

"I don't think so," Bobby replied, guardedly. "He said some investments paid off but never explained himself."

"Drugs," Güero repeated. He eyed the front door. "*Vato*, I don't want some gangsters busting in here looking for their cash and dope. I've seen *Scarface*. They'll cut us up with chain saws."

"*Calmate.* My *tio* Moises is as straight-laced as they come." Bobby eased off the stool and opened the bar cooler. "Look. No beer. Just Coke." He walked behind the bar and grasped the handle of a cabinet. Bottles of wine and liquor sparkled behind the heavy metal screen. He rattled the cabinet door. "Locked." He walked from the bar to the adjoining kitchen and opened the refrigerator. "He left us a bunch of ice cream." He opened another cabinet that was stocked with cookies and bags of chips. "And plenty of snacks."

Güero covered his face with a cushion and moaned. "What are we supposed to do for fun?"

"We got Wi-Fi and cable." Bobby picked up a remote and pointed it at the flat screen.

"TV? Cookies? Ice cream?" Güero whined. "Aw man, this is like a sleepover in middle school."

"I do have this." Bobby reached into his pocket and pulled out a tiny plastic jar.

A smile crept onto Güero's face. "Is that what I think it is?"

Bobby shook the jar. "You bet, *ese.*"

Güero sprang off the sofa. "You got *mota?*"

"The best shit. Purple Train Wreck. It will blow your mind and kick your ass."

Güero hustled to Bobby. "How did you get it?"

"I know a guy who knows a guy who knows a guy."

Güero took the jar and unscrewed the top. The humid aroma of chronic weed wafted out. "*Jesus mio*, this smells like heaven. Let's get started."

"That's the problem. I don't have any rolling papers."

Güero slapped his pockets. "Me neither. Bummer, *ese.* Maybe we could try regular paper."

Bobby shook his head. "I've tried that. And toilet paper. All you do is waste good pot."

Neither he nor Güero were yet eighteen. They couldn't buy papers from the 7-Eleven or even set foot in the local smoke shop.

"We could make a pipe from aluminum foil," Güero suggested.

"I've tried that, too. All I did was burn my lips and didn't even get high."

"How about we call Eddie? Jorge? Wally the Walrus? They're all big-time stoners and probably got tons of rolling papers."

"Good idea," Bobby said. He made the calls. He left messages for Eddie and Jorge. Wally was grounded.

Bobby dropped his phone on the counter. "This sucks. It's Friday night and we got some of the best smoke on the planet and still we got nuthin'."

Güero wandered into the kitchen and rifled through drawers and cabinets. "Don't give up, *vato*. We'll figure something." He waved a bar-beque lighter. "I found this. It's a start."

Inspired by his friend's determination, Bobby headed upstairs to search the rest of the house. He peeked into his uncle's bedroom. Like downstairs, with the furnishings and the artsy paintings, the bedroom looked like a suite in a really swanky hotel. So swanky, Bobby imagined, that if he opened the closet, it would be stocked with gorgeous models.

At first glance, he didn't see anything of interest. Then, as he was about to shut the door, he spied a glass cabinet on the left wall. Something shined inside. Curious, he tiptoed into the room. Moises never said he couldn't enter, but a bedroom was a very private place.

Bobby gazed at the object. A small pitcher? No, more like an oil lamp like he once saw in the museum. The lamp looked made of gold and was ribboned with colored glass inserts.

A thought crossed his mind. Depending on what Güero found, they might be able to fashion this lamp into a water pipe... make it one *chingon* bong!

He tried the cabinet door but it was locked. The lamp gleamed on its glass shelf, beckoning with the potential to deliver a world-class high. All that stood between Bobby and getting loaded was a little ingenuity.

He examined the door. The gap around the door and the cabinet frame appeared wide enough for a knife blade, which he didn't have. But he did have a key.

He inserted his house key into the gap. Working the key, he tried not to scratch the wood but scratched it anyway.

The key caught the latch and it clicked open. The cabinet door swung wide. *Voila compadres!* Success.

Bobby grasped the lamp and lifted. Though not much bigger than a softball, it was surprisingly heavy. Cradling it, he bounded downstairs. Güero piled assorted utensils and what-have-you on the bar counter. Bobby set the lamp next to them. "Güero, you get A's in science and shop class. Figure this out."

Fifteen minutes later, they stared in admiration at their creation. The short aluminum pipe from the basket of a small coffee pot had been slid down the spout of the lamp. A small glass funnel rested in the top of the pipe. They removed the lamp lid and screwed the barrel of a turkey baster into the opening. As an extra measure, duct tape kept everything from falling apart.

"We're fucking geniuses, *ese*." Bobby opened the kitchen sink faucet and ran water through the turkey baster until the lamp was full halfway.

Güero clicked the lighter. "Let's get started."

Bobby gazed about. "We better not light up here. My uncle sniffs any pot and he'll have my ass."

"The backyard?"

"Naw. The *gabachas* are always walking their dogs. They smell us burning this shit," Bobby shook the jar, "they might rat us out. But fear not, *vato*. This place has a rooftop balcony."

Güero picked up their makeshift bong. "What are we waiting for? The ganja express is about to leave the station."

They climbed the steps, singing, "Choo, choo!"

Karam set aside his quill pen and congratulated himself on the day's work. He had just translated high-dialect Babylonian into Aramaic from the third and fourth paragraph in chapter eleven of the second volume of the Apocryphal Sacred Pronouncements of Zahid, Learned Priest to the Royal Court of our Most Exalted Lord Hammurabi. The work was satisfying, but demanding, and fortunately Karam was able

to cross-reference his source text in Egyptian hieroglyphics with a glossary in the original Assyrian cuneiform. Getting this far had taken him twenty-seven hundred years, but not to worry. He had forever to finish this work. For a scholar like himself, this was the upside to being trapped as a genie in a magic lamp.

After letting the ink dry, he gathered the scrolls and pushed away from his desk. He placed the scrolls on a shelf and thought to reward himself with a pot of tea.

He paused to reflect on his good luck that Moises was his new master. His biggest headache as a genie was granting wishes to those idiot humans who would find the lamp, rub it, and try to wish themselves happiness, usually asking for riches or some other nonsense. The joke was on the humans because nothing was free. For the bigger the wish, the more devilish the consequences.

Moises was on patrol outside of Baghdad when he discovered the lamp and summoned Karam, who told him, "Look, I know where this is going. In the end you'll have less than what you started with, the price of your own folly."

"So I don't get three wishes?" Moises asked.

"Actually, you get all the wishes you want. The three wishes tradition comes from people using one wish to discover that my magic works. Then they wish for something spectacular, which comes with a catch. Then they use wish number three to undo the first two wishes and move on. So don't be greedy. Work with me, and I'll take care of you. In return, I want to be left alone to work on my studies."

In all the centuries Karam explained the deal, Moises was the first to get it. What he wanted was: to quit looking like a *sapo*; to return home from the war safe; to own a nice house; and to live comfortably. Simple enough. Once these wishes were granted, he would safeguard the lamp and not bother the genie.

Karam was reaching for a box of tea when the lamp shook. He cursed. Moises was supposed to warn him when the lamp was to be moved.

The lamp jostled again, and Karam tripped over his chair. Then the lamp began to shake. Scrolls and books jumped from the shelves and

fell over him as he bounced on the floor. File cabinets sprang open and regurgitated reams of papers that scattered everywhere. The inkpot rolled off his desk.

The movement halted with an abrupt thump. Karam pushed to his hands and knees to take stock of the damage. Ink puddled over scrolls unfurled around him. In an angry panic, he whisked the turban off his head and used the silk to blot the spilled ink before it could do more damage.

Too bad he couldn't leave the lamp unless he was summoned. The next time Moises called, Karam was going to trick the hell out of him.

A scraping noise caught his attention. A metal pipe appeared in the channel of the oil spout, moving into his chamber at a diagonal, sliding by increments until the mouth of the pipe pushed against the carpet.

Karam grasped the end of the pipe and tried to shove it back up the spout but it wouldn't budge. "Hey!" he yelled. "What the hell are you doing?"

A bright light from above dazzled him. The lamp's lid had been removed. Hands shielding his face, he retreated from the glare flooding the chamber. Then the lamp rocked back and forth as a second tube, this one wider and made of clear plastic, was forced into the opening. Afterwards, strips of material were laid over the colored glass on the walls, and the chamber was engulfed in shadow.

Karam straddled the metal pipe and looked upward, bewildered by the commotion. But until someone rubbed the lamp, he was trapped in there.

The lamp jostled again–*now what?*–and swung through the air. It tipped at an angle. Water sluiced through the pipe above and drenched Karam. He waded through the knee-deep water and shook his fists, vowing vengeance for the harm done to his home and archives. More water doused him.

The lamp swung through the air, water splashing him again and again. He clung to the metal pipe, sputtering like an indignant, wet mouse.

The movement halted. Ruined papers and scrolls floated around him. The air smelled fresh, like he was outside.

Then he smelled smoke.

But not any smoke. It brought an oily, grassy fragrance. Something he had not smelled in decades. Hashish? Not quite. Marijuana.

A second smell overpowered him. The heavy, moist breath of a human. He looked up and saw a mouth planted on the upper end of the plastic tube.

The mouth sucked hard and the air in the chamber was drawn upward. Smoke bubbled from the metal pipe through the water pooled around his waist. A cloud of burning marijuana gurgled into the chamber, choking Karam.

"That was some mighty good shit, *ese*." Güero stared at Bobby, who stared back with eyes red and bleary.

They were back downstairs, slouching in armchairs, having smoked the Purple Train Wreck to ash and tossed the evidence from the rooftop.

Güero pushed to his feet and shambled toward the kitchen. "*Vato*, I'm gonna eat everything your uncle left in the pantry."

"I saw some tamales in the fridge," Bobby said. "Throw those into the micro. And bring the Oreos and Doritos."

He considered the lamp resting in his lap. It had served its purpose well. All that remained was for him to dismantle the bong attachments, put the lid back on, and return the lamp to the cabinet in his uncle's bedroom. No one would be the wiser.

Bobby peeled a strip of duct tape from the lamp. It left a trail of adhesive. He licked an index finger to wet the tip and began to rub the residue, stroking the gold and glass surface.

Smoke jetted from the lamp's spout.

A la madre! Bobby juggled the lamp and dropped it on the coffee table.

The smoke mushroomed against the ceiling, curling in eddies around the dangling lamps. A smoke alarm began shrieking.

Bobby stared incredulously at the lamp, wondering where the smoke was coming from, and worried it was about to explode.

The smoke curled back down to accumulate in front of him, becoming a dense shape, darkening into the silhouette of a person, until it solidified into a man of flesh and blood.

He was dark-skinned, *pocho*-looking. A thin mustache and trim beard adorned his face. However, he wore an Aladdin costume: maroon vest, green baggy pants, and golden slippers with upturned toes, all of which were sopping wet. He brushed aside a lick of damp hair plastered to his forehead.

For a chubby guy he should've been all Santa Claus jolly, but he mostly looked seriously pissed off. Brown eyes burning with fury, he glanced from Bobby to Güero, and his brow wadded in confusion. "Where is Moises? And who are you?"

This bizarre stranger asking for his uncle only fed Bobby's astonishment. "He's my uncle. Me and Güero are watching the house while he's away."

"In that case." The stranger braced himself at attention and crossed his arms. "You summoned me, master?"

Bobby blinked and blinked. Güero watched from the kitchen, his face mirroring Bobby's amazement. He studied the lamp, convinced the apparition was a symptom of the weed.

The smoke alarm screeched painfully loud, souring Bobby's buzz. He cupped his hands over his ears. "Make it stop."

"Your wish is my command," the apparition said.

The room went quiet.

Bobby looked up at the mute alarm, then at the apparition. "You did that?"

The apparition nodded.

"Who are you?"

The apparition bowed. "I am Karam, your generous servant."

Bobby plopped into his chair. He had to be dreaming.

Güero hustled toward them. "So you're a genie?"

"I am."

"Okay, grant me a wish."

Karam pointed to Bobby. "He rubbed the lamp, therefore I serve him."

Güero snatched the lamp off the table and stroked it. "There, now give me my first wish."

In his two-plus millennia trapped in the lamp, Karam never experienced a situation like this before: serving two masters at once. He saw the incredulity ebb from the darker teenager and his blond, green-eyed friend as they realized the power that lay before them. The scheming look was familiar. Karam grinned, mischief lighting in his eyes as he contemplated the lesson he planned to teach the boys.

Güero closed his eyes and a warm look of anticipation settled over his face.

"What did you wish for?" Bobby asked, nervous.

"What every girl wants, *ese*." A bulge started to grow in the front of Güero's pants. The bulge between his legs kept growing, pushing against the zipper until he hollered in pain. "It's too tight." He jerked his belt loose, then undid the fly of his jeans to yank them over the gigantic swell in his briefs. The fabric ripped apart and a penis the size of a young elephant's trunk swung from his crotch.

"What did you do?" Bobby shouted, both amazed by what he saw and disgusted for staring at his friend's junk.

"Stand back," Güero warned. "I don't know how big it's going to get."

"Are you crazy? You wasted a wish on this? You might be an honor student, but you can still be a major league dumbass. No way is some girl gonna let you stick that in her cootchie."

"You never know until it happens." The penis stiffened, growing even thicker and longer. It canted upward, towering above Güero, the glistening bulbous tip swollen to a bright glowing red. The penis kept growing, the skin stretching tight like an over-stuffed sausage casing.

Güero's face blanched white as *queso fresco*. His eyes saucered in terror and he began to shriek when... **Blam!**

Gobs of hot blood pelted Bobby. Güero was still shrieking and he stared at the length of shredded flesh, one end hanging from his crotch and the other wadded on the floor in a pool of gore.

Bobby wiped his face and took in the gruesome scene. Spatters of blood stained the walls, ceiling, furniture, and dripped from the aquarium glass. He trembled in panic. Bobby's penis shrank and turtled into his crotch. Slowly, the shock melted into disbelief, then heated into anger. He glared at Karam. "What did you do?"

"I gave your friend exactly what he wanted."

"Then I wish for you to undo this."

"Sorry, only he can undo his wish."

Bobby grabbed the lamp and tore off the turkey baster. He heaved the lamp, tossing bong water on Güero's face, whose screams dissolved into a fit of gagging and coughing. He gazed in terror at what was left of his enormous member.

"Wish it away, Güero."

"Ok–k–kay," Güero stammered, legs quivering. He whispered, "I wish for my *berga* to go back to normal."

"Your wish is my command," Karam replied.

A blink later, Güero's *chilito* mended itself and shrank into a wrinkled noodle nestled in pubic hair. The blood vanished in puffs of pink smoke.

Bobby looked away, thankfully. He glowered at the genie. After all those good hits on the weed, Bobby was absolutely sober. Clearheaded. Upset. He squinted at Karam, who smirked, waiting.

Bobby hefted the lamp. "I've seen the movies and read the stories. No matter what I wish for, you'll always find a way to trick me." He handed the lamp to Karam. "So here. This is what I want. For you and the lamp to be like you were before I found you."

The genie arched his eyebrows in surprise. "How thoughtful." Instantly, he was in dry clothes with a sparkly blue turban on his head. The lamp returned to pristine condition.

"My next wish. For my uncle to never know this happened."

Karam nodded. "Done."

"What about me?" Güero protested. Still very stoned, he fumbled with his belt as he tried hitching his pants. "Don't forget my wishes."

"No way, bro. You'll get us both in bad trouble." Bobby faced the genie and asked, "Make this night end the way it should've." He blurted an afterthought, "In the best way, please."

Karam bowed and disappeared.

Bobby stared at the fish swimming in the aquarium, little glowing shapes gliding serenely, much like the way he floated in a euphoric haze. Tamale husks and remnants of cookies and chips littered a tray on the coffee table. Güero lounged dreamily on the sofa.

Earlier this evening, in a miracle of miracles, they found a packet of Zig-Zag papers in a kitchen drawer. Uncle Moises wasn't so straight-laced after all.

TAKING
THE
DARE

GARY JONAS

TAKING THE DARE

GARY JONAS

June 1977

"Tell me something about yourself you don't want anyone to know," Brenda said.

All I could think about was the flashes. Brenda was new to the neighborhood, we were both thirteen, and she was my world that summer. Her eyes lit up when discussing comic books, and yet she was athletic and cool. I'd tell her anything, but there were other kids sitting in Tucker's driveway playing Truth or Dare with us, and while Tucker and his sister Sandy were okay, I knew Eric and Larry would be merciless no matter what I said.

Brenda's lips twisted into a grin and my heart sped up. "Don't look so nervous, Alex. It won't go beyond this group." I took a deep breath. "I get flashes."

"My mother gets hot flashes," Eric said.

Brenda rolled her eyes, which made her even more cool.

"I can touch someone and get flashes of the terrible things they've done," I said. "Sometimes they're really bad things and sometimes they're just things the person feels are bad."

"Yeah right," Larry said, glancing at Eric for approval.

I turned to him. "When I met you, I got a flash of you shooting a cat with a BB gun. That's why I don't like you."

"What was the cat's name?" Larry said.

"I don't know. It was a flash. There's no sound or anything, just an image like a snippet from a movie."

"Poor kitty," Sandy said. "Did you really do that?"

Larry grinned. "Ask me when I say 'truth.'"

"You're not making this up?" Brenda asked. "Touch me and tell me what I've done." She held out her hand.

I took her hand in mine. "I don't get anything," I lied. "It doesn't always work."

"I've done terrible things," Eric said.

"I'll bet you have," Brenda said. "But I don't want to hear about them." She turned back to me. "You're lying."

"About what?"

"About the flashes, idiot," Eric said.

"No," Brenda said. "That's true. You can tell by Larry's reaction if nothing else. Alex is lying when he says he doesn't get a flash by touching me."

Eric grinned. "Let me touch you. I'll get flashes."

I shrugged. "I don't want to embarrass you." I leaned forward and whispered in her ear. When I pulled back, I said. "Did you do that?"

"Yes," she said. Her face clouded, and I worried I'd said too much. "But I was nine. I didn't know any better."

"You just told her to say that," Larry said.

That's when Mr. Peabody drove into the cul-de-sac. We all turned to watch him. His garage door raised up and he pulled his black Bronco inside.

"That guy gives me the creeps," Tucker said. "You think he's the one been killing all the kids?"

"What are you talking about?" Brenda asked.

"You haven't heard about the Black Bronco?" Tucker asked. When she shook her head he said, "People say there's a guy who drives around Aurora in a black Bronco kidnapping kids to torture and kill them. Six bodies were found last summer and another this month, mostly in construction sites like the one across the street there."

He pointed toward the site where they were building houses along the street that connected to our cul-de-sac.

"Oh my God!" She looked toward Peabody's house. "He lives next door to me. You don't think he's really a psycho, do you?"

"Come on," Eric said. "It's an urban legend. You know how many black Broncos there are in Aurora?"

"How many?" Tucker asked.

"A lot."

"No," Tucker said. "How many exactly?"

"Tell you what. I'll hit you one time for each Bronco. You can count the bruises and tell me the exact number."

"I was just curious."

"He's not the killer," I said.

"If he's not the killer, why doesn't he ever go outside?" Tucker asked. "Why doesn't he have a wife or kids? Why's he always watch us from the upstairs window?"

"He watches us?" Sandy asked.

Tucker nodded. "I seen him. I think he's the killer."

"No way," I said. "Let's play."

When Eric's turn came he punched me in the shoulder hard enough to hurt, but I refused to let it show on my face in front of Brenda. "Truth or Dare? And you don't have a hair on your balls if you don't say 'dare.'"

I knew what was coming, but I said, "I'll take your bait, Eric. Dare."

He grinned. "I *dare* you to touch Peabody. See if he's the killer."

"That's too dangerous," Brenda said.

"Do you think he's the Black Bronco?" Eric asked.

"No."

"Then why is it dangerous?"

"I'll do it," I said. I didn't want Brenda to think I was afraid of some old man. I summoned my courage and grabbed a soccer ball from the corner of the lawn.

"What are you taking the ball for?" Tucker asked.

I moved to the street and kicked the ball into Peabody's backyard.

"Oh," Tucker said.

I ran to Peabody's door and rang the bell. A dog inside started barking. It took ages for Peabody to answer, but finally, the door opened.

"Back up, Slayer," he said, pushing a big Doberman behind him. "What do you want, kid?" He towered over me. Although he was old, he looked like he still had plenty of muscle on his bulky frame. His gray hair stood out at odd angles and beads of sweat glistened on his forehead. He didn't open the storm door, so I couldn't touch him.

"Our ball went into your backyard."

He studied me for a moment, and I thought he was going to say no, but he nodded. "You can go get it. But be fast about it."

"Okay, can I cut through the house?"

"Use the gate, boy." He pointed and I could have sworn there was blood around his fingernails, as if he'd wiped his hands but hadn't done a very good job of it. That had to be my imagination, of course. It was probably just paint.

I walked around the side of the house and tried the gate, but it was locked. So I jumped the fence and got the ball.

Everyone waited in the street. "Well?" Eric said.

I told them about the blood under Peabody's nails.

Eric tilted his head. "Maybe when you rang the bell he was in the basement carving up his latest victim."

"Hey," Brenda said. "Don't try to scare us. I live next door to the man."

"And you might be next," Larry said, pointing at her.

"Well, the dare isn't over," Eric said. "You have to find out if Peabody is the killer or if he just happens to drive a black Bronco. When you find out, you let us know."

I couldn't sleep that night, so I crept downstairs and went outside. I sat on the driveway with my back against the garage, gazing at Brenda's house across the street. I had no idea which window was hers, but it didn't matter since all the lights were out. I wondered if she'd thought about me before she went to sleep.

My memory drifted back to her flash. She'd been in a hospital hallway, refusing to go into an old woman's room.

I was about to go back inside when Peabody's garage door opened. He backed his Bronco out and drove off down the road.

Curiosity got the better of me. I looked around, didn't see anyone, so I trotted over to Peabody's house.

As I neared the house, I heard a car and saw headlights sweep across the half-constructed houses across the way. I leaped and rolled into the bushes in front of Peabody's door and the black Bronco pulled into the cul-de-sac, slowing as it bumped over the curb onto the driveway. He must have forgotten something. As the Bronco turned into the drive, the headlights passed over me. I tried to become one with the bushes. If he'd seen me...

The garage opened. Peabody pulled the truck inside.

I used the few moments I had to get out of the bushes and around the side of the house by Brenda's place. Slayer started barking his head off.

"Shh!" I said, backing away from the fence.

That only made the dog go wilder.

"What's going on out there?" Peabody called. He walked out of the garage. I dropped to the ground and crawled under the bushes as he moved toward me.

The dog kept barking. A light came on in Brenda's house.

"Quiet, Slayer." His voice was icy cold, and the dog grew silent. He stood five feet from me, looking around. I lay still in the grass as far under the bushes as I could get.

Brenda's porch light came on and Mr. Taylor stepped out in his robe and slippers. "Is everything all right?"

If Mr. Taylor looked at the bushes, he'd see me for sure. I held my breath and tried not to move a muscle. Peabody stepped even closer to me.

"The dog caught a whiff of something he doesn't like."

"Probably a cat or a squirrel." Mr. Taylor walked to the edge of his property.

Brenda came out behind her father. "What's going on?"

"Go back to bed, sweetie," her father said.

Brenda looked over and saw me lying on the ground, but God bless her, she didn't give me away. She said, "Okay, Dad," and took a few steps

back. Once she was out of their line of sight she shot me a look that said, *what are you doing?*

I gave her a weak smile.

"Slayer doesn't bark at cats and squirrels," Peabody said. "He eats them. He only barks at people. That means someone's out here."

"Burglar?"

"Probably just a kid." Crap. He knew it was me.

I should have stayed still. That was the smart thing to do, the only *sane* thing to do. But sanity goes out the window when you're thirteen and in love. This was my chance to be brave in front of Brenda. I worked up my nerve and moved my hand closer to Peabody's foot. Brenda bit her fingers, then waved her hands down telling me to cool it. I shook my head slowly and she grimaced. I reached up Peabody's pant leg and touched his sock-covered ankle.

I flashed on a wild violent scene. Blood splashing and someone falling. I jerked back, startled. Mr. Peabody either heard me or felt me because he looked down.

"What the–?"

I scrambled out from under the bush and rolled to my feet.

"Stop, burglar!" Mr. Taylor shouted.

I ran as fast as I could into the construction site across the street. Peabody and Taylor ran after me.

I dodged around a stack of plywood and vaulted over a pile of two-by-fours. I cut through the foundation for the new house and jumped into the unfinished basement.

Peabody and Taylor stopped a few yards from the opening that led to the basement.

"Did you see his face?" Mr. Taylor asked.

Mr. Peabody sighed, then said, "No."

But I knew better. He'd hesitated as if weighing his options. He must have seen me thanks to the porch light. Panic tightened my chest, and I knew Peabody was probably doing a mental inventory of his knives, choosing the right one to carve me up.

Peabody took a few steps and kicked a loose nail. It rolled and dropped, hit me on the shoulder then clattered to the concrete floor. He'd done it on purpose. He knew right where I was.

"Want me to call the police?" Mr. Taylor asked.

"That won't be necessary. I was right. It's just a kid. I'm sure we put a scare into him. He won't be back."

"Whatever you say,"Mr. Taylor said and walked away.

Peabody walked after him, and I finally relaxed, but then the footsteps stopped and grew closer again. I held my breath. Peabody stepped even closer to the basement opening, and hawked up a nasty old-man loogie, which he spit right on me. It dripped down my face all long and stringy, and I wanted to scream.

"Just so you know, boy, I saw you. And I'll deal with you in good time. Count on it." He turned and walked back to his house.

I stayed in the basement for a very long time.

"He saw you?" Brenda asked.

Brenda and I were at my house waiting for Eric and the others to arrive. "That's what he said." My heart thundered. I didn't tell her everything, of course. I didn't want her picturing me covered in a slimy loogie. Just remembering it gave me the shakes.

"Before work, my dad couldn't stop talking about how Mr. Peabody should have called the police last night."

"He wouldn't. Cops ask too many questions."

"When I saw you reach for him, I about wet my pants!"

"I about wet mine when he chased me," I said, and instantly regretted it because I didn't want her imagining me with wet pants. So I changed the subject. "Who was the old woman in the flash?"

"That was my grandmother. See? I'm a terrible person."

All I wanted was to kiss her. "You're not a terrible person. I think you're wonderful."

Her eyes were shiny as she leaned toward me. Just as Eric and the others showed up. Of course.

"Sorry we're late. What's so important?"

I told them what happened.

Eric frowned. "That doesn't mean he's a killer. Even if he is, the cops won't do anything just because you saw flashes. We need evidence. I say we sneak into his house tonight."

"Are you crazy?" Brenda asked.

"A little," he said. "You aren't invited, though. This will be me and Alex. You guys will stand guard."

"You can't go into Peabody's house," Brenda said. "Especially not after last night."

Eric smiled. "Sure we can. Life without risks is boring."

I watched Brenda. Did she like me more because I was brave? Or did she think I was a complete moron?

"What about the dog?" I asked.

"I'm helping my dad at work this afternoon," he said. "I'll get some tranquilizers and we'll hide them in some raw hamburger meat like they do on TV." Eric's dad was a veterinarian, so he could actually get some, if his dad didn't catch him and kill him first.

"Don't do this," Brenda said. "It's stupid. He already wants to kill Alex." She linked her arm in mine, and I would have given anything for the other guys to disappear.

"Are you a pussy?" Eric asked me.

I couldn't back down in front of Brenda. "I'm in," I said.

Around midnight, we gathered in Brenda's backyard.

She kept trying to talk us out of it, but I was in for the duration.

Eric approached the fence and Slayer growled. Eric tossed the hunk of drugged meat over, and the sound of the dog chowing down made us grin. When we were sure Slayer was out of it, Eric hopped the fence.

I turned toward Brenda, but she just shook her head. "We'll be fine," I said and jumped the fence.

Slayer looked up at us from where he was stretched out on the ground, and whimpered. He dropped his head to the grass and sighed. Eric rushed to the back door. He opened the screen and tried the knob. Locked. He pulled out a bobby pin he'd taken from his mother and tried to pick the lock.

"It looks so easy in the movies," he whispered.

After a minute I shook my head. "Can't get it, huh?"

"No. But I think I saw an open window."

He was right. Eric pulled the screen off with a loud crack. We ducked into the shadows and waited. Nothing. We eased our way back to the window. He motioned for me to go first.

I crawled through, and Eric followed. We stepped down onto a battered old sofa. We took out our little flashlights and clicked them on, keeping the beams aimed at the floor.

All the homes in the neighborhood were built on the same basic floor plan, so it wasn't hard to find our way around. Eric moved through the room and stepped carefully onto the linoleum floor of the hallway. The house was silent. He opened the door that led to the basement.

"I'll check down here," Eric whispered.

"We're not splitting up."

"Suit yourself."

We crept down the stairs into the basement, casting the lights around to check the floor and walls. Off in the corner, a washer and dryer stood guard with folded towels stacked on top.

We moved around a pile of boxes to where the room branched off into an ell. Sheets of plastic hung from the ceiling, reaching all the way to the floor. A fan whirred and sent the sheets waving like a ghost pinned down in a soft breeze.

"Wonder what's back there?" I whispered.

"Only one way to find out," he said and gestured for me to lead the way.

I reached out and pulled one of the sheets of plastic aside. It was thick, at least six mil, and as I stepped through, a blast of foul air hit me.

"Who farted?" Eric whispered, and started chuckling.

I pushed another sheet of plastic aside, and saw a boy, maybe ten years old, hanging upside down from the rafters, his ankles bound by thick rope. Blood trickled down his arms and dripped from his fingertips. His shorts were soiled, and his stomach and chest were criss-crossed with deep gashes.

I dropped to my knees and threw up. Eric's reaction made me want to throw up again.

Eric stared at the boy, a weird grin on his face. He gazed with fascination at the kid and then reached out to poke his finger into one of the gashes.

The boy opened his eyes and screamed.

"Shit!" Eric said jumping back.

"Shh!" I said.

The boy blinked and gave a raspy, loud moan.

"He's going to wake Peabody," Eric said. "Let's get outta here!"

"We can't leave him," I said.

"We'll get out and call the cops," Eric said.

Footsteps sounded above us.

Eric gulped. "What do we do?"

The kid screamed again, and Eric tried to cover the boy's mouth. The kid bit him, and as soon as Eric pulled back, the kid cried out.

"Make him shut up!" Eric said.

The basement door opened, and the overhead light clicked on. Most of the light was in the main basement area, but plenty of it lit up our section, too. I glanced back at the kid, and wished I hadn't. The brighter light made it worse. He twisted a bit and cried out.

"Too late," Eric whispered.

The kid kept screaming.

Eric punched him in the face.

"Stop it," I said.

"He needs to shut up," Eric said, punching him again.

Peabody tromped down the stairs. "Did little Alex come back to play?"

I about shit my pants. How did he know my name? There was no place to hide.

Eric moved back, looked at his bloody fist. Tears welled in his eyes as footsteps crossed the cement floor.

Peabody stepped into view. He held a carving knife. His eyes narrowed to slits. "Hello there, boys. You realize I'm within my legal rights to kill you, don't you?" he said with a grin.

Eric shoved me forward, and made a break for the stairs. I stumbled and ran into Peabody. When I touched him, I saw Peabody carving another kid into little pieces. I froze. He shoved me aside, and lashed out with his blade. Eric was fast, but not fast enough.

The blade sliced into Eric's back, but he didn't seem to notice at first. He kept running, tried to take the stairs two at a time, then tripped on the fourth step. His face slammed into the stairs and he slid to the bottom, groaning.

Peabody walked over to him, bloody knife in hand.

I snapped out of my state of shock, found myself sitting in a puddle of blood beside the boy, sheets of plastic swaying in the breeze from the fan. "Leave him alone!" I said.

Peabody ignored me. He grabbed Eric, pulled him to his feet and shoved him across the room. Eric tripped into the plastic sheets and fell next to the hanging boy.

The boy who wasn't moving anymore.

Peabody glared at me for a moment before checking his carved up victim.

"Dead too soon," he said. He shook his head. "But I suppose a trade of two for one isn't that bad. Eager little Eric killed him before I had the chance to show him how it's done, didn't he?"

"No, you did," I said. I glanced at Eric. He wasn't moving. The bloodstain on the back of his shirt expanded.

"He was alive when I left him," Peabody said.

"You were killing him."

Peabody laughed. "Him or me, him or me, and it will always be him."

"That doesn't make any sense."

"It's tradition," Peabody said. "And now it's your turn. This will go much better for you if you go along peacefully."

"Yeah," I said. "I can see how that worked out for this kid."

Peabody smiled, and before I could take a single step, he swept outward with that blade and sliced my chest open. My reflexes kicked in and I tried to jump back. Instead, I fell backward. I hit the floor hard, and looked at my chest. It didn't hurt at first. In fact, it didn't even look bad for a few seconds. Then the blood welled, and with it came the pain. I grabbed my chest, trying to hold the blood inside, and rivulets of crimson seeped between my fingers.

Eric moaned and started to rise.

Peabody rushed over to him, grabbed his hair and pulled his head back. "You or me, kid, you or me?" Peabody asked.

Tears rolled down Eric's cheeks.

"Looks like it will always be you," Peabody said.

Peabody dragged his blade across Eric's neck, slicing so deep I worried Eric's head would separate from his neck. The blade didn't make a sound, and neither did Eric.

My chest flared with pain, and I did the only thing I could think to do. I shoved myself to my feet and ran.

As I reached the corner of the ell-shaped basement, I chanced a look and saw Peabody release Eric's head. Eric's face flopped to the floor with a sound like a wet washcloth, and the seat of his jeans darkened. Blood spread out on the floor, and when Peabody bolted in my direction, it was Eric's blood that saved me.

Peabody slipped and fell, sliding along the concrete.

I reached the stairs, and raced up them using my hands as bloody supports. My fingers left red streaks on the edge of each step. When I reached the top, I flew through the door, crashed into the wall and left a big crack in the drywall.

My breath sounded terrible, and my chest screamed. Then I realized I was the one screaming. To the left, I could go to the kitchen, or to the right down the hall to the front door.

I was afraid to see what might be cooking in that kitchen, so I went toward the door.

Peabody bounded up the stairs.

I reached the front door, tugged on it, but it was locked. My bloody fingers slipped off the deadbolt. I tried to grab it again, focusing, and the lock turned. I jerked the door open, but Peabody slammed it closed, grabbed me and hurled me into the living room.

I staggered over an ottoman, and crashed into a chair. Peabody stalked into the room, blade held ready.

A stack of magazines stood on the coffee table. *Time* and *Newsweek* sat with pictures of politicians smiling from the covers. Peabody smiled, too.

I kicked the table and sent it smacking into Peabody's shins. The magazines slid off the table, and Peabody bent over, shouting in pain.

As I stumbled past him, he took a swipe at me. I didn't feel it, so at first I thought he'd missed me, but as I fumbled the door open again, I saw blood on my left sleeve. The pain rose up my arm, but I forced myself to keep going.

I shoved the storm door open, and leaped into the night. Bright red and blue lights flashed at me, and I covered my eyes. I crashed into the bush I'd hidden beneath the previous night.

Peabody bolted out the door after me.

"Police! Drop the knife and get on the ground!"

Peabody laughed and reached for me.

Flashes of him killing boys filled my vision, interposed with the sound of gunshots. Time slowed. The flashes ended, and Peabody collapsed.

A policeman cautiously approached. "Are you all right, son?" he asked. He held his gun trained on Peabody's corpse.

I managed to nod. "I don't think Eric..."

He checked Peabody for a pulse then placed a hand on my shoulder, and motioned for two more cops to move in. They entered the house, guns drawn.

A few minutes later, the officers returned.

"Bloodbath down there," one said. "Two dead boys."

They talked about detectives and forensics and kept asking if I was okay. My eyes swept the neighborhood, and I saw Brenda standing with her father at the edge of the lawn, bawling her eyes out. I wanted to kiss those tears away.

An ambulance pulled up to the curb. Two paramedics rushed over to me. They poked, and prodded, applied bandages. The whole time they worked, I stared past them at Peabody's open, blank eyes.

How was it that, mere moments before, his body had been alive and focused on killing me? Now it was just an empty shell.

The paramedics loaded me onto a gurney and carried me to the ambulance. As they moved, I saw Brenda angling toward the back of the vehicle.

"Wait," I said, and nodded toward her.

They let her through.

"You were gone so long, I had to call the police," she said. She tentatively touched my face. I didn't feel the wounds when Peabody slashed me, but I felt her fingers like tingly, electric shocks.

"You saved my life," I said.

"The police saved your life."

"No, you did." I took her hand in mine, kissed her fingers, and watched her face turn pink.

Then I remembered. "Eric didn't make it."

She nodded. "But you did. And thanks to you, no one else will die, and I don't have to live next door to a murderer."

"We need to get him to the hospital, miss," one of the paramedics said.

"Sorry," she said. She leaned down, planted a kiss on my lips. "Heal fast."

The flash when she kissed me was of all of us in the backyard. In her view, the worst thing she'd done was let me go into that house. As if she could have stopped me.

MELANIE TEM: HUBBLE'S CHILD

EDWARD BRYANT

W ell, no, not literally. If you want to be a stickler, Melanie was born to Mr. and Mrs. Kubachko in Saegertown, PA, in 1949. I'm clumsily building a metaphor and all will eventually come clear.

Right up front I must declare that Melanie Tem was my friend for something like forty years. More than half my life.

I met her when she joined the Northern Colorado Writers Workshop back in the early '70s. When Steve Rasnic joined the NCWW a little later, I introduced Melanie to her future husband and partner. In 1979 I was honored to preside at their wedding in a beautiful mountain park setting west of Denver. Soon after the wedding, they each adopted the carefully chosen surname Tem. If you've ever wondered, that's the name of the Egyptian generative deity and, as a bonus, the Romany word for free country. Thirty years later, Melanie and Steve asked me to assemble a small-press tribute to the celebration of their pearl anniversary. As lagniappe, I got to perform the wedding celebration for one of their daughters.

But what really jogged my orbit into increasing inter-section with that of Melanie and Steve was my crazily erratic health. Two decades ago, I awoke one morning to discover both my shoulders had been mysteriously shattered in the night. That medical conundrum was followed in short order by a quadruple cardiac bypass

and then a string of other medical challenges. A mutual friend of us all, concerned she wouldn't be able to keep close track of me once she left Denver, sat down for an urgent confab with the Tems. All agreed they would keep a watchful eye on me and my well-being, particularly by having me in for supper several nights per week and sometimes *every* night. I think for them both it was like taking in a feral boy who'd been living among the savage wolf-dogs on the pampas.

I exaggerate. I was more like the creepy uncle who lives in the attic, but ventures down at night to forage. But seriously: I got to see their kids grow up. I was privileged to join them all for their birthdays. Discovering that Melanie loved to pop the air cells in Bubble Wrap, I gave her a giant roll of the stuff for one of her birthdays. I also discovered she had an obsessive love for staled marshmallow Peeps at holiday time.

We took endless neighborhood walks after supper with a succession of family beagles and we talked. As her illness developed, we talked about how she was coping. Melanie was a woman who was never in denial. She knew how to wrestle fear to the ground. In the last two years, she incorporated eastern spirituality into her coping armory.

She also remembered to call me on all the trip-ups I committed in my mundane life and I was increasingly willing over the years to pay heed to her counsel. When I hit bottom in my own life a while back, Melanie was a prime mover in putting together Friends of Ed, an informal but highly effective group who contributed advice and support, problem-solving savvy and tangible resources to help me back on my feet. I could have had no better friend. What a gift, that friendship.

I even found myself occasionally serving as husband Steve's proxy for events he preferred to avoid. So I escorted Melanie to see performances by the likes of Bruce Springsteen and Halden Wofford & the Hi Beams, and some live theatre and jazz events, all Melanie enthusiasms. Because her limited vision restricted her ability to appreciate vivid colors, she asked to see the brilliant pyrotechnics in the skies on Independence Day.

Then there were the times Steve was out of town. Hold on, cowboys, this isn't a salacious tell-all. See, Steve's a picky eater. So when he left for a convention Melanie didn't want to attend, Melanie and I would

concoct menus of all the foods Steve disdained: mushroom gnocchi, mixed fruits, tuna casserole, Waldorf salad.

But stale Peeps and mushroom gnocchi do not a full life make. Melanie was so much more. She was a mother whose devotion to her children and grandchildren was immense. She took pride in their accomplishments and then offered an unconditional love at their occasional missteps. There was no false sympathy or empty platitudes. She handled her kids with the same tough, unwavering sensibility she employed with her professional colleagues and her students.

Melanie's day job for most of her adult years was as a social worker and an administrator, first working with adoptive services, then directing a non-profit that helped the seemingly helpless find essential resources and paths to independent living.

As a writing teacher, both singly in a continuing workshop at home in Denver and in tandem with her husband Steve at Jeanne Cavelos's famed Odyssey Workshop in New Hampshire, she honed the no-bullshit skills that inspired students to extraordinary efforts and earned their fierce loyalty. The Tems have collaborated on an instructional book about the act of creative writing that should instantly become a seminal text once a publisher has the wit and vision to publish it.

In the meantime, writers and readers alike should pay heed to the collaborative (again with Steve) *The Man on the Ceiling*, both the multiply honored novella version (American Fantasy, 2000) and the novel length expansion (Wizards of the Coast Discoveries, 2008). In each case, the reader finds an unflinching analysis of imagination and creation told through both fiction itself and a painfully honest meshing with family autobiography. Some facts are malleable within, but truths, never.

The same can be said of the truths in all Melanie's writing. In the '70s NCWW, I encountered a project Melanie never actually let the rest of us read. She'd set a murder mystery in a nursing home with an elderly woman, sunk in dementia, as the protagonist. Imagine Miss Marple with Alzheimer's. Melanie then calmly and heretically suggested that dementia might be not so much a terrible and debilitating disease as it could be an alternate but legitimate means of apprehending consensual

reality from a different direction. Gutsy stuff, and indicative of what was to come in the following decades.

While her writing career was simmering in the '80s with stories highly regarded by both critics and readers, her novels debuted auspiciously with *Prodigal* for Dell's Abyss line in 1991, a book that earned her a Bram Stoker Award and a British Icarus Award. *The Wilding* (1992) followed, along with *Revenant* (1994), *Desmodus* (1996), *Deceiver* (2001), and *Slain in the Spirit* (2002). With fellow writer Nancy Holder, she wrote *Making Love* (1995) and *Witch-Light* (1996).

Other novels included *Blood Moon* (1997), *Daughters* (2001, written with Steve), *Black River* (1997), *Tides* (1998), and her story collection *The Ice Downstream* (2001). Her most recent novel *The Yellow Wood* came out from Chizine early this year and Melanie was able to see the first copies.

Publishing soon will be *Singularities*, a comprehensive selection of her short fiction in an exquisite edition from Centipede Press. Centipede also published *In Concert* (2010), the collected collaborations with her husband. Much like the classic collaborations of such couples as C.L. Moore and Henry Kuttner, and Leigh Brackett and Edmond Hamilton, the joint stories were seamless literary partnerships.

Though her work was often published as horror, science fiction, or fantasy, she never adopted any of these rubrics. "Fantasist" might have been closest. Melanie simply considered herself a writer. And so she was.

That writing appeared in many forms. She wrote poetry and put together accomplished oral storytelling presentations. As a fan of live theatre, she ambitiously tackled the stage as a playwright, grappling such edgy social issues as killing young psych patients with trendy but dangerous therapies (*Fry Day*), language and voice (*The Society for Lost Positives*), and aging and memory (*Comfort Me With Peaches*). That last script even saw an off, off, *way* off Broadway production mounted in Melanie's home state of Pennsylvania.

While Melanie could decline the pigeonholing of being classed as a genre writer, it still must be recognized that she was a master of the cool fantastic. She knew very well the cold cosmic horror of even the H.P. Lovecrafts of literature and didn't shy away from plumbing the terror

of chilly human relationships. She knew grief intimately. Readers didn't generally find her tales cuddly at all, but they also couldn't turn away from stories that engaged with sometimes painful honesty.

Her words provoke and stimulate, triggering all the complex reactions readers feel when they interact with a storytelling virtuoso.

Now then. About that enigmatic initial notion of the child of Hubble. The first reference is to Edwin Hubble, the famed astronomer who is honored by having his name attached to the near-Earth orbital space telescope. Most of you have seen the galleries of wondrous and awe-inspiring cosmic images beamed back to us on this planet. Some of those images, such as the Pillars of Creation, defy easy superlatives.

But here's the point. The images reflect realities that lie hundreds of millions of light years away. The originals were born, lived, and died, but what was once created still courses across the universe and now it's our turn to see those quasars, pulsars, exotic nebulae, and all manner of stellar phenomena from the past. New observers are constantly illuminated.

It's similar with human art. We'll never personally meet sixteenth century playwrights, eighteenth century artists, or nineteenth century novelists. They are long at peace. But we continue to appreciate and be inspired by their works.

This is why the Hubble image for Melanie. We can no longer directly converse with her. But her legacy still exists. Her work will radiate through space and time to find new generations, to widen their eyes and open their minds.

Okay, are you now accusing me of being a touch hyperbolic? Shucks, I eat hyperbole for breakfast. But I'm not here to defend my dietary habits.

Just don't ignore the essential reality of the ripple effect. Whether as quiet concentrics or wild tsunamis, the ripples spread.

Literary Hubbles will relay Melanie and her creations through the universe. And to those who have yet to encounter those creations, I say to them:

Keep watching the skies.

ACKNOWLEDGMENTS

ABOUT THE AUTHORS

Mario Acevedo is the author of the bestselling *Felix Gomez* detective-vampire series from HarperCollins. His debut novel, *The Nymphos of Rocky Flats*, was chosen by Barnes & Noble as one of "The 20 Best Paranormal Fantasy Novels of the Decade" and was a finalist for a Colorado Book Award. Acevedo was named one of 100 Colorado Creatives by *Westword*. His novel, *Good Money Gone*, co-authored with Richard Kilborn, won Best Novel: Adventure or Drama–English in the 2014 International Latino Book Awards. His short fiction has been included in anthologies from Arte Publico Press. He is a former president of the Rocky Mountain Fiction Writers and was voted as their 2009 Writer of the Year. He is also a past-president of the Rocky Mountain Chapter of the Mystery Writers of America. He teaches Genre Fiction at Lighthouse Writers Workshop and Writing the Graphic Novel at Front Range Community College. Mario lives and writes in Denver, Colorado.

The ongoing theory that it was a severe neurochemical event that switched **Edward Bryant** from writing sizzling science fiction to mildly unsettling horror still hasn't been overturned. Bryant's written a few decades' worth of short fiction, nonfiction, Hollywood stuff, and the occasional novel. He lives in Denver, where he's preparing *On the Road to Cinnabar*, a huge retrospective of his life's work.

Dustin Carpenter is an author, cinematographer, and IRONMAN Triathlete, but feels most at home in a good story. Currently, he is working on the second book in the *Apollo Pentalogy* series, *The Mask of Andrean*, as well as laying the groundwork for *Natrola*, a transmedia experience. Carpenter works as a creative media generalist, and has been typesetting for just over a decade. He is the author of *Azimuth Falls*.

Sean Eads is a reference librarian living in Denver, Colorado. His first novel, *The Survivors*, was a finalist for the 2013 Lambda Literary Award. His second novel, *Lord Byron's Prophecy*, will be released in October 2015 from Lethe Press. His short fiction has appeared in various anthologies, including *Zombies: Shambling Through the Ages* (Prime Books), *Kaleidoscope* (12th Planet Press), and *Equilibrium Overturned* (Grey Matter Press). Besides writing, he enjoys playing golf and watching University of Kentucky basketball games. His favorite writers and influences include Herman Melville, Ray Bradbury, and William Faulkner.

Keith Ferrell has written more than a dozen books, fiction and nonfiction, including bestseller *History Decoded*, which he co-wrote with Brad Meltzer. His short fiction has appeared in *Asimov's*, *Black Mist*, and *Millennium 3000*. From 1990-1996, he was the editor of *OMNI Magazine*. Ferrell lives on a small farm in southwestern Virginia.

Warren Hammond is known for his gritty, futuristic *KOP* series. By taking the best of classic detective noir, and reinventing it on a destitute colony world, Hammond has created these uniquely dark tales of murder, corruption and redemption. *KOP Killer* won the 2012 Colorado Book Award for best mystery. Hammond's latest novel, *Tides of Maritinia*, was released in December of 2014 (Harper Voyager). His first book independent of the *KOP* series, *Tides* is a spy novel set in a science fictional world.

Jason Heller is the author of the alt-history novel *Taft 2012* (Quirk Books) and a Senior Writer for The Onion's pop-culture website, The A.V. Club. He's also a former nonfiction editor of *Clarkesworld*; as part of the magazine's 2012 editorial team, he received a Hugo Award. His short fiction has been published by *Apex Magazine, Sybil's Garage, Farrago's Wainscot*, and others, and his reviews and essays have appeared in *Weird Tales, Entertainment Weekly, NPR.org, Tor.com*, and Ann and Jeff

VanderMeer's *The Time Traveler's Almanac* (Tor Books). Additionally, he wrote an official *Pirates of the Caribbean* tie-in book, *The Captain Jack Sparrow Handbook* (Quirk). He lives in Denver with this wife Angela amid a dearth of things that aren't books.

Gary Jonas is the author of the *Jonathan Shade* fantasy series, which includes the novels *Modern Sorcery, Acheron Highway, Dragon Gate, Anubis Nights, Sunset Specters*, and *Wizard's Nocturne*. His other novels include *One-Way Ticket to Midnight*, and *Pirates of the Outrigger Rift* (co-authored with Bill D. Allen). He created the *Night Marshal* western vampire series, and wrote the first volume before turning it over to other authors. His short fiction has appeared in anthologies and magazines, including *Robert Bloch's Psychos, It Came from the Drive-In, Prom Night, 100 Vicious Little Vampire Stories, Sword and Sorceress VII*, and many others. The best of his short fiction is collected in *Quick Shots*. As if that's not enough, he's also written screenplays, and has had a couple of them optioned in Hollywood.

Stephen Graham Jones is the author of fifteen and a half novels, six collections, and well over two hundred stories, many of which have been selected for annuals and anthologies and textbooks. Stephen's been a Colorado Book Award finalist, a Bram Stoker Award finalist, a Shirley Jackson Award Finalist, and he's won the Texas Institute of Letters Jesse Jones Award for Fiction, the Independent Publishers Award for Multicultural Fiction, and been an NEA fellow. Next up from him is the werewolf novel *Mongrels* (William Morrow), in May 2016. Stephen lives in Boulder, Colorado.

J.V. Kyle is the pen name for Keith Ferrell and Joshua Viola.

Aaron Michael Ritchey is the author of *The Never Prayer* and *Long Live the Suicide King*, both winners in various contests. His latest novel, *Elizabeth's Midnight*, is now available through Staccato Publishing. In shorter fiction, his *G.I. Joe*-inspired novella was an Amazon bestseller in Kindle Worlds, and his story, "The Dirges of Percival Lewand" was recommended for a Hugo. He lives in Colorado with his wife and two ancient goddesses of chaos posing as his daughters.

Jeanne C. Stein wears two writing hats. Under her own name, she writes the national bestselling Urban Fantasy series, *The Anna Strong Vampire Chronicles*, and as S. J. Harper, she writes *The Fallen Siren Series*. Both can be found at the FallenSiren.com website.

Steve Rasnic Tem has won the Bram Stoker, International Horror Guild, World Fantasy, and British Fantasy Awards for his work. Tem's new novel, *Blood Kin*, is a Southern Gothic/Horror blend of snake handling, ghosts, granny women, kudzu, and Melungeons. His previous novels are *Deadfall Hotel*, *The Man On The Ceiling* (with Melanie Tem), *The Book of Days*, *Daughters* (with Melanie Tem), and *Excavation*. His next novel, *Ubo*, a dark SF meditation on violence, will appear from Solaris in the spring of 2016. Steve has published over 400 short stories. They've been collected in *Ombres sur la Route*, *City Fishing*, *The Far Side of the Lake*, *In Concert* (collaborations with Melanie Tem), *Ugly Behavior*, *Onion Songs*, *Celestial Inventories*, *Twember*, and *Here With the Shadows*, a collection of traditionally-inspired ghostly fiction from Ireland's Swan River Press. In 2015, Centipede will publish a giant collection of the best of his uncollected horror: *Out of the Dark: A Storybook of Horrors*.

Dean Wyant is acquisitions editor and co-founder of Hex Publishers. He is a forty-year resident of Colorado with a decade of retail bookselling experience and a deep network of author contacts. *Nightmares Unhinged* marks Wyant's short fiction debut.

ABOUT THE ARTIST

Aaron Lovett is lead artist for Hex Publishers. His work has been published by Dark Horse and is in the pages of *Spectrum 22*. His art can also be found in various video games, books and comics. He paints from a dark corner in Denver, Colorado.

ABOUT THE EDITOR

Joshua Viola is owner and chief editor of Hex Publishers. He is an author, artist, and video game developer (Capcom, Disney Interactive, and Konami). In addition to creating a transmedia franchise around *The Bane of Yoto*, honored with more than a dozen awards, Viola is the author of *Blackstar*, a novel based on the work of acclaimed electronic-rock musician Celldweller. He lives in Denver, Colorado and can be found on the web at: www.joshuaviola.com

Made in the USA
Lexington, KY
03 February 2017